SAVAGE BONDS

by

ROXANE BEAUFORT

CHIMERA

Savage Bonds first published in 2000 by
Chimera Publishing Ltd
PO Box 152
Waterlooville
Hants
PO8 9FS

Printed and bound in Great Britain by
Caledonian International Book Manufacturing Ltd
Glasgow

All Characters in this publication are fictitious. Any resemblance to real persons, living or dead, is purely coincidental

Copyright © Roxane Beaufort

The right of Roxane Beaufort to be identified as author of this book has been asserted in accordance with section 77 and 78 of the Copyrights Designs and Patents Act 1988

SAVAGE BONDS

Roxane Beaufort

This novel is fiction – in real life practice safe sex

'In the far off days before the Great Deluge changed the face of the world, there lived giants and trolls, dragons and mighty sorcerers, slaves and masters, and heroes who were the stuff of legends. None was braver than Varna, the warrior Princess of Trokles. Her beauty inspired lust in every man who beheld her. All wanted to subdue her, but she would bend the knee to no one. She defied her enemies even when a captive, despite the harsh chains that bound her and the savage whips that bit into her flesh.'

Mezentius, the Chronicler.

PRELUDE

He lay there, watching his slaves.

They were beautiful, each and every one, male or female, his spoils from battles, pillage and plundering. Some were commoners, others vanquished royalty. It made no difference once they were in his ruthless hands.

He was filled with lustful thoughts, and proud of it. He stretched his magnificently honed, muscular body, his skin responding to the feel of purple silk. His robe was open down the front, displaying a rock-hard belly, a thatch of wiry black hair, and his erection. He rubbed it, working his fingers round the rim where his foreskin had rolled back from the shiny dome.

The divan was on a dais, deeply cushioned, and canopied in cloth of gold. It took pride of place in his private apartment, a setting devoted to pleasure. He sometimes invited guests to partake of the feast of flesh on offer. As tonight, for example: the king was in an expansive mood.

Like every other part of his vast palace, this room was awesome in its immensity.

Great white candles wept waxen tears in their floor-standing, wrought-iron holders, their light dancing across frescos of life-sized scenes of debauchery where gods and goddess, nymphs and satyrs indulged in lascivious play. Furnished in sombre black and crimson, the atmosphere was oppressive, despite arches that gave on to a terrace.

The carved ceiling was supported by basalt pillars, their starkness relieved by the naked bodies chained to them. Garlanded girls drooped there, eyes cast shyly down, the light glinting on the curling hair between each pair of thighs, and the pink nipples crimping on perfect breasts. There were handsome youths too, their cocks kept erect by straps drawn up tight round the base and circling their balls.

The king chuckled as he noted how vulnerable and subservient this made them. He gestured imperiously and a huge bull of a man strolled along the ranks of tethered slaves. His head was shaven, and his teak-brown skin glistened with oil. His chest was wide, his shoulders rippling with muscle. He wore leather boots and hide breeches with an open codpiece from which his twelve inch penis projected, swaying as he walked, a throbbing bough knotted with veins, its head bare and fiery. His teeth flashed as he grinned at the slaves and flourished the pliable whip clamped in one brawny fist.

The guests chattered, laughed and made comments. They took their ease on couches beside low tables loaded with food and carafes of wine. The gentlemen eyed the bound girls, and the ladies openly speculated on the sexual stamina of the young men.

It could have been a respectable gathering with the tinkle of harp and trilling of flute, the fabulous jewels and exotic silks, were it not for the freedom with which they lavished kisses and caresses on one another. Hands cupped opulent or pert breasts and teased rosy nipples, fingers sought out genitalia: no one seemed particularly fussy about the gender of those they fondled.

Their host signalled to his servant again and the whip fell across the thighs of the youngest of the new batch of female slaves. She screamed and tugged at the chains fastened through a ring bolt in her wrist manacles.

'Bring her to me, Aswad,' the king ordered.

He had been anticipating this moment. His cock twitched and lengthened an extra inch as he thought about her buttocks reddening under the cut of the lash, or the leather coiling around and slicing into the tender flesh of her lower belly. She was fresh and innocent, a virgin, so they had assured him, her initiation about to begin.

He sat up as she approached. She looked terrified. She was forced to her knees near the king's bare feet. He placed a hand under her chin and raised her face, looking down into soft dark eyes framed in a mass of unruly hair.

'You're trembling, my child,' he said, his voice deep and cultured. 'Are you afraid?'

'Yes, sire,' she faltered.

'You have need to be,' he assured her, in a deceptively kindly manner. 'Though you were once a noblewoman, here you will learn to be humble, your sole object in life to bring about my pleasure. Do you understand?'

'I'm trying to accept it, sire,' she sobbed, the tears coursing down her cheeks and hanging from her breasts like dewdrops.

'Do I hear a hint of rebellion, slave?' he said in a clipped tone, his eyes cold. 'This will be punished.'

'I'm sorry, sire...'

'Master!' he shouted, and grabbed at the thin gold chain linking the rings piercing her nipples, tugging at it mercilessly. 'You will call me master!'

'Oh... oh!' the girl cried, sliding forward on her knees, propelled by the pain shooting through her breasts.

'Say it!' he demanded, his face set in harsh lines as he gave an extra pull on the chain, her nipples standing out, engorged with blood.

'Master!' she whimpered, and wept harder.

'I don't think she means it... yet,' murmured the woman on the dais beside him. She reached up to wind her arms round his neck. 'She needs to be taught the pleasure of submission, and the joy to be had once one has passed through the barrier of pain.'

'You are right, beautiful one,' the king said, and caressed his consort and sister who was his equal in wickedness and sorcery.

Bizarre and lovely, her hair was the colour of copper, of autumnal beeches, of the sunset, that burnished mane contrasting with her alabaster skin. The pendants that dangled from her ears flashed like crystals splashing from an ice-cold waterfall. Her breasts were full, and her voluptuous body was nude, except for a jewelled waistband, thick bracelets and gem-ornamented studs fastened into her labial wings. Her pubis was shaven, the area smooth and inviting, and a diamond glinted in the hood of her clitoris.

The king smiled sardonically and pushed the girl down till her face was pressed to the obsidian tiles, knees drawn under her, rump raised high, showing her hair-fringed crack from clit to anus. He stood up, towering over her, considering that tempting morsel, measuring the area with his eye.

He held out his hand. It closed over the plaited leather butt of the whip Aswad proffered. The girl moaned and shivered, her shoulders on the floor, her slender back and rounded buttocks helpless and at his mercy.

He heard the excited exclamations of the spectators, caught the sweet aroma of his consort's arousal, and the bitter smell of fear rising from the girl. Yet, as he examined her, parting her bush and running a finger over the pink folds within, it was to find her wet. The sight of her white thighs caused a jolt in his phallus. Her innocence was intriguing. There was nothing he liked more than robbing a captive of his or her virginity.

He stood back, let her wait for a moment, and then with a quick flick of the whip, snapped at her buttocks. She shrieked and tried to draw herself into a ball, but Aswad kept her in position.

The guests had forgotten protocol, and even the fear that made them wary of the king's mood swings. They were straining to see what he would do next, longing to witness his ravishment of a virgin. When he repeated his stroke on the girl's rump her anguished scream joined that of others as the crack of whips on flesh resounded, some of the crowd seizing canes and paddles and laying about the tethered slaves.

He was in control, yet hit her hard and fast, his arm becoming an extension of the punishment tool. It acted like a channel feeding back her terror, agony, and the beginning of an unwilling pleasure.

The whip landed on places as yet untouched, making her body jolt. Red lines appeared on her fleshy bottom, and then on her thighs and up across her shoulders. One blow curled round her ribs and left a crimson mark on her right breast. She trembled as she cried and he smiled as he listened to the high, keening note that was creeping into her voice. Despite her tears and entreaties something dark and dangerous within her was responding to the energy he was pouring out. She wanted more.

He laid one last powerful lash across her welted hindquarters. Her feet beat a tattoo on the floor and he moved to her side as she stopped gyrating wildly. Her breathing calmed and she stared up at him. In her eyes he read fear and a drooling admiration. He placed a palm on her rump and she twisted round, thrusting her cunt at him.

He cupped it in his hand, long fingers finding the slippery crack of her arse and thrumming on her swollen clit. She flung back her head and screamed and he felt the vibrations as orgasm thundered through her.

'She's not had a man's weapon in her cunny, sire, nor yet in her anus,' Aswad informed him.

'I should hope not,' the king answered forcefully, dipping a finger into the copious juice flowing from her vulva, then lifting it to his nostrils and inhaling the strong, oceanic odour. 'Your head will be on the block if she's been tampered with in either orifice.'

'I want to watch you take her, brother,' his consort urged with a kind of panting eagerness, her slanting feline eyes feverish and bright. 'Then turn her over to me so that I can make sure she's suitably stretched with larger and larger lingams, till she's ready to receive you in her fundament.'

'And you want to play with her, too? Confess it. She's delectable, isn't she?' he said indulgently, running his wet finger down her cheek and letting it hover over her mouth.

She licked it, relishing the taste of the girl, her tongue coiling round it as if she sucked his cock. Then she replied, 'But of course. I'll teach her the sacred arts of love. Have I ever neglected my duty, lord?'

'Never, adored one,' he acknowledged. 'But now stand aside. I have another purpose for our throne. This is where the virgin shall be deflowered.'

She smiled, kissed him and stood on the steps, an arm resting across the shoulders of a sullen-looking youth. Her hand played with the chain attached to a studded collar banding his neck. Thongs hung from this, passing tightly across his ribcage, through an onyx ring in his navel, and down to form a harness for his cock.

'You may pleasure me while I watch, Jat,' she ordered and, grabbing one of his hands, thrust it between her legs.

Fury blazed in his eyes, his bearing still haughty in spite of the weals, both old and new, that scored his body with a ladder of stripes. She laughed, lips drawn back from her teeth like a wild-cat and, pinching his nipples till he grimaced, rode his hand in frenzied lust as she observed her brother.

The girl struggled, but Aswad soon had her sprawled among the damask cushions, holding her arms above her head while the king positioned himself between her widespread legs.

A drumbeat pulsed in the air, and voices rose in unison, chanting, 'Do it, lord king. Let her blood flow.'

Taking his erection to her pubis, he stared down into her eyes. Her lips formed the words, 'No. Please, sire. Don't.'

He slid to his knees between her thighs, placed his hands each side of her crack, widening the slippery wetness, then pushed his cock into her with full force. He felt a moment's resistance, then her hymen ruptured and he entered her tight passage, the pressure, the narrowness, the luscious juice which her body had produced in spite of her protests, making him groan with pleasure.

She thrashed and struggled still, but her cries were not those of a woman in torment, rather they resembled the yowling of a female cat on heat.

The audience went wild, cheering and whistling, inspired to throw aside all restraint and indulge their own desires, seeking gratification any way they could. Glancing up, he saw his sister clinging to her latest slave, one leg lifted to rest around his waist, rubbing her pubis against him.

The king paused, stayed still, let his phallus throb within the girl. She quivered beneath him. He could feel the heat radiating from her cunt. It seemed to clasp him like a velvet glove. Now that she wanted him his fire died a little. He never had found satisfaction in willing bedmates. He liked to use force, to exert his power, to make his victims suffer and break their spirit. The more they despised him, the more he relished the conquest.

He pulled out of her, signalled to Aswad who dragged her from the couch and, with a burly knee in the small of her back, made her sink to her knees again. The king stood there, legs wide spread, his strong thighs supporting his body, buttocks clenched, his cock standing out from his groin. He grabbed the girl, using her hair like a halter and dragging her against his crotch.

'Suck me,' he ordered.

He looked down, relishing her confusion and disgust, then felt her generous lips opening, taking part of his helm inside the warm wet cavity of her mouth. The surface of her tongue played round the stem. He pumped his hips and she gagged as his glans jabbed the back of her throat. His grip on her hair tightened and he controlled her motions, the fire rising in his loins, along his spine, into his brain. His cock throbbed as orgasm overwhelmed him, his ejaculation shooting out, filling her, choking her.

As he withdrew he was still spurting, his spunk spilling out over her face, her hair, her breasts. No disgust now. She was licking it in, cleaning the last of it from his shaft with her tongue.

He pushed her roughly away from him.

Later he lay in bed with his consort and she uncoiled from his body long enough to say, 'You subdue everyone, my king. But there is one woman who would resist you.'

'And who is that?' he said gloomily. Despite that evening's indulgences there remained a maggot of discontent within him.

'The daughter of the Northlander king.'

'Harcon? He should have yielded to me months ago. He refuses to join the confederacy. Silly old fool! How can he hope to withstand the power of my allies and myself.'

'He's a proud man, beloved, and his only child is even more stiff-necked. It would be nigh impossible to subdue her.'

He sat up restlessly, needled by this slur against his all-powerful might.

'No one can resist me,' he insisted.

She sat back on her haunches and regarded him with

violet eyes, the tip of her tongue roving over her scarlet lips. 'She's a warrior princess and no man has yet penetrated her body,' she added in her honeyed voice. 'Ravishingly beautiful, too, so my spies report.'

'Show her to me,' he growled, reaching for his whip, and her skin smarted with the remembrance of its kiss and her clitoris pulsed in anticipation of yet another climax. He was her master as well as that of the slaves.

'Jat!' she shouted into the dusk of the room. 'Bring me my scrying-glass.'

'You've trained him into obedience?' the king asked. Her methods of subduing slaves never ceased to amuse him. She did not stint on whip or rod, bondage and confinement. Not many withstood her.

'To an extent,' she said, her arched brows drawn down into a little frown. 'But he can still be defiant. He's not yet forgotten he's a prince.'

Jat returned, carrying an object covered by a black silk shroud.

She had him place it on a low carved table by the bed, then whipped away the silk, revealing a skull carved from a single large crystal. A wave of power emanated from it, very wise and very ancient and, like a sleepwalker, she turned the empty eye-sockets away from her and gazed at the domed cranium.

'What d'you see?' her brother asked.

'Wait. Give me time.'

Silence filled the room and, as they both stared, the skull appeared to sway and move and lose all shape. In its place came a thick grey mist that spread until it enveloped the crystal. Slowly the blackness receded and they were looking into a chamber, white and light and translucent. Diaphanous curtains stirred in the slight breeze. They hung from brass rods, draping a shell-shaped couch.

The king drew in a sharp breath and leaned closer, the

vision so rare and lovely that even he was overawed. This was quickly replaced by desire which, heavy and urgent, weighted his loins and roused his libido.

'That's her... the dark-haired beauty,' his witch sister murmured. 'See how she enjoys the caresses of her companion.'

His throat thickened, his phallus too, as he looked at the naked brunette. She was, perhaps, the most perfect creature he had ever seen, and his experience was legion. Her shapely limbs were wrapped around those of a lissom blonde woman, also very lovely, but none could compare with the dark one.

Lust for possession threatened to swamp him as he watched them caress one another and heard their moans of ecstasy smothered by passionate kisses. Lovely limbs twined and parted; slender hands explored breasts and labial folds; fingers fondled the hard little pleasure buds that crowned their clefts. They cried out when they climaxed together.

'Her name?' he gasped.

'Princess Varna.'

'And you say she's the daughter of my enemy, King Harcon?'

'That's right.'

'Put away your crystal – I've seen enough,' he stated, the grooves each side of his hard mouth deepening. 'He's been given warnings aplenty. Now I'll conquer him and possess her.'

Chapter One

She woke with a start, her skin cold and clammy, mind still snared in the most horrible nightmare.

A man, or something more than a man – an entity from other dimensions – had locked her will with his in an agonising mental duel.

Still petrified, she recalled every feature of his viciously handsome face, ruthless and imperious, with a full-lipped mocking mouth and eyes that blazed with the dark secrets of aeons.

Recently, when making love with Phila, she had experienced the uneasy feeling that they were being watched. This could not be, of course. The palace was too well guarded for interlopers, and yet it had been disturbing. It had happened again last night. Then, when she fell asleep, she was set upon by a being who she had felt to be evil incarnate.

Now, with a tremendous effort, she surfaced quickly. For an instant the other world clung stubbornly, that terrible vision more tangible than the reality of the dawn. Varna shuddered and slipped out of bed quietly so as not to awaken Phila. She slept on, sprawled across the tangled sheets, head buried in her arms like a slumbering child.

Varna caught a glimpse of herself in the oval wall mirror. Her face was pale under the healthy tan acquired through hours in the saddle, hunting, hawking and racing. There were mauve smudges below her amber eyes. Many said she was beautiful, but she took little notice. It was a far greater compliment when some renowned swordsman told her she wielded her weapon with skill or handled her javelin expertly. Then she would blush with pleasure, valuing her warrior expertise above all.

Suitors came courting her, but she had no interest in them and her father was not one of those despots who insisted his daughter marry someone of his choosing. King Harcon was a beneficent ruler, and Trokles had lived in peace with its neighbours for three hundred years. Varna intended that it should stay that way, her interest in arms purely those of any young athlete who wanted to enter tournaments and win contests. She balked at the idea of using them for war.

Yet something had changed her during the nocturnal hours, and she paused to stare more closely at her reflection. Her features were classical, a straight nose, wide brow and high cheekbones. Her mouth was generous and easily moved to laughter, but capable of great passion and hauteur.

'You have your mother's eyes,' her father often said, his bearded face softening. 'I always said they were the colour of sunshine pouring through wine, golden and sparkling.'

Sadness tinged any reference to his queen who had died when Varna was a baby. He had never married again, preferring to live a celibate existence filled with memories of the woman he had loved so deeply. Varna was his heir, and Trokles would be hers in the fullness of time, that peaceful country of rich soil and thriving crops, healthy cattle and a population who lived in harmony in the temperate climate. King Harcon encouraged the arts and funded universities. He was head of a tolerant, democratic government where all were free to worship whatever gods they chose and travellers were made welcome.

But though he rarely mentioned it, Varna knew he wanted to see her settled before he died. He thought she needed a husband to help with the responsibility of ruling, and children, too, heirs to the throne.

Varna sighed and moved back to the bed, looking down at her friend, companion and lover, the loyal Phila. The aroma of her body was sweet, reawakening Varna's passion. She reached down and ran a hand over Phila's pubis, her fingers tingling at the feel of those crisp fair curls, her own sex ripening again at the thought of being touched like that herself. Her hand drifted over Phila's breasts and the nipples hardened, even though she slept.

Growing up together, they had explored sexual desire and satisfied each another's bodily cravings. They talked of men and were curious about the act of love, wondering how it would feel to be penetrated by an erect phallus. To date, they shared a free and easy comradeship with the soldiers and squires with whom they sparred in the fencing schools and gymnasiums. Neither was given to flirtation, unlike the other ladies in which the court abounded.

Varna needed to talk to someone about her bad dream, but did not want to disturb Phila – only perhaps to make love again.

She would reserve that pleasure till later, she decided, and moved away. The marble floor was cool under her naked feet. It shone like opal in the rose-shot light. She shrugged on a cream robe. It clung to her slender body, the twin peaks of her nipples lifting the delicate fabric, the dark triangle of floss outlined at her mound. She walked out between arches into the garden. The breeze was heavy with spices. The morning hymn of praise to the day carolled from a hundred bird throats. The sick feeling of presentiment lessened as she raised her face to the sky.

The sun was rising in the east, blinding the sickle moon and dissolving the pale wisps of cloud. It came up in a burst of glory – gaudy greens and purples and orange. Flaming through a haze of gold and delicate greys, its great amorphous bulk was like a melting mirror, dribbling and spreading over the heavens, banishing the night.

Varna, leaning an elbow on the balustrade, had almost gained control of her panic. Surely evil could not flourish where there was so much beauty?

She comforted herself with this thought, gazing down over Ciophos. The buildings of the capital were designed so that they appeared to float, ethereal and spacious, blending with the muted greens of gardens and parks. Situated on the edge of a lagoon the palace overhung the water in some places, upheld by slender pillars rooted in the blue depths. The sound of water was everywhere – the gentle sucking of waves, the rain-spray fall of fountains tumbling into ornamental pools.

On the shore the silver sand met the sea. The forests skirting the spit were emerald, shimmering as the light increased, a heat haze already beginning to form. There was activity in the harbour; trawlers under sail and ferries and barges and pleasure-craft, too, as late-night revellers returned home. Several galleons rode at anchor in the harbour, richly adorned with gilded carvings, King Harcon's own vessel among them.

Ah, yes, Varna assured herself, the citizens are happy and prosperous, secure in the knowledge that my father and I are dedicated to preserving their future and that of their offspring. Our forebears grew weary of corrupt rule and treachery, and the ravages of war with its aftermath of plague and famine. All that is past history.

Happier now, she returned to her room, bending over to kiss Phila and wake her. She seemed confused at first, then arched her agile body, opened her hazel eyes and looked up at her with a smile.

'Good morning,' she murmured sleepily.

'It is a good morning, yes,' Varna agreed, every passing second restoring her faith and banishing that cold prickle of foreboding. 'And we've much to do. I've arranged to meet Duke Edorta to finalise details of the tournament.

We only have a month in which to prepare.'

'Oh, do you have to go so soon? Can't you come back to bed?'

It was too tempting to refuse and Phila moved, sensuous as a cat, making room for Varna. She half-sat, half-knelt, while Phila's hands explored her breasts through the silk robe, then eased it from her shoulders. The ache of desire made her brownish-pink nipples pucker.

Phila's hand travelled down to Varna's triangle and, 'You're very wet,' she said with satisfaction. 'So am I. Feel me.'

She rested back on an elbow, one knee raised, the other slack, the smell of arousal, like cinnamon and sandalwood, escaping from between her legs. Varna stared at her aware, as if for the first time, of those small tip-tilted breasts, strong hips and flat belly.

Reaching out, she made those breasts tremble as she stroked them with the back of her hand, and then pressed her face to them. Her own quivered in response.

Phila's cleft parted as Varna explored it. The sensation of soft wet smoothness was similar to when she masturbated, running her fingers over her own silky delta. Phila leaned forward and kissed her.

It was an intense kiss, filled with passion, and Varna slithered down till she could take one of Phila's nipples between her lips and suck it. The skin tasted nutty, the teat enlarging as she sucked and nipped and sucked some more, as a babe might at its mother's dug. At the same time her own were swelling, and she dived a hand down amidst Phila's luxuriant floss, finding her clitoris and rubbing it, the swift passage of her fingers bringing her to a rapid climax.

With her lover shaking and moaning under her hands, Varna's own needs were swamping her. Sensitive to this, Phila made love to her slowly, hearts beating close, moved by a common pulse. She lay between Varna's thighs, mouthing her clit and cunt as if she was devouring her partner's pleasure. And Varna angled herself to give her greater access, thrusting upwards. Phila's tongue flicked over the fat bud protruding from its cowl.

Varna strained to reach her crisis, her hands in Phila's hair. It was almost too intense. She was stranded on the plateau, unable to reach the longed-for peak. Phila's fingers joined her tongue and she pinched Varna's clitoris, coaxing her up and over.

'Oh... oooh,' Varna cried as she reached the acme of bliss.

Now they played a different game, going further, deeper into one another, lying belly to belly or back to buttocks, rubbing their slits together, the air ripe with musky female sap. They scooped at each other's cloven inlets, drank the flesh and the fluids, the very quintessence of their womanly parts. Varna was intoxicated with the savours, scents and tastes that entranced her till, momentarily exhausted, they rested among the tangled sheets.

They were roused by hurried footsteps outside followed by frantic hammering at the door.

'Princess, open up,' a male voice shouted. 'The king requires your presence urgently.'

Varna swung her sun-browned legs over the side of the bed and grabbed for her robe, dragging it on as she crossed the room and flung the door wide. Her father's equerry snapped his heels together and saluted, though his gold-frogged blue uniform was awry and his expression one of extreme alarm.

'What is it, Count Gentza?' she demanded, all those bad feelings returning tenfold.

'A messenger rode in at daylight... near dead from his wounds. He'd managed to escape and ride here through the night.'

'What's happened? Tell me, man!'

'The eastern border was attacked at dusk.'

'Attacked? By whom?' Varna blurted out. Her brain did not seem to be functioning properly.

'Valdivian soldiers, my lady.'

'But why? I thought the matter settled. My father refused to enter into an alliance with them. We entertained their envoys and they accepted his decision. They returned to King Lagras and he hasn't troubled us since.'

'I doubted his sincerity at the time, princess,' Gentza said. 'Your father is too trusting. He trusts everyone. They say Lagras is a sorcerer, and has used dark powers to subdue the other states, swallow them whole and make them part of his empire.'

Varna's heart sank, but she remained outwardly calm as she replied, 'Tell me exactly what happened. I'll see this messenger and question him.'

'This isn't possible. He died an hour ago. It seems that three towns along the border were attacked simultaneously with much slaughter and destruction. No one was prepared for such a thing.'

'This is outrageous,' Varna stormed. 'Has anyone informed the Valdivian ambassador? No? Then do so at once. Lagras shall pay for this outrage. Out of my way, sir. I must go to my father.'

The humid air was thick with the clamour of battle. A lurid glow enveloped the plain. The heavens had opened and rain cascaded from black thunderclouds. Forked lightning blasted the scene in an unnatural blue-white glare.

In that morass of mud and blood men were locked in deadly combat. Their shouts rose above the roar of the storm – fierce battle cries – yells of rage – screams of agony. Horns blared, arrows sang, and steel belled on steel. War horses reared and wheeled, as intent on maiming as were their riders. Their iron-shod hooves trampled the mushy earth and their teeth snapped savagely.

Varna was cornered. She had been driven towards an outcrop of rock. She stumbled over heaped corpses, her sandal-boots squelching in the ooze. Her breath rasped and sweat trickled into her eyes from beneath her helmet. Her sword arm was numb, but she continued to deflect blows, protecting herself with her round shield.

The voice of her instructor seemed to ring in her brain. 'That's it! Strike! Hold the sword steady! Now! Whirl it over your head. Slash! Cut!'

'By Tammuz, the wench can fight,' one of her assailants grunted in a foreign tongue. He was of an alien race who prayed to alien gods, but Varna was familiar with the language.

She stood her ground, adrenaline pumping, every nerve and sinew tingling. She had never felt more alive. A savage yell came roaring up from her belly and out through her snarling lips as her broadsword ripped open the speaker's throat. Blood spurted from the jugular vein, spattering Varna's short leather kilt and metal-studded jerkin. She wore bands on her forearms to give added strength to her wrists, and greaves to protect her legs from ankle to knee. But even so her figure-hugging armour left no doubt that it was a woman who wielded the weapon.

There was a drumming in her ears, a fiery mist blinding her eyes and a white-hot excitement within her. Had she been a man, she was sure she would have had an erection. As it was her secret lips were swollen, and her pleasure bud hard.

The four remaining enemy soldiers stepped over their fallen comrade. They were tall and olive-skinned, with square-cut black beards. Their shields were gone, their breastplates dented, and their helmets showed the marks of fierce strokes. Blood smeared their clothing and crimson gouts dripped from their swords.

'What are you doing on the battlefield, bitch? You fight like a veteran,' growled the leader. 'Tell me your name so that King Lagras may know who it was I raped before beheading her.'

'You'll tell him nothing,' she grated. 'But when you reach hell inform the monster who guards the gates that you died at the hand of Princess Varna, daughter of King Harcon.'

'Not I,' the man boasted, grinning wickedly. 'I'll get a medal, I shouldn't wonder, for it's said that you're a cold virgin who's never been fucked. Open your legs and yield, then when me and my mates have finished shafting you, we'll kill you.'

'Never!' Varna hissed.

The Valdivian leapt, his sword curving in a deadly arc. Varna side-stepped. The blade glanced across her helmet in a shower of sparks. As she recovered balance she thrust upwards. Her sword slid beneath her opponent's raised arm. The point bit through chain-mail, flesh, bone and heart. He dropped like a felled oak.

His mates closed in on Varna. She backed away, grinding the face of a corpse deeper into the mud with her heel. She struck out, hearing one of them yelp and beating down the weapon of another. How she wished Phila was at her side, but they had been separated early on. The battle had raged all day and she was tired. Her limbs felt like lead.

The soldiers renewed their attack and she was horrified by the lust in their eyes. They looked mad – cruel – determined to ravish her. Surely fate could not have ordained that she surrender her virginity and her life to such as these?

She felt herself falling, tripping over a body wearing the blue colours of her own side. His dead hand still gripped the hilt of a broken sword, his head thrown back, chin tilting towards the sky. A Northlander, like herself.

The courage was draining out of her. There were too many blue clad corpses, the field littered with them, while the scarlet and black clad Valdivians seemed as strong as ever.

That pause cost her dear. The soldiers seized and disarmed her. Something struck her across the brow, dislodging her helmet. It fell to the ground and her sable-hued hair tumbled free.

'Ye gods! What a find!' exclaimed one of the ruffians. 'I'll have first go at her, lads, seeing as I'm your sergeant. We'll do it in order of rank.'

'But we're foot soldiers,' grumbled the others. 'How'll we decide?'

'On the turn of a coin,' he advised, barely heeding them as he leaned over Varna.

He was a mercenary from somewhere beyond the seas, but for the moment he was in Lagras's army. He was shorter than the rest, and stocky, his skin the colour of well-tanned hides, and he peered down at her with dark eyes set in a network of wrinkles. He held a razor-sharp dagger in one hand, the point pricking her throat.

'I reckon you'd better do as I say, girl. Princess or no bloody princess, I intend thrusting my cock into you,' he said in a guttural accent.

It was the first time she had ever been helpless and under a man's domination and the sensation was not pleasant. He stank of sweat, mud and ale. He was scarred, he was crude. He had obviously done his full share of murder and rapine. But the dagger tip warned her not to resist him – if she wanted to go on living. And she did. Most definitely.

'Let me go,' she said with freezing calm. 'I'll ask my father to pardon you.'

He flung up his head and bellowed with laughter. The rain saturated his face and formed runnels over his hairy chest and down the arms that held her captive. 'King

Harcon?' he roared. 'And what will he do? The battles lost, sweetheart. We're victorious. You'll be sold into slavery, and will thank me for taking your maidenhead. I'll be more merciful than some perverted toss-pot who buys you at the slave auction, or a whorehouse bawd who'll want to get her money's worth.'

'Get on with it, sergeant,' one of his men urged, the front of his breeches already undone, his cock poking out. He was rubbing it vigorously, little drops of pre-come wetting the end.

Varna remained passive, but her mind was whirling. She recalled every one of the moves her martial arts teacher had taught her. She brought up her knee, ramming it into the sergeant's testicles, then, when he yelled and doubled up, rolled out from under him.

'No, you don't,' shouted one of the others, younger than the rest, a fledgling soldier but strong and wiry. He thrust a foot between Varna's and brought her crashing to the mud again.

His hand was under her bottom, widespread across the fleshy globes, and he kept her still with the force of his muscular legs tangled with hers. Varna gasped as he pressed his pubis to her belly, making her aware of the heat and thickness of his cockstem through the coarse woven trousers he wore.

She could not get her breath as their combined weight pressed her buttocks into his opened palm. To accommodate this her thighs were forced wide, cramping the inner muscles. His middle finger penetrated upwards, pushing aside the thong that protected her sex lips, sliding along her wet crack and finding her clitoris. It pulsed, making her hips jerk. He smiled knowingly into her face. Shame burned within her. She should be grasping her knife and plunging it into his back, not experiencing arousal. But when he rubbed her again the feeling could not be denied, rooted between her legs, strong and sexual.

She had never been touched like that by a man before.

'No!' she cried, and threshed beneath him. 'Get off me, you bastard!'

For answer he tore at the lacing of her jerkin, baring her breasts and pinching the nipples. They stood out like ripe berries and he stared at them avidly.

'Hold the bitch!' he shouted and she felt her arms dragged above her head, while he pushed up her kilt and tugged at the thong. The side fastening snapped. He knelt over her, his stiff cock already bared for action. It was big – bigger than she had ever imagined a man's weapon to be. She could feel it pushing against her opening as he struggled for penetration.

A scream rose in her throat, the desperate scream of a woman being violated. What use her warrior training now? As if illumined by the savage flash of lightning that crackled overhead, she was horribly aware of the weakness of woman-flesh that made her the victim of men.

'Go on. Spear her. Drive it into her,' his comrades urged, and each one had his penis out.

Varna glimpsed a row of cocks, tumescent and ready, their owners polishing them, rubbing the shiny red heads. The sight held a horrible fascination, and her feelings of fury were being transformed into a heat that fanned through her loins.

The young soldier was panting with exertion, his cockhead at her vulva. She struggled furiously, but now they had been joined by others who held her wrists, making movement impossible.

Suddenly everything changed. A shock went through them – through her, too.

They grunted. Astonishment blanked their eyes. The young rapist gasped and slumped on her. The others toppled and fell, arrows protruding from their shoulder-blades. The blindness cleared from Varna's sight. Hands were there to raise and support her. Other soldiers, but big-boned, ruddy-skinned, fair-haired. Her father's men.

'Highness,' said Duke Edorta, covered in muddy and bleeding from many wounds. 'Are you hurt?'

'No,' she said, managing to keep her voice steady as she adjusted her kilt. It was a brief garment, designed for action and speed, but with the thong gone her naked sex showed at almost every move. The duke handed her a cloak which she shrugged around herself, then retrieved her helmet and placed it on her head.

'The king is asking for you,' Edorta said, and in his eyes she read defeat. Her heart plummeted like a stone.

She followed him behind the boulders, ducking and weaving to avoid arrows. He led her back to the field, the din and the slaughter, to where a circle of men were struggling to protect the blue and silver standard of Trokles. They were attacked relentlessly by the enemy whose leather armour was scaled with iron and who were equipped with axes, broadswords and spears.

King Harcon lay beneath the tattered banner that swirled in the storm. Varna crouched at his side, blinded by tears and rain. 'Father, oh, my father,' she sobbed.

With a groan he raised himself, and she stared, appalled at the gaping wound in his chest, and at others renting his mail. An arrow was embedded in his thigh, his powerful body bleeding in a dozen places.

'Listen to me, Varna,' he said, gripping her arm. 'This is a black day for Trokles. King Lagras has beaten us, but all is not lost... not forever. You can save the country.' Death was etched on his strong features but the light in his eyes was undiminished.

She could not believe that he was dying, her wise father who had never stinted in his affection for her. 'How can I do that, when you and your army have failed?' she whispered, bowing her head.

The circle was growing smaller as one Northlander

after another fell. 'The Valdivians are winning, crushing all who stand in their way,' Harcon said. 'Under the leadership of their emperor, Lagras. He's a magician, a madman, a tyrant who has resolved that Trokles, the last kingdom on the continent to stand against him, should be vanquished.'

'Then all is lost. How can I resist his power?' she whispered.

He struggled to sit up. Count Gentza supported him. The faithful aide was battle-stained and near death himself, his eyes bleak as they sought hers.

'You can do it,' the king insisted. 'But the way will be hard. You'll need allies. Run for the forests. Hide yourself. Don't let Lagras capture you. Help will come. The gods have promised.'

'Hush, my lord, don't distress yourself,' Gentza pleaded, holding a leather water bottle to the king's lips.

'I must speak with my daughter of the prophecy,' he muttered, blood trickling from the corner of his mouth.

'I don't understand,' she said. 'What must I do? What is this prophesy?'

'"When night eats the sun, when the old wolf is slain, then the she-cub shall conquer,"' he murmured hoarsely. 'Run, Varna, run. If you fall into Lagras's hands he will enslave you. Go deep into the wilderness. Put your faith in the gods and all will be revealed.'

He started to choke and blood frothed from his mouth.

'Do something!' Varna shouted to Edorta and Gentza, but they shook their heads. Harcon's eyes closed. His head fell to one side and they laid him back on the trampled sod.

'Go, princess... Go!' Gentza urged.

The bodyguards were dying round their chieftain, and Varna snatched a sword from one of the slain and crawled towards a heap of large rocks that lay between her and the brooding forest that spread out at one side of the plain. She crouched there, peering between a gap, watching the final destruction of the Northlander army.

Horsemen bristling with weapons seized the Trokles standard and circled the dead king. None was mightier than the man on an ebony stallion caparisoned for war. He was motionless. An awe-inspiring figure, he wore black armour. His mail was of woven gold, and a scarlet cloak swept down across his mount's sweating flanks.

Varna could not see his face. This was hidden by the visor of his helmet. Sombre and quiet he sat, and his men became still, too, awaiting his command. Nothing broke the silence except the distant rumble of the retreating storm and the cries of men in their death throes.

Overhead vultures wheeled.

'It is done, lord and master,' shouted one of the commanders, leaping from his horse and approaching Harcon's body. 'Would you have his head?'

The sun came out, beating hot on the bloody field. The earth began to steam. The storm was over, as was the battle on the Asgrid Plain. Lagras lifted a black gloved hand and his deep voice rang out.

'Bring it to me!'

Mercifully the broad backs of Lagras's henchmen blocked Varna's view, but in the next instant a cheer rang out and she caught a glimpse of something held aloft – something bloody that swung by its long greying hair.

The soldiers roared, chanting one name only. 'Lagras the Dark One! Lagras! Lagras! Death to his enemies! Power to his sword! May he live forever!'

They were silenced by a gesture from him. 'The king of Trokles is slain,' he boomed. 'He had a daughter... a girl who fought like a man. Find her and deliver her into my hands, dead or alive.'

Varna flattened her back against the rock and searched desperately for somewhere to hide. There was no cave, not even a crevice in that smooth surface. The forest was a distance away. Even if she ran her hardest it would be impossible to escape the enemy horsemen. There was no help for it. She would stand and fight and die, taking as many of Lagras's soldiers with her as she could.

She could hear them coming, shouting, hunting their human prey. She remembered her near rape, the feel of sweaty male flesh, the hardness of their cocks and her own shameful response.

'Udin,' she whispered, evoking the All-giver, the mighty god of Trokles. 'If you have a purpose for me to fulfil, then help me now.'

It was suddenly too much; her weariness, her wounds, the death of her father. Dizziness filled her head, a sensation of falling, but slowly, peacefully, sinking into the rock which seemed to melt under her hands. She felt herself drawn into it as if by protective arms. She slept, but did not sleep, held in an enchantment. She was surrounded by darkness, yet could see. What seemed to be a sheet of transparent water lay between her and the Valdivian soldiers who clumped round a corner.

They started ferreting about, their swords glittering in the sunshine as they looked for her. One of them stared straight in her direction, then turned away. She heard him speak to his companions, but his voice was faint.

'She's not here,' he said. 'We'll have to search among the corpses.'

'We've got to find her,' one of his mates replied, his face fearful. 'Lagras will flay us alive if we fail.'

'There she goes!' shouted another from the top of the rock. He was pointing into the distance. 'Look! It's like she's on a demon horse.'

'After her. Catch her,' they chorused as they vaulted into their saddles.

Varna heard the thunder of hooves and saw with her new inner sight. A fugitive was galloping across the plain, a girl on a piebald mare. She looked exactly like herself.

Varna knew this to be a mirage, but the cavalry were in pursuit. Hardly anyone remained on the battlefield except the scavengers detailed to bury the Valdivian dead and rob the Trokles cadavers before leaving them to the jackals and raptors.

'That's got rid of them rather neatly,' said a voice from somewhere above her. 'Useful that. A sleight of hand, my dear. A conjuring trick. Soldiers are stupid brutes at the best of times. Not strong in the brain department.'

She found herself in the shadow of the rock, no longer absorbed into it. She shaded her eyes with one hand and stared up.

Standing on a ledge was the most amazing vision she had ever seen. An armoured figure – a man, perhaps? Yet he seemed as insubstantial as smoke. His hair, flaxen with a blue sheen, flowed from under a winged helmet and his mail-coat shone with the iridescence of a dragonfly's wings.

'Who are you?' Varna challenged, her fingers tightening round the sword hilt.

'Asvald, the messenger of the gods. You asked for help, didn't you?' he replied nonchalantly.

He was so beautiful that she was almost speechless. But all this talk of gods? She was not sure she believed in any of it. Her prayer to Udin had been out of habit more than faith.

'I've heard of you,' she said cautiously. 'Aren't you also named The Prankster?'

'That's right. And you didn't really think I existed,' he answered, smiling. 'Not to be wondered at, Princess Varna. The gods and their realms are invisible to most humans, but these are exceptional circumstances. You've inherited second sight from your mother's mother. Some say she was a great friend of the elves, and they gave it to her.'

'D'you expect me to believe all that?' Varna said loftily.

'Who are you really? How do I know you're not one of Lagras's spies?'

'Don't be foolish!' he snapped, and the blue aura that surrounded him was shot with crimson. 'Use your gift.'

'You talk like a madman,' she replied disdainfully. 'I'm no seer. I'll leave rune magic to old women and crazy hermits. I wish for no part in it.'

'Wish or no, it's there. Much good fighting has done you. Time to try other methods.'

Those twilight blue eyes looked into hers and she felt as if she was drowning in them, forced to recognised truths she had always struggled to ignore – dreams that came upon her willy-nilly – an affinity with animals, forests and the strange creatures that inhabited them. This had always been there since her earliest memory.

'How is magic going to help me?' she continued. 'My country will now groan under Lagras's tyranny. My people will be enslaved.'

'Don't despair.' Asvald was on her level now. He looked solid: a warrior in a glittering breastplate, a silver-hilted sword in one hand, a spear in the other.

'That's one reason why I'm here. Most inconvenient. There I was, enjoying an orgy with some of the minor gods and goddesses, when along comes one of those ravens belonging to Udin. It flapped and squawked and made a frightful din. Said it had a message from him. I was to go and assist you, at once.'

'And who is that person being chased by Lagras and his men?' she asked, so disoriented that she wondered if she was suffering from the blow to her head.

'Nothing but a mirage, princess. The Valdivians are a misbegotten crew who owe their allegiance to gods other than Udin. Oh, I know Lagras is a sorcerer and commands cohorts of demons, but he's no match for me.'

Asvald swung round on his heel, whistling softly. He was answered by the whinny of a splendid horse who, like him, was made up of a strong, yet not quite fleshy, substance. Its coat was blue. Its mane and tail floated like golden gossamer, finer than spiders' webs. It was shod in sparkling silver.

Asvald sprang into the saddle and Varna mounted behind him. Then they were off, those glittering hooves skimming the ground and rising into the sky.

Looking down, Varna could see a long line of horsemen as the Valdivians continued to chase her double. Then the forest loomed up on the horizon.

The horse touched down, snorting and pawing the ground as he was reined in. Varna slid from his back. Asvald looked at her thoughtfully. 'Goodbye, princess,' he said.

Loneliness choked her. 'You're not coming with me?' she asked.

He shook his head, his smile faintly mocking. 'I can't enter here.'

Her head was aching and she passed a hand over her tear-streaked face, saying, 'I'm afraid. It's awful. My father's dead.'

He suddenly appeared beside her, though she had not seen him move. 'Don't mourn him. He's with your mother now.'

She stared into the blue mystery of his eyes and then it seemed that he was kissing her, gently at first, then harder. She wound her arms round his neck, or thought she did, but he was so translucent she could not get a grip on him.

She felt him, though: the hardness of his magical phallus pressed against her pubis, and her clitoris pulsed. It was as if she was naked.

Now he was everywhere, nipping her breasts, lapping her navel, working his way up the back of her legs, that warm wet tongue-tip finding the crease of her buttocks and dipping into the amber crack to find her quivering anus. He circled and played, then concentrated on her dark floss, parting her moist labia and stroking her clitoris.

She writhed and murmured under the torture of ethereal caresses that felt solid and real. She saw them as colourful patterns dancing in her head, and the dance grew more frenzied. Her body shook, and the narrow division between pain and pleasure blurred completely. The sensation seemed to go on forever, and she did not know if she was dying slowly or erupting into orgasm, caught up in the awesome explosion as she rubbed herself against his tongue, his lips, his teeth.

She wanted him, crying out, 'Take me, Asvald. Take me!'

And instantly, abruptly, she was aware that he had gone.

She fell to the forest floor. Her clothing was in place, but her vagina spasmed as the waves of pleasure receded. She clutched her arms about her, doubting her sanity. A voice whispered on the breeze, promising to return. Then it was in her head, shifting timbre, becoming a woman's voice calling her name, a voice she knew.

'Varna! Are you there?'

Phila came through the trees, but Varna was too dazed to reply. She stared down at her dusty armour and ran a hand through her tangled hair.

How long had that beautiful episode with Asvald lasted? It seemed to have absorbed her entire life. And how could she have been brought to climax by a being such as he? Had this, too, been a dream, like that nightmare she'd had not long ago which had presaged disaster?

Chapter Two

The forest was dense. It was a place of swamps and dripping gloom and decaying vegetation. The trunks of the trees rose straight as lances towards the hidden sky where interlacing branches formed a canopy, festooned with sickly-perfumed flowers and fleshy-stemmed creepers.

'We must find shelter before dark,' Varna said, walking carefully, muscles tensed, fist balled round the cross-guard of her sword. 'I've never seen such a loathsome spot.'

'Didn't your heavenly messenger warn you, this Asvald you've been raving on about?' commented Phila pithily.

'No, he didn't, and I wish I hadn't mentioned him,' Varna retorted.

'D'you know what I think?' Phila said briskly.

'No, but I suppose you're going to tell me.'

'I think you were overwrought, had a smack on the head and imagined the whole thing.'

'It was real. *He* was real. The pleasure he gave me was real. But does it matter? We're in mortal danger. Lagras is after us and we've landed up in this hellhole.'

'You're not wrong,' Phila agreed, shuddering as she looked around her.

Unhealthy, fever-ridden, the forest breathed out a miasma of death. The rotting remains of fallen trees harboured aggressive insects. Flies rose in clouds, and everywhere was a tangle of undergrowth. It crept over the ground, scaled the trunks, and hung web-like overhead, as if spun by some ghastly spider lurking there to trap its prey.

'Udin!' Varna breathed aloud, chilled with superstitious dread, though her jerkin was soaked with sweat. 'Have you any idea which way we're heading?'

'No,' Phila said, and then gave up trying to be brave. She clung to Varna's hand, her big eyes shining in the dimness. 'But I'm so glad I found you. I was worried to death. I thought you'd been taken prisoner, or killed. Oh, Varna, what are we going to do?'

They hugged each other, and Varna gave up the struggle to control her grief. Her father was dead, and the hurt inside her like an open wound. The feel of Phila's body brought a measure of comfort and she longed to lie in her arms somewhere safe, to cry her heart out and be soothed and petted and brought to completion. Even now, even *here*, the familiar heat of passion coursed along her veins and into her belly.

The bareness of her mound attracted her attention constantly; it was damp and warm, the kilt offering scant protection. She was unaccustomed to being without a cache-sex of some sort, be it never so brief, when she donned fighting gear. It was too humid to wear her cloak. This was slung across her back.

'We'll survive. Asvald won't let us die,' she promised, with more confidence than she was feeling. 'Come along. Maybe we can find a dry cave and light a fire.'

'I'm hungry,' Phila moaned.

'So am I.'

'And I want you.'

'I know.'

They moved on. There was no sound except the sucking noise as their feet crossed the boggy leaves and matted grasses, but Varna had the unnerving feeling that they were being observed by invisible eyes. It was an ominous silence. No bird calls, no chatter of parrots, no jaguar's cough.

The ground started to rise, but they had not travelled

far when they suddenly halted. There were noises ahead, shouts and burst of raucous laughter.

'Valdivians?' Phila whispered.

'Let's take a look.'

The undergrowth had thinned. Where several gargantuan trees had crashed down, the last of the sun's rays poured through the gaps. Varna crept closer and quietly parted the bushes. In the centre of the glade a brushwood fire crackled, illumining the scene with leaping flames.

Dread gripped her gut. The noisy beings she had heard were trolls. She had encountered them before. They were a dying breed, part human, part monster, thick-witted, cruel and mean.

Broad and squat, with bandy legs and splayed feet, these were dressed in animal skins and pieces of tarnished armour. Their skin shone with a grey-green hue. Some were bald, while others had shocks of thick, wiry hair. All were intensely ugly.

Stocky horses with shaggy coats and feathery forelocks jingled their harnesses and whinnied restlessly in the background. Their saddlebags bulged with plunder. Varna guessed she had stumbled across a troll raiding party.

In a high state of excitement they waved their spears and choppers, barking and grunting and baring their teeth at the girl who confronted them. Her legs were as long and supple as a dancer's, and she wore a jerkin of gilded leather over a short linen skirt. The sight of her lithe and lovely body was driving the trolls crazy.

She stood there defiantly, eyes snapping with fury, both hands clasped round the pommel of her broadsword. Her limbs were sun-bronzed, rendered darker by the flames. Her boots were tightly laced about her calves. A headband crossed her brow, restraining the tawny hair that cascaded over her shoulders. Several dead trolls lay at her feet.

The rest capered around her jeering, but keeping well

out of the way of her weapon. Then one feinted with his spear, aiming at her breasts. She knocked it aside with the flat of her blade. Another took his place, a grin twisting his flat-nosed face. Swinging her sword, the girl yelled a battle cry and fetched him a blow that severed his hand from his hairy arm. He backed off, howling, blood spurting from the stump.

'Get her, you fools!' bellowed their leader, his thickset form clad in a torn surcoat many sizes too small. He had a helmet cocked to one side of his skull-like head. 'By Hraesvelgur, the swallower of dead men's flesh! Are you afraid of a girl? I want to see her stripped naked and bound to a tree. I want to flog her arse and whip her breasts. I want to ram my prick into her cunt and up her arse. I want to hear her scream. My cock's ready. Look. Have you ever seen a finer one?'

He was hopping about like a great toad, his gnarled appendage swinging and bobbing as he displayed it lewdly, his balls dangling in their hairy purse.

'I'll do it, Krill. I'll catch her, and when we've all had our fill of her hole, I'll kill and cook her for you,' one of his minions cried, and released a stone from his sling. It hit the girl on the shoulder, spinning her round.

The trolls swept forward like a muddy tide, hallooing triumphantly. Krill lumbered after them, brandishing a stone mallet mounted on a shaft the size of a small pine. The girl fell, but Varna did not attack. There were too many of them. She must wait for the right moment.

Now Krill dragged the girl to her feet, his dirty hands exploring her body lecherously. He tore at her clothing till it hung around her in tatters. She outfaced him, as proud in her nakedness as she had been when covered. Varna's loins stirred. The girl was slim, with the muscular look of someone who trained hard to keep in trim. But her breasts were large and high, crested with dusky nipples. She had a flat belly and hips that flared out from a narrow waist, and her flaxen bush was neatly trimmed.

Krill leered and, while she was held by others, took his cock to her pubis, rubbing it over her clitoris. The girl did not flinch, merely stared at him contemptuously. He forced her to her knees and inserted his phallus in her mouth, holding her head firmly in his massive paws and forcing it up and down over his meaty stem. He groaned as he used her, but did not take his final pleasure, holding back.

The trolls roared and urged him on, but he shouted, 'Not yet! Not yet! She must suffer first. This will make it all the sweeter. Tie her up. She's to be punished. She killed some of my men.'

They marched their prisoner to where two saplings grew close together. She was turned towards them, her arms seized, forced wide, and tethered by the wrists to the trunks. Then her legs were spread apart and her ankles bound. This exposed the rounded cheeks of her backside and bared the furrow between.

Krill drooled as he fingered her. She flinched, but could not escape that rude handling. He drove two fingers into her vulva, drawing them out, then pushing them in again, imitating the movement of coition. And his other hand, big as a shovel, reached round to the front and squeezed her breasts and tweaked the nipples.

'You like that, don't you, deary?' he crooned, spittle hanging in strings from his mouth. 'Your cunny is all wet for me. I can feel it, slippery as a serpent's trail, and smell it, too. Lovely ripe pussy smell!'

'You filthy bastard!' the girl shouted, the disdain in her tone cutting like a knife.

His hideous face turned livid. He used her brutally, pinching and slapping her. His hands tortured her breasts and his fingers forced her open and lifted her high. Her toes scrabbled for a purchase on the pine carpet as he impaled her.

He let her go abruptly and unwound a horsewhip from his paunchy waist.

Varna, hidden in the scrub, tensed as he flung back his arm.

The whip whistled and the girl bucked as it landed on her buttocks. A vivid red line formed almost at once. Krill grunted and the lash bit deep again. She writhed, jerking at her bonds in a futile effort to escape the pain. He braced himself and let fly another blow. And another. His men were beside themselves, staring fixedly at the vivid lines that marked the girl's fleshy hinds. They grasped their crotches, licked their thick lips in anticipation, and dribbled strings of saliva on to their erect cocks, rubbing themselves vigorously.

Varna could take no more, appalled to see the welts darkening, blood-red where they bisected the girl's buttocks at the widest part. She could hear the breath rasping in the captive's throat, and felt every blow as if it was her own cringing body being abused.

'Ready, Phila?' she muttered.

'Aye, ready.'

'Then let's go!'

As one they leapt into the clearing.

The magic had begun. Sandor could feel it, taste it, smell it. It touched the crown of his head, penetrated, darted down his spine and settled in his loins, making his cock thicken. He recognised that sensation. Something exciting and significant was about to happen.

He strode along the woodland path, a striking young man, six foot six inches tall, with strong features and straight brown hair. His aquiline profile and wild green eyes made him look like an arrogant bird of prey; beautiful, but dangerous.

Alert, waiting for the magic to manifest, he found his favourite place, a waterfall that crashed down into a natural basin. He undressed and dived in, then surfaced, throwing back his soaking hair. He stood beneath the torrent letting it pour over him, lifting his face to the invigorating sting and washing the sweat from his body, working up over his thighs and massaging his bottom hole and genitals.

This had the inevitable result. His wet penis swelled into a stiff erection between his fingers. He removed himself from the waterfall to a more tranquil section of the pool, then lay on his back, his balls floating, his hair drifting around his head. He dreamed, staring up to where the sun dappled through the leaves, and his dreams did not feature glory or adventures, but women. He could almost feel their lips on his mouth, his body and his cock, their hair forming a curtain over his face, a perfumed cloud wherein he might lose himself.

He knew so little about them, and they fascinated him. Instinct told him there was an exploit just around the corner. Would this include them? Was he about to learn the mysteries of their bodies, a thing so far denied him?

His cock pointed towards the sky, and he began to work his loosely curled fingers up and down its length. This was good. This was perfect. This would suffice until he was able to find a girl who would let him touch her breasts and bury his manhood in her quim. He was not familiar with the courtship rituals of human beings, but had watched animals mating. He was confident he would know what to do when the time came.

He could feel his balls starting to tense but, wanting to enjoy every last ounce of pleasure, he waded to the pool's edge and stretched himself out on his wolf-skin cloak.

Eyes closed, he let his right hand stray down to his tumescent shaft. He lost all awareness of anything save the ecstatic sensation as he touched the ridge of his rolled-back foreskin and anointed his glans with the juice seeping from its eye. His hand was big, but his cock filled it, a large organ that matched the rest of him.

Passion was taking over, gathering in his groin, bubbling and boiling in his cock. He could no longer control it. He gasped and worked himself frantically, feeling the onset of bliss. His cock twitched and his semen shot forth, bedewing his fingers – once, twice and a final jet that sprayed his chest and belly.

He did not let go at once, fondling the tip gently to encourage the last bit of sensation, then he lay supine and flung an arm over his eyes, replete but not quite satisfied. He needed a woman, and soon.

After resting, then washing away his spunk, he put on his clothes, fastened his sword-belt and bundled up the cloak. A glance at the sun told him he was heading homewards.

He had tracked bears, wild boar and tigers through the mountains, endured the bitter winds and snows of the peaks, battled with the Frost-Giants and creatures of the netherworld but, though he knew this forest like the back of his hand, it was hazardous. Always ready for action, he was passing beneath a particularly dense leafy canopy when he heard a slithering sound above his head.

He froze.

With a rush something shot down and wound itself about his body.

He looked up into the cold yellow eyes of a serpent, a double-fanged abomination, its venom-dripping jaws gaping wide. Part of its twenty-foot length had an unbreakable grip on a tree. The rest was fastened round him in a bone-crushing grip. His left arm was pinioned, but his right was free.

Feet planted firmly, Sandor braced himself against the monster's strength, whipped out his sword and sliced at that scaly, mottled skin. The serpent writhed and knotted, striving to throw a coil round his arm, but the blade rose again, hacking off its head. It flew into the bushes. Sandor was showered with stinking black fluid. The pulsating coils fell away.

In the serpent's place stood a beautiful woman. Her hair melded with the flora – greens and reds and fiery chestnut. Her body undulated like the serpent she had just inhabited, her diaphanous garment revealing spherical breasts with nipples the size of cob-nuts, and a pubis that was high and clearly defined. He knew who she was and put up his defences.

'Cragfor. Why are you here?' he cried angrily.

The enchantress laughed, a low-pitched sound that stirred his cock into life again. 'Sandor, my pet. That's not very welcoming,' she scolded, her voice husky. Then she fixed him with her magnetic golden eyes. 'When are you going to let me enjoy that magnificent body of yours? I ache for your fresh young prick.'

'Never,' he said grimly. 'I want a real, flesh and blood woman, not a treacherous nixie.'

Her smile grew cold, more icily sensual. 'That's an insult. I'm no water-sprite. Too powerful by far. You'd best beware, Sandor, and do as I ask. Come now, it won't be so bad, will it? I can show you pleasures you've never dreamed existed. I watched you bringing yourself off just now. You're dying for it, aren't you, sweetheart.'

He could not drag his eyes from her, though this was not the first time she had tempted him. He stood and stared and was possessed of a burning need that culminated in his loins.

'Why did you try to kill me a moment ago?' he asked, succeeding in looking away and regaining some of his control.

She laughed again, a brittle sound like breaking glass. 'I wouldn't have hurt you. That wasn't my intention. I wanted you to take notice of me, to stop mooning about after human women. I can give you eternal life – make you my king – the king of the Forbidden Mountain.'

'I don't want your gifts. Let me pass.'

'You don't mean that,' she whispered, and her eyes went down to his stone-hard dick that strained at the lacing of his codpiece.

She sank to her knees, positioning herself before it.

Desire worked like yeast within him. Why shouldn't you enjoy her? urged an insidious voice in his brain. Yet he knew she was a witch. If he gave in to her persuasion and his own needs, then he would be hers forever.

'No,' he said, and pushed her away.

'Why not? Want to play the noble hero, do you?' Her frustrated rage crackled and burned. He could feel it scorching his flesh. 'Want to become involved in another adventure that will one day become a legend?'

'Leave me alone, Cragfor,' he shouted. 'I'll never belong to you.'

'We'll see about that!' she hissed, then vanished, leaving a small glowing halo behind her. It popped, and there was nothing left.

Sandor cleared his throat, but no sound came. Beads of sweat broke out on his face. He knew Cragfor was a cunning enemy and had probably been sent to divert him from his real purpose, whatever that might be.

He wiped his sword clean on a handful of grass, slipped it back into its scabbard and continued his journey, convinced that this was where the magic was leading him.

It's your fate, your destiny, something whispered in his mind. Go. Accept the challenge. Who knows? It may lead you to your bride.

Varna launched herself into the attack. She caught Krill off guard, striking at his back. He swung round with a curse, then grabbed up his mallet. It swished through the air. Varna ducked. The mallet smashed into the ground.

She leapt towards the girl and cut her bonds. Though

weakened by her ordeal, the young amazon grabbed for the nearest spare weapon and, still naked, joined in the fray. Trolls were falling, yelling, some recovering, others staining the forest floor with their slimy, stinking blood.

The girl shot Varna a quick glance. 'I don't know who you are, but thanks. I'm Merrisan,' she gasped, sinking her sword into a troll's obese belly.

From the corner of her eye Varna could see Phila holding her own, but they were hopelessly outnumbered. More trolls were pounding into the clearing, attracted by the din. Everywhere she looked Varna could see a seemingly endless tide of them, bristling with weapons. Arrows twanged, bounced off trees and quivered in the ground. Troll marksmanship was poor, but they were tremendously strong and she could see that both Phila and Merrisan were tiring under the assault.

She redoubled her efforts, her sword a dazzling point of fire. She could not allow herself to be beaten! She was an outcast, a fugitive, but she had a sacred duty to perform. Her father must be avenged and her country saved. She bent swiftly and snatched up a knife from one of the slain, holding it in her left hand. With two weapons she could wreak twice as much havoc.

Yet every time she slaughtered a troll another took its place. Bones fractured under her blows. Her dagger darted like a snake's tongue and Merrisan and Phila were fighting valiantly, but they were gradually losing their strength. Varna's mouth set grimly. She knew that a terrible fate awaited them if they were captured. The trolls would rape them, slaking their low-grade lusts, and then roast them alive and eat them.

She was face to face with Krill again. His mallet came down, giving her sword arm a glancing blow. Had it struck full on he would have broken it. She raised her knife but Krill suddenly stood stock-still, nose up snuffing the air, ears cocked.

An unearthly yell rang out. Dark shapes swung down from the trees landing on the trolls with rending teeth and claws. Primitive men? Varna wondered, while thought was at all possible. No. These were apes. A man led them, tall, broad and recklessly brave. His broadsword was invincible, his long-knife a flashing streak. He seemed to be everywhere at once.

The fight was short and bloody. The trolls had met their match in this warrior who dispatched them with ease and the apes who tore them apart and beat their brains out. Krill flung himself on his horse and fled, followed by any trolls left alive.

Varna, Phila and Merrisan closed ranks. It was possible that the man would turn his attentions to them.

He stepped through the carnage of the now silent glade, his weapons already sheathed. Varna registered that he was above average height and broad shouldered, had long mahogany-brown hair and a haughty mien. He wore clothes made from coarse hempen material and skins – a jerkin that left his muscular arms bare, and a pair of trousers bound about the legs with wide thongs. They fitted closely, and she was very conscious of the pronounced bulge at the apex of his thighs.

She could feel a blush rising across her throat and into her cheeks, and tugged at the hem of her kilt. She was embarrassed in case he should catch a glimpse of her mons.

'Who is that?' she murmured to Phila, and felt her clutch at her arm.

'A god, maybe? Or a brigand?' Phila answered, eyeing him suspiciously.

He ignored them, however, moving from one group of apes to the next, speaking to them softly. Then under the leadership of their silver-backed alpha male, they melted into the forest.

Now he turned to Varna. Close up, she found him even

more devastatingly handsome. He held out his right hand. She grasped it in greeting and salutation, a thrill shooting up her arm at the contact with his warm palm. The feeling tingled along her shoulders and down her spine, into the very heartland of her being. She could feel her labial wings pulsing, and fresh dew gathering at her vulva.

'My name is Sandor Deva,' he said, and his accent was strange, neither Northlander nor Valdivian. He seemed reluctant to let go of her hand. It was numb by now but she did not care.

'And I'm Varna, princess of Trokles,' she stammered, vexed because she was rendered almost speechless, just at the very moment that she wanted to appear bright, intelligent and, above all, in command of herself.

'I'm Phila,' her friend put in gruffly, still suspicious of the stranger and unmoved by his charismatic good looks. 'You and your monkeys arrived just in time. We were about to be cooked meat.'

His arched brows drew down in a frown and he released Varna's hand. 'They aren't monkeys. They're great apes. They came to help you when I called. I hate trolls and so does every forest creature. Trolls are merciless. They hunt down and torture the animals.' Then his gaze encompassed the third girl. 'And who are you?'

'Merrisan,' she replied evenly.

'I won't ask you all why you're here,' Sandor said, hands resting on his hips, his hawk-like gaze returning constantly to Varna. 'Strangers are usually reluctant to discuss their past. This forest is dreaded. Only those in dire need venture into it.'

'I've nothing to hide,' Varna said, chin lifted haughtily. 'My father was King Harcon, and today his armies met those of King Lagras on the Asgrid Plain. We were beaten and my father was killed.'

'Lagras. I've heard of him. He's evil. He'll even recruit trolls to swell his ranks,' Sandor said slowly, and his green eyes shone with a peculiar intensity. They reminded Varna of polished steel.

'I've sworn to make him pay,' she grated.

'You say your warriors were defeated?' Merrisan asked, her face pale. 'My brothers fought with them. They made me stay at home, but I ran away. I too hate Lagras. He has already enslaved my youngest brother, Jat. I was looking for the battlefield when I was attacked by the trolls. Oh, Varna, were all your side slain?'

'I don't know. I had to get away fast.'

'I saw prisoners being rounded up by the Valdivians,' Phila put in.

'My poor brothers. They'd be better off dead than in Lagras's clutches,' Merrisan said grimly. She turned away, found her pack, pulled clothing from it and started to dress.

'Who whipped you?' Sandor asked, pointing to the stripes on her back and hindquarters.

'The trolls,' she said abruptly, then slung her knapsack over one shoulder and limped towards a break in the trees. It was obvious that she was bruised and sore from her beating.

'Where are you going?' Varna called.

'To Quexol, the capital of Valdivia.'

'You'll never find the way,' Sandor said quietly. 'The hyenas will be feeding off your carcass before dawn.'

'I'll take that risk. I must find my brothers. If they've been killed, then I'll concentrate on freeing Jat.'

'Wait. We'll go together,' Varna said. 'Three can fight better than one.'

'Not three rash females who are tired out,' Sandor stated.

'You can't stop me,' Merrisan declared.

But Varna thought Sandor was talking sense. They were hopelessly lost. The terrain was wild and hostile. They needed to rest, eat and make plans.

'He's right, Merrisan,' she said. 'Though my father's blood cries out for vengeance, I must heed Sandor.'

'I'll take you to where I live,' he offered, and there was something in his eyes when he looked at her that made Varna shiver – not with fear, but with passion.

For the first time in her life she was experiencing the chemistry that draws a woman to seek a mate. But why now? And why here? There was no answer to this. All she knew was that if he asked her to couple with him, penetrating her virgin place with his penis, she would do so gladly.

Phila was looking at her in a puzzled way, and Varna wondered if she had guessed. Neither she nor Merrisan seemed to share the lustful thoughts about Sandor that were making her wet between the thighs. They walked along together, talking seriously, and Varna was in front, trying to match her stride to Sandor's, though his length of leg made this impossible.

It was dark now, the forest alive with the rustle of night-hunting things. The tortuous track wound upwards, strewn with rocks and slithery gravel. The trees were stunted, twisted out of shape by the wind that gusted over the ravine. A cliff towered on one side, rising sharply from the black abyss.

Varna looked down into space, her heart in her mouth. There was the thunder of unseen water below and a mist swirled up, dampening her hair with clammy fingers. It was cold on the heights and her clothes were inadequate, the draft lifting her kilt and playing with her bare crack like impudent fingers. She wound her cloak round her, but it did not warm her delta. She was sure that nothing would ever heat it now except the feel of Sandor's hand.

'We're almost there,' he said beside her, the rich timbre of his voice adding to the mayhem in her belly. She yielded, melting into him as he pulled her against his body. She could smell him, an intoxicating mix of leather and the personal odour of his hair, coupled with male sweat and the damp heat of his crotch.

'Don't you feel the cold?' she asked, shivering more with excitement than chill.

'Rarely,' he answered with a chuckle. 'And now I can't feel anything but you.'

His arm was so strong, his chest and side so hot. She wanted more of him, wondering if she dared drop down her hand and press it to the front fastening of his trousers.

She was shocked at such a thought, but aroused, too. There had been too much fighting and sorrow that day. She needed something to restore her. Not a woman's body – not Phila – but the hard planes and angles of a man's with all its untapped secrets.

She sensed that Sandor was not quite sure of himself. He held her as if she was made of spun glass, and this was strangely reassuring. She had imagined so confident a warrior would be perfectly at ease with women, used to them being only too eager to unite their bodies with his. She perked up and, though not quite daring to touch him intimately, was aware of her own feminine power. Even such as he could be awed by her.

Without relinquishing his grip, Sandor guided her along a perilously narrow path, round some rocks, and on to a small, grassy plateau. A cave mouth yawned ahead, lit by ruddy firelight. Varna glanced back to make certain Phila and Merrisan were following, then stepped inside. The cavern was large. Smoke spiralled upwards to disappear on the darkness.

'Welcome to my home,' Sandor said, as they moved towards the fire.

'Thank the gods for shelter,' Phila exclaimed, spreading her hands to the blaze. 'And that smells wonderful. Can we have some?' She gestured to where a cauldron hung from a tripod over the flames.

'Hey! Keep your thieving hands off my stew,' shouted

a grotesque figure who leapt from the shadows.

'Be quiet, Rion, you double-dyed spawn of a pig's bladder!' Sandor snarled. 'These are my guests, and I expect them to be treated well. No treachery or you'll answer to me.'

'Guests? *Women* guests? Well, that's a different matter, Sandor,' answered Rion, and he grinned at them, showing broken, blackened teeth. 'Lovely women. Oh, my goodness! Visiting my cave! You'll be kind to poor Rion, won't you, my dears? You'll kiss his cock and press it to your breasts. Oh, yes. Yes! I'm ready to shoot my load at the very thought!'

He moved agilely on his short legs, circling Varna, Phila and Merrisan. His arms were stubby, his head large, and sparse hair straggled round his wizened face. He wore a dirty robe over deerskin pantaloons. He perused the women from top to toe, and the look he gave them made the outspoken lechery of the trolls seem innocent by comparison.

'Be quiet, you rogue. You'll treat them with respect,' Sandor warned.

'Of course, Sandor, my son. But you'll share them with me, won't you? You'll not be cruel and selfish. There's plenty for all. Six breasts, three cunts, three arseholes, three mouths and lots of lovely arms and legs,'

'They are not to be violated,' Sandor retorted and, seizing Rion by the throat, pinned him up against the wall. 'And I'm not your son, so stop calling me that. D'you think I want kinship with a reptile like you?'

'Ungrateful,' Rion muttered, massaging his neck when Sandor plonked him down on his feet. Then he grinned ingratiatingly at the women, asking, 'Will you tell me your names, pretty ones?'

'You don't need to know them. This is the law of the forest,' Sandor reminded heavily.

'Oh, all right. Keep your secrets,' Rion said, in a huff.

'You treat me so badly. And I saved you as a baby, reared you, cared for you. You'd have died without me.'

'And have you ever let me forget it?' Sandor responded with a scowl. 'You never do anything unless there's something in it for you. But I'm no longer a child, as I keep telling you. I shall go where I want and do as I please.'

'Oh, how harsh, how cruel are the young,' Rion wept, dabbing at his eyes with a corner of his disreputable garment.

'Silence, you old babbler, and get us something to eat,' Sandor shouted angrily. 'Or d'you want me to call the apes?'

'Hush, now. Don't lose your temper. Leave them out of it,' Rion begged, grovelling almost to the sandy floor. Then he scurried about, fetching wooden bowls and taking them to the cooking pot.

'Be seated, if you will,' Sandor said to the women, indicating tree stumps that acted as stools. 'Take no notice of Rion. He's cunning. But I can take care of him.'

The rich gamey smell rising on the steam from the pot made Varna's mouth water, and she ate eagerly when Rion handed her a bowlful. Even the way he continued to look at her could not put her off. She was starving and for a while concentrated on nothing but filling her empty belly.

She sat cross-legged on a rug near Sandor, glancing across at Phila and Merrisan now and again. They had their heads together, talking warfare, and she was happy to see that Phila was looking at Merrisan with shining eyes, touching her every so often. Varna was sure that, friends now, they would soon be lovers.

She was warm and full and comfortable and could not stop staring at Sandor. The firelight flickered over his features, outlining the strong nose, high cheekbones and slightly slanting eyes.

'Where are you from?' she asked, transgressing the forest rule of anonymity.

'The west,' he said, tracing a pattern in the sand with a stick. 'Mine is an odd tale. Rion found my mother wandering in the woods. He brought her back here for she was about to give birth to me. She died shortly after, but Rion has told me she confided that she was Lady Carmel and had fled her homeland when enemy forces overran it. Lost, half-mad with grief, she had given up the will to live, for my father, her beloved husband, Ledro, was killed in the fray.'

'Like my father,' Varna said quietly, and without realising what she was doing, laid her hand on his arm. The muscles were iron-hard, the skin lightly furred.

Sandor said nothing for a moment, arms clasped about his humped knees as he stared into the fiery embers, then he continued, 'Rion is devious, but I think he spoke the truth when he said that my mother told him Ledro was a Durani Knight. He ruled the province of Veledy.'

'The order of Durani? My own father belonged to this secret sect,' Varna broke in, and dared tighten her grip on his arm. They now had a common bond.

She was not aware that Rion had sidled closer until he suddenly said, '"When night eats the sun, when the old wolf is dead, then the she-cub shall conquer."'

Varna was on her feet in an instant, her dagger at his ribs. 'What d'you know of the prophesy? Tell me or you're dead!' she cried.

'Leave him to me,' Sandor said, lifting Rion and shaking him. 'Answer the lady, rat-face!'

Rion wriggled and spluttered, beating at him with his fists. 'Put me down! I'll not say a word till you do.'

'Right. Now talk!'

Rion straightened his shoddy old robe, glaring from one grim young face to the next. 'You youngsters are all the same,' he grumbled. 'And as for you, Sandor, you're a swaggering bully. I've been like a father to you, had you from a newborn babe. And what thanks do I get? None! I might as well have sheltered a poisonous adder. It's not fair.' He began to snivel, shaking his grizzled head and wiping his nose on the back of his hand.

'Shut up!' Sandor shouted. 'You're a bag full of wind and lies.'

'Will you listen to that?' Rion wailed, appealing to the women who remained stony-faced. 'Fed and sheltered him I did. Warmed pap for his baby mouth. Clothed him. Taught him how to use a sword. Oh, the ingratitude of him!'

Varna took a step towards him, the light slanting off her dagger. 'The prophesy,' she insisted. 'Is there more? What must I do to conquer Lagras?'

Rion had retreated to a ledge of rock and sat there hunched up and sulking. 'Why ask me?' he muttered. 'If Sandor's to be believed, I'm good for nothing but to fetch and carry, work my fingers to the bone for a selfish wretch of a boy!'

Varna looked enquiringly at Sandor who shrugged in response. 'Ask away,' he advised. 'He'll be unable to resist telling you, but don't trust him.'

Going over to the huddled figure in the corner, Varna tried again. 'I didn't mean to upset you. I need your help. When he lay dying my father told me that only I could save Trokles from the sorcerer's power. I don't know where to start. I could use the counsel of a wise man, like yourself.'

It stuck in her craw to flatter him, but this worked. He squinted over his shoulder at her, saying, 'You're a polite young lady. Maybe you can teach Sandor some manners. He spends too much time among the beasts.' He clambered down from his perch and hobbled closer to her.

She managed not to move back in disgust as one of his

hands closed over her breast. His eyes shone lustfully as he added, 'What will you give me if I help you? Can I expect your hand on my prick? Maybe, your lips? And will you instruct your friends to sleep with me tonight?'

Varna was desperate for information. When he produced an unexpectedly large cock from the depths of his filthy pantaloons, she allowed her hand to close over it. 'This is all I can give,' she said, her voice filled with loathing. She squeezed the repulsive mottled flesh, then let it go. 'And no more till you tell me all I want to know.'

'Bitch!' he cried wrathfully. 'D'you promise to satisfy me?'

'I might,' Varna lied.

'Stop pestering her, Rion,' Sandor said, looming over him. 'Just tell her what she wants to know.'

'I'll do what I can, but it's not a lot,' the dwarf conceded, fondling his fully erect member. Varna was surprised at its size. Limp, it must have reached his knees, but in this stiffened state it was as impressive as a sceptre.

'Go on,' she urged, glad that Sandor was there to protect her. The sight of Rion's phallus was repulsive yet intriguing, too. Was Sandor's anywhere near as big?

Going over to the fire, Rion poked about in the ashes. The flames leapt into renewed life. 'The prophecy is an ancient one,' he said, and continued to fondle his cock. 'It was told to me by a warlock. You are she whose coming was predicted in the runes, but your task will not be easy.'

'I don't mind,' she said, leaning forward eagerly. 'Where do I start?'

'First, you must find the sword,' he pronounced solemnly, enjoying her attention.

'What sword?' Varna asked, wondering if he was inventing this in the hope of a sexual reward.

'Welgard. The Sword of Victory, of course. Don't you know anything?' he said scornfully. 'It's a magic sword, made by skilled craftsmen. Its blade is carved with wish-hopes, the runic signs for good fortune, and it shines like the sun. It makes its owner invincible.'

Hope surged in Varna's breast and vague memories filled her mind. Somewhere, she didn't know when, she had heard of such a weapon. Perhaps her father had spoken of it but she had assumed it to be a fairytale.

'Where is it?' she asked urgently, approaching him, almost prepared to bring him to orgasm if he would reveal the sword's hiding place.

'Patience, patience, we haven't completed our bargain,' Rion said, his eyes hooded as he glanced lasciviously from her to the other girls. 'I can't tell you that.'

'Can't or won't,' Varna said.

'Not unless you're especially nice to me.'

'Enough of this,' Sandor shouted, blazingly angry.

'Hush, please. Leave him to me. I must learn more,' Varna said, though the smell of Rion's scabby body was making her feel sick. 'Now, good Rion,' she continued. 'Where is the sword?'

He was on his knees, his cock burgeoning, filling his hands with its hugeness. He suddenly howled and writhed and ejaculated in a pearly stream over her feet. She shot back with an exclamation of disgust, aimed a kick at him and shouted, 'The sword! Where is it?'

He lay in a heap on the ground. Then gasped, 'I don't know.'

'You cheating rogue,' she cried.

'But I can give you the name of someone who does,' he whimpered.

'Who is it?'

'The witch, Cragfor.'

'No!' Sandor exclaimed, raising his fist to strike him.

Rion cringed and buried his head in his arms. 'It's true. You'll have to give in to her, Sandor. You know she's had her eye on you since your balls dropped. It's the only way forward on the quest. The road is long and fraught with danger. You need Welgard. Only Cragfor can tell you where it's hidden.'

'I'll go to her,' Varna declared. 'Tell me the way and I'll leave at daybreak.'

'Impossible,' Sandor said. 'She lives in a terrible region, at the top of the Forbidden Mountain. I'll go with you.'

'And I,' put in Merrisan. 'Find the sword, Varna, and then we'll go to Quexol.'

'Bravely spoken, my dear,' wheezed Rion, removing himself from Sandor's reach. 'Find the magic sword, the slayer of giants and monsters...'

'I know what you're up to, Rion,' snapped Sandor, and a look of pure hatred passed between him and the dwarf. 'You want me to wield Welgard and kill Firestorm the dragon, so that you can get your greedy hands on the treasure it guards. This is what you've always wanted. Why else did you look after me, if it wasn't that I should bring you wealth untold?'

'Well, maybe that was a tiny part of it,' Rion admitted slyly. 'But I did it mostly out of the goodness of my heart and genuine love for you.'

'More lies,' Sandor said grimly. 'I should chop your head off.'

'No, no. You misunderstand me,' Rion persisted, grabbing Varna's hand. 'Don't listen to him, lady. You're a brave girl and when you've accomplished the task on which you're bent, then you'd let him borrow the sword, wouldn't you? To kill the wicked Firestorm and give me a little nest-egg for my old age?'

'Don't heed him,' Sandor grunted, and spread his cloak on a heap of furs, adding, 'Sleep here, princess, while I keep watch. At first light I'll take you to meet Cragfor. Pray to whatever gods you believe in, for she is steeped in guile and will demand a price in return for her help.'

Varna snuggled under the cloak, wishing he would join her, but he sat by the fire while Rion occupied a corner, having tried unsuccessfully to interest Phila and Merrisan in his bent and hideous body. They had treated him to a torrent of abuse when he suggested sharing their bed. In the darkness, Varna could hear him muttering and groaning and his stealthy movements as he continued to stimulate himself.

Chapter Three

Lagras, King of Valdivia, Warlord of Cutha and Emperor of the six states of Shamash, rode at the head of the triumphal procession through the broad, straight thoroughfares of Quexol.

People thronged the route, hailing the conqueror.

Beautiful women leaned from carpet-hung balconies, showering rose-petals on him and the glittering array of arms, pennants, horses, camels, chariots, bowmen and spearmen, and carts bearing booty. They jeered and spat at the line of prisoners who shuffled along, shackled to one another.

Lagras permitted himself a sardonic smile. He knew the citizens dare do no other than praise him. The streets were lined with guards. They had been carefully selected for their physique and fearsome aspect, wearing crested helmets and iron-plated hauberks, their muscle-knotted arms folded, hands grasping naked scimitars. Lagras did not believe in loyalty. Obedience could only be obtained through fear of the whip, the torture chamber, and the executioner's axe.

He knew that spies employed by his efficient system mingled with the crowd. The smallest criticism of him or his methods was punished by a brutal public death. But this was a rare occurrence and the populace gave little trouble, controlled by Lagras, his sorcery and his priests.

Quexol had been constructed hundreds of years before, built on the site of a city belonging to a civilisation that had existed in the very distant past. It occupied a prime spot at the mouth of an estuary and was practically impregnable. The walls were thick and high and it was surrounded by a deep moat watered by the River Akkad.

Its civic buildings were overpoweringly large and built of solid blocks, and its main temple was a ziggurat, a stepped pyramid that pointed towards the sky. The atmosphere of Quexol was heavy. Laughter was rarely heard. Even the children were subdued, and the eyes of the inhabitants were mostly dull. It was a city held in an enchantment.

Lagras observed that nothing had changed during his absence. Those left in charge had performed their tasks admirably. He glanced back at his army as the cortège rumbled and clanked through his capitol. What fighters! Most impressive of all were those flanking him on either side – the Cutha Lancers – his élite bodyguard.

Lagras rode as if born in the saddle, a commanding figure, yet he seethed with unrest. King Harcon was dead. His head topped a pike borne in front of the miserable train of captives. But his daughter had escaped. This thought rankled, and Lagras's lust smouldered like an ember in his belly. Since seeing her in Naram's scrying-glass she had haunted him, night and day. He had taken his pleasure in a dozen orifices since then, but had been unable to forget her.

Now the saddle beneath him chafed against his testicles and tantalised his cock. The tip rubbed the supple leather of his breeches, and he imagined her fingers tugging at the lacing restraining it, then palming his shaft, and the feel of the silken lips of her mouth – or her labia.

His fury and desire mounted. She was denying him. He was not used to being kept waiting. When he found her, and he was convinced he would, she would be severely chastised for this misdemeanour. He'd take sublime pleasure in carrying out her punishment himself. He allowed his imagination to play on what form this should take, and his cock stiffened, the glans bedewing his waistband.

The procession was taking too long. He needed relief – and now!

He leaned over and spoke to the leader of the Lancers, 'Hurry it up, Captain Cafless.'

The captain touched the peak of his plumed helmet, saying, 'Yes, sire,' then turned to his men and issued a brisk order.

His command rippled down the ranks and the horses trotted faster, the foot-soldiers marched that much quicker and those in charge of the prisoners used bullwhips mercilessly. If any were too weak to keep up they were dragged along by their chains.

Lagras's foul mood lifted a little when they arrived at his palace fortress. It loomed ahead ominously, its aspect one of grim power. The embossed, copper-studded gates swung open, and he passed beneath the towering archway and down an avenue lined with huge effigies of winged serpents with human heads.

Lagras dismounted and climbed a series of wide, shallow steps to his own quarters. He gave scant heed to the banqueting halls and reception rooms that stretched into infinity on either side. Accompanied by his guards he walked swiftly, hardly pausing to touch his forehead and chest in acknowledgement of the bronze figures of gods that stood in niches en route, attended by black-robed priests. The all-pervading aroma of incense wafting from their censers was potent, making the senses swim.

Varna will be forced to make obeisance to them, too, forsaking all others, Lagras vowed. She'll worship the vengeful, blood-hungry deities I revere.

Leaving his guards posted at the door, he strode into his private suite. Naram had adorned it for his return. She had not used flowers or laurel wreaths or any of the usual displays that welcome a conquering hero. Instead she had arranged a series of artistically presented tableaux in which only the most perfect specimens of beauty appeared.

She's so clever, my sister-queen, he said to himself.

In the first one a lovely young woman with a mane of curls was on her knees, her full breasts swinging, her haunches raised high, her curling pubic hair barely covering the split fig of her sex. Bright pink blotches were spreading across her bare buttocks. Aswad stood behind her, driving at her with a leather paddle. The sharp thwacks as it landed and her moans of pain punctuated the air.

'I see you've tamed her,' Lagras said. 'At one time she was wild and defiant.'

'I do my best, your majesty,' Aswad answered smugly.

Lagras leaned over the panting girl and slid his hand under her belly, cupping her pubis. She gave a long shuddering sigh as he opened her wide and started to masturbate her. Her hips began to gyrate to his movements and Aswad held one plump breast, the nipple stiffening. Then his big hand encompassed both, circling and fondling them. She could not hide her excitement, a fresh trickle of pleasure juice oozing from her. Lagras dipped into her pool and spread her wetness over her clitoris. His cock was rampant inside his breeches, but he was not about to let go.

'That's it, Aswad,' he said huskily. 'She's trying to resist, but won't be able to.'

He pressed harder on her nubbin and, with his other hand, explored the tightly puckered mou of her anus. She squealed as his slippery index finger pressed against it. There was a moment's resistance, then he felt her sphincter yield and his finger entered her deepest, most secret recess. He wriggled it, made her squirm, his friction on her clitoris unrelenting.

'Oh, please... please,' she moaned.

'You want it?' he whispered, his voice bland as milk.

'Oh yes, yes!'

'Then ask me properly.'

'Please, master.'

Lagras registered that her arsehole needed stretching. Naram must attend to this, but there was superb satisfaction to be gained through fingering such a tight aperture. She moved her hips higher, driving back on it, driving against the hardness of his phallus, seeking she hardly knew what.

He felt her clitoris throb and her body jerk and shudder. A rush of juice gushed from her, wetting his hand. She collapsed, curled in a heap on the floor, and Lagras smiled.

'Hang her up and flog her,' he said to Aswad, and her arms were stretched above her head, manacled at the wrists and attached to a meat hook suspended from high in the rafters. She screamed as Aswad's flail landed across her rump.

Lagras contained his lust. Sometimes pleasures should be savoured. This could only increase the ecstasy when at last it swept over him. He needed Naram, the author of this side-show.

He paced across the room, enjoying the other little treats she had prepared. Two young male slaves wearing only chains and spiked collars knelt with their hands strapped behind them. A couple of Aswad's assistants were caning them. At the same time, another dropped in front and used both his hands on their cocks.

Lagras liked seeing the pain and confusion on their faces, the way their bodies jerked as the canes struck, and how their pricks went soft, then hardened again under the caresses of those experienced hands. At one moment they were moaning on the point of climax and in the next they were squirming under the force of the rod.

Naram, with her wanton knowledge of his preferences, had ordered a coffee-skinned beauty to be strung up like a fowl. Her arms had been yanked high and chained, and her legs raised, knees bent, her body doubled up.

Lagras spent some time examining this trussed victim, running his fingers over her exposed genitals. He was fascinated by the scrub of inky crimped hair, and her full sex where the folds were the colour of pewter, her anus a little black dot and her clitoris a large red bud poking out boldly. He tickled it, amused to see the sap glistening at her vulva.

The chains and leather creaked as she wriggled, and he guessed that she hated his touch but longed for orgasm. He left her, going to the next unfortunate, a young man this time, similarly bound, but with pale skin and fair hair. That which sprouted from his pubis was of a darker shade. His eye caught Lagras's and the king knew with a certainty that sent darts of desire to his cock, that this one was only interested in being shafted by men.

He let his gaze bore into that of the slave's and the boy's phallus thickened, the pink glans shiny, a drop of dew dangling from it. Lagras fingered the prisoner's bare perineum and stroked his taut balls. The boy's cock wept even more. Lagras moved on.

'Where's the queen?' he demanded restlessly, troubled by that peculiar itch which only Naram could ease.

'In the bathhouse, my lord,' Aswad answered.

Of course, she would be, Lagras thought. She'd know he'd be travel-stained and weary, needing to cleanse himself of the sweat and grime of war. She'd be eager to hear about it, too, especially the bloody bits. Later, he'd show her King Harcon's severed head, before he had it staked to the battlements, food for the crows.

He walked across the polished granite floor and entered his *hamman*. It was large and tiled in lapis lazuli and terracotta. Light poured down from a central cupola, brilliant, rainbow coloured, adding to the sybaritic luxury. In the middle was a sunken bath with graded steps stretching the entire length of one side.

Naram sat there, half-submerged, her shapely breasts buoyed by the scented water, tiny emerald hoops sparkling in her pierced nipples. Her flaming hair was piled on top of her head, secured with jewelled pins, but with little tendrils at her cheeks and the nape of her neck. Slaves attended her; gorgeous girls and virile young men. They scurried to do her bidding under the watchful eye of a gaunt woman clad entirely in a uniform of black leather and silver chains. Her height was exaggerated by a towering head-dress shaped like an ibis, and she carried a cat o' nine tails which she did not hesitate to lay about their backs and buttocks, breasts and cocks.

She cracked her whip as Lagras entered and the slaves dropped down, foreheads pressed to the tiles.

Naram inclined her head, saying, 'Welcome, my lord king.'

He stood at the edge of the bath under the glow from the silver and gold lamps standing in alcoves. He did not need to say a word. Naram gestured to Rana, her slave-mistress, and the woman shoved two girls forward. They knelt at Lagras's feet and, while they disrobed him, he caressed them as and where he fancied.

His cock, released from the restriction of his breeches, uncoiled and thickened. He gripped one of the girls by the hair and pushed her face down to his crotch. He felt her mouth open and suck him in till every last inch was out of sight and his hairy thatch pressed against her nose.

Naram's carmine lips curved in a smile. Jat, her personal toy and the most recent of her acquisitions, sat sullenly beside her, tawny hair damply tousled, his arms spread out on the steps, back pressed against the tiles, his body semi-floating.

'Why aren't you hard?' she said shrilly, rounding on him, slapping his face and then clamping her hand on his penis. 'Haven't I ordered that you should always be ready for me?' She turned pleading eyes towards her brother, complaining, 'He's still rebellious, my lord. If he can vex me by a refusal, then he will. I found out that he was masturbating frequently to keep his cods drained with nothing left for me. Isn't that so, you impudent varlet?' she snarled, squeezing Jat's testicles fiercely.

'You have no right to keep me here. I'm not your plaything,' he gasped, trying to push her off, but her hold merely tightened. 'I'm a prince, I'll have you know.'

'I don't care if you're a god,' she stormed and, still grasping his balls, she commenced teasing his cock. In spite of his resolve, it swelled at her touch.

'D'you want me to devise a punishment?' Lagras asked, stepping down into the water. It lapped round his legs, deliciously warm and fragrant. Just for an instant he wondered if he was getting too old for fighting. The prospect of spending more time here amidst the delights of his harem were decidedly appealing.

But no: there was at least one more task ahead, and that was possessing Varna.

'She escaped,' he said angrily, without waiting for Naram to reply. To soothe him she acted the odalisque, pouring a puddle of liquid soap into the palm of her hand and spreading it over his back and dark-furred chest.

'I presume you mean Princess Varna?' she replied, one hand going lower, sliding over the slippery wet length of his phallus, and lower still, till she was cleansing his balls and worming the tip of her little finger into the tiny outlet of his anus.

'Yes, the bitch. I know she's run away. Her body wasn't among the dead.'

'You couldn't bring better news, tyrant,' Jat shouted recklessly. 'I'm glad she's given you the slip and I pray that you'll never find her.'

'Be quiet, Jat!' Naram cried, and added, 'Rana, deal with this fool, but here, where the king and I can watch.'

Aswad came to help and, between them, he and Rana hauled Jat from the bath. He was manacled and a gag stuffed in his mouth. His muffled protests, like his struggles, were useless. A snap of the fingers and another slave came forward, going down on his knees and sucking Jat's penis.

'He can't stop it. See how it's growing,' carolled Naram, and she ran her thumb up Lagras's stem, then circled the circumcised head.

'Has he been sodomised yet?' Lagras growled, following her gaze to where Jat stood defiantly, his face anguished as his cock betrayed him.

Lagras's excitement burned like a brand. Perhaps he would slake his lust in Jat's rectum rather than the cunt of some shrinking piece of girl-flesh. There was nothing quite like a tight male hole for coaxing the final iota of joy from a man's prick. His cock throbbed with the need to abuse Jat.

Relaxing under Naram's tender administrations, he feasted his eyes on her favourite slave who was sturdily built, his skin golden-brown, his hair streaked by exposure to that self-same orb, his eyes a brilliant blue that bordered on amethyst. He stood stock-still under the sexual torment, his thighs slightly parted, water trickling over his tight buttocks and balls and running down his legs.

'He's not been buggered by my orders, sire. Who knows how he took his pleasure in his former life?' Naram murmured, her voice as honey-sweet as her tempting touch.

'I'll ask him,' Lagras said, smiling grimly in his beard. His cock was ready to release its tribute, but Naram knew how to control this. Her fingers pressed hard on its base, preventing the rush of seed escaping him.

'Do so, my liege. Perhaps you will be the first to take him,' she whispered dreamily.

‘Aswad, remove the gag. You there – what d’you call yourself? Prince Jat,’ Lagras shouted, his voice echoing under the dome. ‘Have you a virgin arse?’

‘I don’t know what you mean,’ Jat groaned, half-bent over, his bound hands preventing him from avoiding the attentions of the kneeling slave suckling at his cock.

‘Have you been fucked by a man?’ Lagras continued, taking malicious delight in the prince’s confusion.

‘No! Never!’ Jat protested, the sweat standing out on his brow as he fought to conquer the pleasure that was sweeping over him.

Lagras’s balls ached with wicked anticipation. ‘Is that the truth?’ he questioned.

‘I never lie,’ Jat declared, and his cock was ramrod stiff and dribbling.

‘Let him go,’ Lagras commanded, and rose from the bath, water cascading from his strong tanned body, the skin marked here and there with the scars of old wounds.

Aswad and Rana obeyed, standing to attention either side of Jat. The man who had been sucking him was pulled off. Still manacled, Jat could not defend himself when Aswad suddenly gripped him round the back of the neck and made him bend over. Then he held him in an iron grip as Lagras scooped a finger of oil from one of the unguent jars and inserted it into Jat’s nether hole.

Passion was running strong in him now, a fierce passion that roared down his spine like serpent fire. He probed within the narrow passage, entering inch by painful inch, ignoring Jat’s outraged cries as he tried to clench his muscles to prevent this invasion. Lagras’s cock was rigid, and he inserted the helm into Jat’s rectum, then, with a thrust, drove it home, oblivious to his yelp of pain.

‘He’s fully erect! Let’s play the hump-backed beast!’ Naram exulted. She left the bath and presented her wet and shiny bottom to Jat. She drove herself on to his penis, and then pumped vigorously.

He gasped, his eyes tight shut, his flesh responding instinctively to the feel of her velvety, pulsating love-channel. Lagras pushed harder and his cock shot into Jat's rear. The wave of sensation that had been building up in him reached its peak, roaring up from his toes to his loins. His semen jetted from him in hot bursts and, as he came, he was dimly aware of Jat shuddering and bucking as he ejaculated into Naram.

She cried out in ecstasy as her own fingers brought her to orgasm, and Lagras was almost satisfied, would have been entirely so, were it not for the niggling annoyance of Varna.

He pushed Jat away, then shrugged his shoulders into a magenta robe handed to him by Aswad.

'You're still angry, sire?' Naram said languorously, coiled at his feet, caressing his legs with strands of her tangled wet hair.

'Yes, and shall continue to be so till we catch Varna,' he replied dourly, turning his heavy-lidded gaze to her.

She jumped up, signalled to Rana who swathed her in a semi-transparent wrap, then took Lagras's hand, saying, 'We need to consult the oracle, my darling, and talk with Chedon, the soothsayer.'

'What does your scrying-glass tell you?'

Nagras's expression darkened and her eyes flashed. 'It's cloudy, impossible to read. Someone is tampering with it, preventing me from seeing. It has never happened before. Varna must be protected by powerful magic.'

With her fingers laced with his, Lagras went with her, reaching a room at the top of a tower, accessed by a spiral staircase. The light was diffused. Here and there gleamed a sliver of gold or silver, or the milky polish of ivory.

In the centre was a white dome with an aperture through which a slice of the sky was visible. Beneath it a telescope was mounted on an axis, so finely balanced that it could be moved at the touch of a finger to follow the stars in their courses. Lagras gritted his teeth. He needed more than astrology to help him.

Naram undulated her body against his, the nipples poking through the exquisitely soft silk of her wrap, two points of sensual pleasure chafing his chest. She wound a leg about his, pressing her pubis upwards and he could feel the plump contours of her vaginal lips.

'Don't despair, beloved,' she murmured, her tongue flicking across her lips. 'Do you really want her? Am I not your queen and lover?'

'Of course. You are my treasure, my consort and my wife. Nothing can alter that,' he vowed, and it was true. A strange passion united them: it was as if they were twin-souls, alike in wickedness – violent, cruel, self-willed and arrogant.

'But never your slave,' she reminded, and reaching inside his robe, dug her talons into his scrotum.

He seized her wrist, bending it back, forcing her to release him. 'You are, when I command it.'

'Yes, *master*,' she replied sarcastically, and kissed him, teeth nibbling at his lips and tongue.

A sound drew Lagras's attention away from her. He looked across the room to where a stove had been built into a recess, sheltered behind a glass screen. His nostrils caught a succession of strong odours, some aromatic, others foul.

'Chedon, what have you for me?' Lagras demanded.

The magician closed the door of the stove and rearranged a set of glass vessels shot with green and amber. The light cast fantastic colours over him. He looked so frail that it scarcely seemed possible that blood still circulated beneath his skin, stretched like parchment over the bald forehead, hooked nose and furrowed face.

'I have much, oh illustrious king,' he replied in a reedy voice. 'Didn't I foretell that you would have a great victory? More is to come... much more.'

'You did, wise one,' Lagras said. 'But there is one thing that hasn't been accomplished. The capture of Princess Varna.'

'Ah, yes... the princess. I read of her birth in the stars. She was born to be a thorn in your side, majesty.'

'Tscha! I know that! But I need to catch and subdue her. She *shall* bend to my will.'

Chedon stirred one of the vessels. Fine vapours, poison-scented, rose and circled. There was a weird bubbling and simmering, like songs in different keys.

'Hark to them,' Chedon said with a smile. 'There's your answer, sire. A concert for you. New tunes. New brews. There isn't a plant that doesn't have its own voice, its soul-song. I don't encourage good little souls, only bad ones. Oh, yes. There's enough in this crucible to make helpless idiots or dead flesh of a hundred lusty men. Don't I keep the citizens passive with my distillations of the black Lethe flower? Wouldn't they, perhaps, rise up against you, were it not for their craving for dreams, which I satisfy?'

'You do, but I'm not seeking poisons or drugs at this moment in time. I need answers to vital questions. Where is Princess Varna? Who dares shelter her? What plot is she hatching against me?'

'Aha,' said Chedon, his eyes shining keenly in that ancient face. 'We must visit the sacred pool.'

'You think it will reveal anything?' Naram sneered. 'My glass is useless.'

Chedon shot her a look of undiluted venom, then shrugged and added ironically, 'Perhaps you have offended one of the gods, my lady. Inadvertently, of course. You're of too sweet and mild a nature to upset anyone, knowingly.'

'I'll upset *you* if you don't get on with it,' Lagras growled, his hands flexing with the desire to fasten them round Varna's body when, at last, she was his helpless prisoner.

'Patience, sire, patience,' Chedon chided gently. 'First I must select herbs that will please the goddess Izar, for it is she you will need to propitiate.'

His cassock, embroidered all over with cabalistic signs, rustled and his slippers flip-flapped as he crossed the floor. He opened a carved black cabinet. Inside were shelves containing phials and tubes and packets of herbs. He rubbed his hands together as he made his selection.

'Hurry!' Lagras snapped, and a great rage possessed him, his impatience with Chedon and Naram sending the blood pounding in his head. Had he been armed, he could have murdered both of them.

At last they descended the winding stairs and reached the temple used exclusively by the royal family. It was dark inside, with no chink of daylight to flush out its shadows. Waxen candles burned in torchières around which bronze serpents writhed. The black basalt walls gave back sombre reflections.

And above all towered the brazen image of Izar, supreme goddess of chaos. Four arms sprouted from her body and in each hand she bore weapons. Her eyes seemed to glare wrathfully. Her mouth was open over a lolling tongue. Her hair was made up of asps. Smoke drifted over them from chafing dishes, and they appeared to move, sinuous and deadly.

Do I believe in her? Lagras wondered as he prostrated himself. Goddess of my ancestors, she to whom I pray before going into battle. But what proof do I have that she's no more than an invention of kings who sought control over the masses?

This was neither the time or place to entertain doubts. He turned to the high priest who stood in the shadows behind the altar. Below this lay a circular pool, its rim guarded by entwined serpents with golden scales and rubies for eyes.

'Are you ready?' Lagras asked him curtly.

The priest nodded, the hood of his black habit concealing his face. One of a dozen acolytes who attended the goddess came closer, carrying something wrapped in a cloth. The priest took it and placed it on the altar at Izar's feet. He pulled aside the covering, raised his arms and started to chant.

Lagras knew that the next move was up to him. He was the one begging a boon of the goddess and he must provide the sacrifice. He lifted the sacred knife and plunged it down into the heart of the victim. The day-old infant died without a whimper.

The chanting was louder, a monotonous plain-song, rising to the vaulted ceiling as if bearing the soul to Izar's realm. Now it was Chedon's turn and he mixed blood with the potion he had brought with him and sprinkled it over the smouldering brazier.

Lagras stood before the image and declaimed, 'Great goddess. Accept my offering. Answer me. Where is Princess Varna?'

At once Naram repeated the question, her head thrown back, her russet hair reflecting the flames, her eyes filled with mysteries. 'Great Mother of Abominations, answer him. Where is Princess Varna?'

There was a moment's silence, then the temple shuddered. A wind came from nowhere, howling round the room. The incense smoke billowed, and the candle flames lay flat under the sudden blast. There was a sound that rose in volume till it hurt Lagras's ears. It stopped abruptly and a tomblike quiet descended, a watching, waiting quiet, filled with unnameable things.

He feared nothing and no one, human or immortal, but could feel the sweat running down his body. There was something poisonous in the vapours that rose from the water as he leaned over the pool.

At first he could see nothing except his own reflection and that of Naram pressed close to his side. Then there was blankness. The still water began to sway and move. A thick inky mist spread swiftly and, in the blackness, he saw a tiny glow of hellish green. It grew, solidified, became the warped and terrible features of Izar. She was animated now, filled with dreadful life. The snakes hissed about her grinning face. Her mouth was smeared with blood and her fangs gleamed as she spoke.

'I accept your gift, Lagras,' she said in a low, grating voice. 'See what you wish to see.'

The vision faded and in its place were ravines and the peaks of a mountain. Through razor-backed ridges a path wound dizzyingly as it dropped down to an abyss filled with mud. Bones lined the trail, and vultures fought over decomposing remains.

The scene became clearer, nearer. Lagras drew in a sharp breath as figures appeared, groping along the track, inch by perilous inch. The one in the lead meant nothing to him, a wild-looking, tall young man. Then there were three women, dressed as warriors and carrying weapons. He scanned them eagerly and found Varna bringing up the rear. His heart skipped a beat and then raced on.

'There she is,' he said jerkily. 'Look, Naram. I want her, and nothing is going to stop me getting her.'

Naram stiffened, alert as a stalking panther as her eyes fastened greedily on the man. 'I'll help you get her, and in return I want *him.* An enemy? Not for long. He'll join my slaves.'

'Not if Cragfor decides otherwise,' suggested Chedon, hovering near her elbow.

'Cragfor the Witch!' Naram shouted, her face a mask of fury. 'What has she to do with it?'

'The Forbidden Mountain is her territory,' Chedon replied. He looked at Lagras under his bushy brows and added, 'Even you can't break her spells, lord.'

'Why is the princess going there? And who is that young barbarian?'

'A forest dweller, but destined to become a hero.'

'I can see that,' Naram broke in, her lips shining crimson as she plucked at her nipples with one hand, while burying the other between her legs, the silken fabric quickly stained with her love-juice. 'He's magnificent. Just let me get my hands on him and he'll become our ally.'

'Be silent!' Lagras thundered. 'She thinks to escape into the Forbidden Mountain, but she's wrong. I'll deal with her and her companions and that inferring hag, Cragfor. Izar! See to it!'

He stepped forward and stamped his foot. The floor shook with a rumble that became a grinding roar. A gap opened and out of it seeped a green cloud. It span like a top, widening and spreading. Vague forms materialised within it, contorted, nightmare images, oozing slime and shooting out tentacles.

'There's a price to pay, king,' the goddess cried, her voice deafening.

'I sacrificed to you.'

'I need more.'

Lagras was dragged into her embrace. His cock pulsed and kicked, like a separate entity attached to his groin. He felt her nails ripping at his skin, the curved talons of a demon woman, but he wanted her to continue, wanted it more than he had ever wanted anything. The movements of her hands drove rivers of ecstatic sensations through him. She was everywhere – in his blood – his nerves – his heart. She smothered him between her thighs, rubbing the whole of him against her massive clit. He heard himself bawling in mingled agony and bliss, pouring out his libation in a cataclysmic orgasm.

He clawed his way out of the blackness, swaying on

his feet, his face triumphant. The gateway to hell remained open. The shapes swirled round it.

'You'll not summon the forces of the Were-demons?' Chedon gasped.

'Izar has promised me. Her creatures will help me vanquish Cragfor,' Lagras said, and the expression on his darkly-bearded features was awesome.

Chapter Four

'I've done it, mistress,' Rion said, lisping in his excitement, spittle flying. 'He's on his way to you.'

'Get away from me, you louse,' Cragfor retorted, roused from her half-dream, lolling on an elbow among the silken sheets of her enormous bed.

As she came more fully awake, so she changed. In slumber she was ugly, reverting to her own hideous shape, offspring of an ogress and a troll. She kept this at bay by sheer willpower and strong spells, designing for herself the most alluring body and exquisite face, perfect teeth and gorgeous hair, the colour of which she changed as fancy dictated. But she could never disguise her eyes – upward tilting at the outer corners, and topaz hued, the eyes of an untamed beast.

'But surely, my goddess wants her plaything, doesn't she? The young and lusty Sandor? And there are females with him. Oh yes, three amazons for your pleasure,' Rion added, bent double in his earnest desire to curry favour.

'Tell me something I don't already know. What d'you think I've been dreaming about if it wasn't the events taking place, or those about to happen?' Cragfor said, and booted him in the midriff. 'It's a pity my guards weren't more alert. They'd have stopped you pushing your way in here, impaling you on a spear, I shouldn't wonder.'

'I came by underground passages,' he muttered, winded, fawning on her but deeply resentful. 'Ways known only to myself and my forebears who worked the diamond mines.'

Cragfor yawned widely. 'You think? I know

everything,' she said.

'Then you'll reward me? Let me have one of your slave-girls. A tall one with big breasts. A statuesque one with ebony skin who'll bully and torment me and piss all over me. Will you do that, omnipotent one?' he implored.

'I might,' she conceded, amused to keep him dangling, her reactions slightly human but mostly animal. She'd play with the dwarf like a cat with a mouse and then bite his head clean off.

She made an expansive gesture which embraced the slaves in attendance. They were many and varied, each selected for his or her particular feature; a shapely bosom or dark-skinned sex-lips; an unusually curved cock or intriguing anal hole. Like her archenemy, Lagras, she never curbed her lust or did other than satisfy her craving for sensation and power.

The cavern formed the centre of her domain. It was of cathedral-like dimensions. Stalactites hung from the roof like the pipes of a mighty organ, formed over a hundred million years by water percolating through limestone. Everything was gargantuan; massive ledges upholding lamps that glowed with a sulphurous light; furniture chiselled from solid rock, and the bed in which Cragfor lay, carved with sinuous plant forms and weird reptiles. The humid temperature was constant, the mountain enfolding the witch's realm in its volcanic maw.

She looked round her restlessly. There was one thing missing. A man who would be her equal, her king and fellow warlock, and when Sandor was born Cragfor had overseen the birth from the distance of her eyrie and determined that this hero should be hers. She had examined Rion's soul, seeing it as black and wizened as a walnut, and was fully aware of his motives for harbouring the boy. Very well. Let him believe that his greedy ambitions might be realised soon. She had other fish to fry.

She beckoned to a tall woman of monumental proportions, and said, 'This dwarf seeks to satisfy his base desires. You will do whatever he asks, Leila. Understood?'

The woman bowed her stately head, and the beads in her multitude of little braids clicked rhythmically. Her peat-brown oblique eyes brimmed with mockery as she loomed over the little man. 'I understand, mistress,' she answered in a deep, mellifluous voice.

Her near naked body was enough to addle a holy man's brain – long-limbed and with protruding breasts, the nipples jutting out, and hips like slices of watermelon. Her lower belly was hidden by a dense black thicket. She parted this and opened her fleshy lips wide, rubbing them firmly as she stood astride Rion. He sighed, drawing in a great lungful of her spicy musk, staring as if mesmerised at the rich promise of her delta.

'Can I really have her?' he stammered, rolling his eyes at Cragfor.

'You may, for as long as I find it entertaining,' she answered lazily and snapped her fingers at three of her women.

Two knelt over her, massaging perfumed oils into her body, paying special attention to her breasts. A third crouched between her relaxed legs, combing the luxuriant growth of hair that covered her mound, then parting the deep red slit and working her engorged clitoris.

Cragfor arched her hips, holding her pelvis upwards, her skin tingling, her nipples aching with need. It would be so easy to reach a climax, but she wanted to save it until Sandor arrived. She groped for the thick strap that lay near her pillow and the slave pleasuring her clit shook beneath the terrible crack as the leather hit her bare hinds. Inspired by her scream, Cragfor rose, lashing out mercilessly.

'Attire me, and I'd better look stunning or you'll suffer,'

she shouted, striding ruthlessly among her slaves, the strap whirling above her head and landing where it willed.

Soon she shimmered and glittered, her robe a sheath of golden tissue that undulated round her body as she moved, emphasising the slim hips and waist, the generous rump with its deep crease, the large firm breasts with the permanently erect nipples. She raided the overflowing jewel caskets, running avaricious fingers through priceless gems till she found ones that scintillated at her neck and wrists and ears. Then she had her attendants sprinkle gold dust over her skin and hair.

This did not quite satisfy her and, by thought, she changed the colour of her thick locks and pubic floss to a vivid royal purple. Ready at last, she looked at her image in a sheet of mirror-glass, and nodded. 'That will do,' she said. 'Now open the gates. My guests are here.'

She seated herself on a gilded throne, elbow resting on the velvet padded arm, chin in her cupped hand, brooding as she waited, yellow eyes fixed on the entrance. Within a few moments the high stone doors slid back and Sandor strode across the threshold.

Varna ached all over. The journey had been unspeakably difficult. Not only had a storm arisen, but it had seemed they were beset by invisible forces that did their best to topple them from the treacherous path. It was only the thought of Asvald that kept her going – that and the strength and purpose of Sandor.

Somehow they had won through, crossing the final rope bridge spanning a gorge and reaching the gates of Cragfor's kingdom. These had opened as if on oiled hinges and they had traversed a long passageway, and down countless steps leading into the bowels of the mountain. They felt as if there were guards on either side, but could see no one.

'Cragfor's a witch,' Sandor had reminded grimly.

'Beware of her enchantments.'

'I'll try, but I've never met a witch before,' she had protested.

'Don't believe anything she says,' he advised brusquely.

And now she was in Cragfor's presence, overwhelmed by the vast rocky chamber with its bizarre and savage ambience. Her eyes went to the subdued men and women who appeared to be the witch's servants. Some were clothed, but the majority were nude and, when she saw that they wore chains, she realised they were slaves. Her sense of justice rose up in revolt.

She followed Sandor's upright back till he halted before a great carved throne with a brocade throw and serpentine legs. There lounged the most exotic and lovely of women. She was haughty, her gossamer thin robe covered in sparkling jewels. Her head-dress was a conical crown so lavishly ornamented that it hurt to look at it for long. Varna was startled by the vivid purple of her hair and the black-lined, mauve lidded eyes gazing at her so intently.

At the same time she was excited by glimpses of her voluptuous flesh beneath the transparent gold tissue, and the way it slipped from her sloping shoulders, displaying her deep cleavage and the hard studs of her nipples.

Who was this lady? A courtesan or an empress? And why had she taken up residence in a witch's lair?

'On your knees, Sandor!' the woman said, in a ringing tone that echoed under the roof.

'No, Cragfor,' he said firmly. 'I'll not kneel to you.'

The sweat broke out at Varna's armpits and trickled slowly down her ribs. So this was the dreaded sorceress. She was suddenly aware that she was shabbily dressed, her clothing torn and dirty, though Merrisan had found a pair of linen breeks in her pack that offered privacy for her sex. Even so, she quaked inside, fearing that she looked a sorry sight, but she held her chin high and her spine straight.

The witch gave a sultry smile and leaned forward. 'Very well, Sandor, my hero,' she said, her voice husky with welcome as her hand stroked the side of his cheek, then dipped down to caress his chest between the opening of his jerkin. 'I admire your spirit, as well as your superb body. You will service me yet. Meanwhile, you have a boon to ask of me.'

'I have. Or rather, Princess Varna has.'

Varna felt herself coming under the scrutiny of a pair of blazing eyes – the colour of citrons, or the sun at certain times of the year.

'Step forward, child,' commanded Cragfor.

Sandor stood to one side and Varna could feel invisible fingers creeping all over her. Not only externally, but inside as well. They seemed to probe into her virgin passage, making it throb, to coil along her sex lips and distend them, to push back the fleshy hood and expose her nubbin, tickling and tormenting it to aching desire. At the same time a tongue slipped past her anal ring, making her jump at this invasion, then settling down to fondle the tight aperture till her womb churned and she was almost sobbing her pleasure.

Then, as suddenly as they had started, the unseen fingers stopped, leaving Varna doubting her own sanity. Yet, drowning in the acid fire of Cragfor's eyes, she knew that the witch had been examining her with astral agility.

She gripped the cross-hilt of her sword and stared back boldly. 'I was told that you would know the whereabouts of Welgard,' she said, keeping her voice steady.

'And who told you that?' Cragfor asked, extending a hand and placing it on Varna's breast. Her palm burned through both leather and metal.

'Rion, the dwarf. I have a duty, Cragfor. A duty to my country and the memory of my dead father.'

'Very commendable, I'm sure,' the witch observed.

'And there's no need to explain. I'm aware of your circumstances. Rion is here. He's already taking his reward. Look,' and she pointed to an alcove where the dwarf lay spread-eagled and chained across a boulder.

He was naked, a rictus of joy distending his mouth. His cock pointed upwards, hard as a lance and bursting with juice. A black woman was lashing him. There were livid welts across his lantern-chest and withered thighs. The woman climbed above him, knelt astride and held open her cleft. A stream of urine gushed from her, splashing his face and trickling into his mouth. Varna heard his gurgles and panting cries and saw his semen spurt, creamy white and forceful.

Cragfor's harsh laughter reverberated through the cavern. 'What a fool!' she exclaimed disdainfully.

'Why do you encourage him?' Sandor asked, anger darkening his brow.

'He serves a purpose,' she answered pensively, and rose to her full height in order to link her arms round his neck and tug the curls at the nape of his neck. 'He reared you, my dear. I knew your mother, Lady Carmel, and promised to protect you.'

'My mother? What about her?' He had seized her wrists in order to free himself but now he paused. She pressed against him, her pubis digging into his groin.

'She was a woman of rare kindness,' she said, her voice low. 'She never judged anyone by outward appearances. All were her friends, human and immortal. She didn't despise me for what I was. The world is mostly made up of wicked self-seekers, but not Carmel. I already hated Lagras, but can never forgive him for his part in the downfall of her province.'

'Lagras was behind the death of my parents?'

'He was a young man then, around your age, but yes, Lagras is behind everything that is bad, and so is his bitch-queen, Naram.'

'Then you'll tell Varna where the sword is?'

Cragfor lifted her eyes to his, an amused smile curving her scarlet lips. 'Wait a moment. I've not become a crusader in shining armour all of a sudden. A leopard doesn't change its spots overnight, nor a witch become beneficent. Just because I respected your dam, doesn't mean my plans for you are forgotten. Oh no, dearest boy. The price for information will be high, but not unpleasant.'

Varna hated the familiar way in which Cragfor handled Sandor's body. As if seeing with her fingertips, the witch ran them all over him, then settled at his lower-belly and crotch, feeling his cock through the supple leather. He stood there like a statue, his mouth set in a grim line, but Varna could see that no matter how he fought for control, his wayward phallus responded to Cragfor's experienced touch, as if it had a life of its own.

The witch purred deep in her throat, laughing up at him, confident of success. Then she turned and clapped her hands, crying, 'We must feast. It's not every day that I have distinguished visitors. A princess and a Durani Knight, plus valiant she-soldiers.'

Phila and Merrisan had closed up behind Varna, alert for trouble, but they were helpless against Cragfor's enchantments. A gesture from her and food appeared on the long stone table; capons and wild-fowl, venison and boar, vegetables swimming in butter, pyramids of succulent fruit, and grapes glowing on beds of dark green leaves. Silver and crystal wine jugs stood between gold candelabra, and perfumed oil warmed in jewelled burners, the scene as extravagant and wondrous as any banquet designed for the highest of kings.

'Be seated,' Cragfor said graciously, sinking on to a divan placed at the head of the board.

Varna glanced down, discovering to her astonishment, that her dirty garments had been replaced by a tiny sequinned bodice that barely hid her breasts and a diaphanous skirt slit to the thigh on each side. A wide belt girded her waist, with a panel dangling from the front, barely covering her mound. Her sable bush was visible through the sheer material. Her boots had been replaced by toe-post sandals of gilded leather. The breeks had vanished and her pubis was completely naked, honeydew seeping from her to wet her inner thighs. There was a heavy sense of arousal warming her clit, and this increased every time she glanced at Sandor.

'Here, sit by me,' Cragfor cooed and patted the damask upholstery of the couch.

There was nothing Varna could do to resist her, nor could she stop leaning against Sandor on her other side. He was heart-stoppingly handsome, his clothing transformed into that of a nobleman; a midnight-blue velvet tunic, lavishly embroidered, and baggy pantaloons ending in finely crafted knee-boots, also jewelled and adorned. His hair fell to his shoulders, a gold circlet clasped about his forehead.

She could see Phila and Merrisan nearby, and they were looking at each other in amazement, deeply suspicious of the change in their apparel. Both wore the vestments of army officers, with much use of rich cloth, frogging and braid. Their broad-brimmed hats were heavy with ostrich plumes.

'You approve of the clothes? I thought up things that would suit your personalities,' Cragfor said, and gestured to her slaves to pour wine into engraved goblets.

'I didn't expect this. All I want is the sword,' Varna said suddenly, aware that she was in danger of being seduced from her purpose. 'And I don't like being waited on by slaves. I assume that is what these unfortunates are. There were no slaves in Trokles. All were free.'

Cragfor chuckled ironically. 'And look where it's got you? Trokles has been defeated. This is one thing about which Lagras and I agree... the value of the slave system. But he's rather jealous of some of the ones I own. These for example; my hermaphrodites. Rare these days, though I understand the human race started out this way. Why else would you possess such a delicious set of wine-red nipples, Sandor, my love, if it wasn't a left-over from an experiment by the gods?'

She dived a hand into the opening of his fine linen shirt and tweaked his nipples. He slapped her away, fury working on his face, but she merely laughed and had the hermaphrodites move closer.

Cragfor kept such rarities stripped and on exhibition. In spite of herself, Varna could not help looking at them. They were fair of form and face, one dark, the other redheaded. Their features were refined, their bodies muscular, their hands and feet delicate. Cragfor handled them as if they were favoured pets.

'See their breasts?' she said, lifting her hands and jiggling them. 'Fully formed and feminine. And look lower. They both have cocks and balls, but behind these lie vaginal openings.' She lashed them with a belt, adding, 'Bend over, slaves, so that we can see.'

They dropped down from the waist and clasped their hands round their ankles. Their rumps were fully exposed and their unusual genitalia everything Cragfor had described. Compassion swept over Varna, but also an ignoble curiosity of which she wasn't proud. But she could not help reaching out a hand and touching those fascinating parts. The cocks were stiff, with bulging plums, the balls twin sacs burgeoning with seed, yet between them and the puckered anal mouths were wet pink vulvas.

'Incredible,' she breathed, and was ashamed yet excited by the visions of weird couplings these two inspired.

'Interesting and fulfilling. Let me demonstrate.' Cragfor clapped her hands again and two more slaves, a male and a female, crawled across the floor to her feet. 'Do it,' she commanded.

The male slave, a well-muscled man, stood behind one of the hermaphrodites and thrust his cock into the proffered vagina. The other, a nubile brunette, lay on the floor and the second hermaphrodite parted her thighs, knelt between them, and took her with as much force and enthusiasm as any man.

'You see?' Cragfor remarked, her hand resting on Varna's knee and sliding upwards towards her bare cleft. 'It is as I said. Both of these creatures have been delivered of offspring and suckled them at their breasts, and both have fathered children. Isn't it fascinating?'

Varna was experiencing nausea coupled with that uncomfortable edge of desire which was making her long to embrace Sandor. It was the witch's fingers wreaking havoc on her inner thighs, but he was the one she wanted. There was so much she yearned to know about him; his heart, his mind and, above all, his lovemaking.

'Were the children normal?' she managed to enquire.

'You mean, were they male or female, not both?' the witch replied, leaning her head against the scrolled back of the couch and having one of the most handsome of her boy slaves hold a bunch of luscious green grapes to her mouth. His sun-browned skin contrasted sharply with her white breasts and arms. She bit into the fruit greedily, then pushed her face into his smooth groin and transferred her juice-slippery lips to his scrotum, sucking at his tense balls.

Varna was finding it increasingly difficult to concentrate but, 'Yes, I suppose that's what I want to know,' she managed to blurt out.

Cragfor straightened, dismissing the boy with a resounding slap on his tight buttocks. 'One was like them, the other a female with a clit instead of a penis and no balls. But I'm tired of this.'

Music filled the air, the lilt of a flute, the throbbing of a tambour and a troupe of dancers leapt into the circle of light. Wearing bird masks, they started to gyrate wildly. They formed a dizzying kaleidoscope of thrusting breasts, gilded nipples, feathers and spangled drapes floating open to reveal dark slits or erect phalli. Incredible creatures, their virile strength, breathtaking agility and passion ravished the senses.

Every movement was designed to be intensely sexual, female curves flowing and mingling with male musculature, lovely legs locked round their partner's waists, cocks thrusting between slender thighs, nipples straining to meet lips, mouths swooping to suck at bulging glans or lick at the silvery moisture seeping between swollen labia.

Varna was enthralled. She could not resist pushing aside her skirt and finding her own secret wetness. Her fingers glided through her bush, enticing her clit to emerge, feeling it stiffen at her touch. Her breasts were so charged they felt sore. She yearned to feel the pressure of Sandor's cock rubbing against her buttocks. The desire for something hot and hard penetrating her love-channel was almost unendurable.

'You're not eating, princess,' the witch said, and Varna's cheeks burned like her sex as she knew Cragfor was reading her mind, even as she grabbed a knife and hacked slices from a steaming haunch of venison. 'It's essential you keep up your strength, if you're about to fight Lagras.'

'Does this mean you'll lead me to the sword?' Varna asked eagerly.

Cragfor speared a succulent morsel of roast deer meat and placed it between Varna's lips. 'We'll see,' she murmured, with a smile that made Varna shiver. 'Be a good girl and do as I say.'

She replaced the knife on the table and her mouth

followed the trail of the meat, licking the gravy from Varna's lips and inserting her tongue between them. Varna closed her eyes under that seductive caress. Whatever Cragfor was – clever charlatan or gifted enchantress – it was nigh impossible to resist her blandishments.

The meat was tasty, the wine strong, the music hypnotic. Her sight blurred as she watched the whirling dancers. Now they were performing the sex act, with no pretence at art, the naked women were lifted in the strong arms of the males and impaled on the jutting cocks.

Everything in the witch's cavern enhanced the feeling of abandon. Pleasure was all important. Varna could see Phila and Merrisan succumbing to its spell. Alert warriors though they were, their carnal feelings had gained supremacy. They coiled around one another on the opposite couch, fingers seeking, lips tasting, lost in a sensual world of their own.

Cragfor laughed to see them, and chortled with delight as she observed Rion struggling along on hands and knees like a dog, Leila tugging at the lead fastened to a leather collar round his scrawny neck.

'Doesn't it do your heart good to see him thus?' she asked Sandor, turning from playing with Varna's breasts to toying with the front lacing of his breeches. 'Don't you want to humiliate the runt?'

'I'll not be free of him till he's dead,' he growled, slumped low on his spine, a beef bone held between his sinewy fingers, his long legs stretched out under the table. He did not take his eyes from the dancers.

'This can be arranged,' she answered carelessly.

'Nothing dishonourable, Cragfor. No dark alley and knife in the back. You'll leave him to me,' he warned, and wiped his fingers in her hair. It crackled and sparked under his touch.

'Whatever you say. I love it when you're being

masterful,' she mocked, squeezing his crotch. 'But come, there are other diversions. Varna wants the sword and I want to enjoy your bodies in return – virgin maid and virgin man. What could be more delectable? Do you agree to my terms?'

'No, it's monstrous,' Varna cried and tried to stand up. It was impossible. She seemed to be restrained by invisible bonds.

'That's not very flattering. Mind your manners and remember who you're talking to,' Cragfor reprimanded.

'But I don't want you. Don't you understand? I've never believed I could traffic my flesh for gain, any more than I could endure being a slave.'

Cragfor smiled maliciously. 'You may find yourself doing both, if circumstances dictate. You're only a human and have little control over your destiny. I, however, have arcane powers and wisdom. So, alas, has Lagras. You'll have to resort to your physical charms in order to enlist my aid and vanquish him. There's no alternative.'

'Then I'd rather die. Forget I asked your help,' Varna said coldly, gripping the edge of the table to steady herself against the giddiness making her head swim.

'And what about the vow made to your father? I think we can help one another,' the witch said slyly. 'You can't hide anything from me, girl. You love Sandor, don't you?'

Varna glanced at him, blushing hotly, but it seemed this conversation could be heard by no one but Cragfor and herself.

'I don't know what love is. I've never experienced it,' she said.

'It's an aberration, a madness known only to humans. We're more practical immortals who can see it for what it really is... lust. But you have to go and dress it up in fancy sentimentality, write poems and songs about it, perform valiant deeds, act like moonstruck idiots,' Cragfor said scathingly, yet Varna caught the faintest hint of envy in her voice.

What was this mysterious element so strong that even a witch might desire it?

'I think my father loved my mother,' she said quietly. 'He mourned her all his life.'

'There you are then,' Cragfor snapped pettishly. 'Foolish fellow. He could have had his pick of a thousand concubines. That's what I mean. Humans are daft when it comes to that moony, romantic thing they call love. I suppose you'd die for Sandor?'

'Yes,' Varna said without hesitation.

'Would make any sacrifice for him? Want to mate with him for life and bear his children?' The witch's tone was decidedly edgy.

'Yes, all those things.'

'Then, dear heart, you have a gift from the gods that far exceeds anything I or Lagras possess.'

'Magic?' Varna asked, puzzled.

'Oh, yes. A great and powerful magic. Some say the greatest in the world.'

Varna stared at this woman who was universally feared and read in her eyes a deep, abiding sorrow. Did she regret that she wasn't human, able to love as mortals do?

'You shall have your lover for this one night,' Cragfor's voice murmured in her brain. 'And I shall share the experience, though you won't know I'm there.'

'And Welgard?'

'By dawn you'll be told where to find it.'

'And if Sandor won't agree? How do I know he feels the same about me?'

'He does. He burns for you. Like you, he's still a virgin. This promises to give me a unique experience.'

Cragfor cast her spell.

Sandor and Varna were alone.

He did not know how they had got there, but he wasn't grumbling. The woman he adored, revered, respected and wanted so badly that his cock was permanently erect, was sitting in a great copper bathtub with him.

'Varna,' he said hoarsely, the warm water slopping around them as she sat facing him, her legs between his, her toes curling round the full scrotal bag between his opened thighs. 'Why are we here?'

'Don't ask,' she whispered and leaned towards him, the tips of her breasts brushing his chest. She placed wet fingers over his lips.

'It's to do with Cragfor, isn't it?' he said suspiciously, catching her hand in his and tickling her palm with his tongue.

'Yes, but not a wicked enchantment as you might think. We are but fulfilling our desires. At least, I am,' she added, looking at him shyly. 'I hope you feel the same.'

'Oh, Varna... princess, of course I do,' he cried in an anguished tone as her arms crept round his neck and pulled his face down to hers.

He kissed her awkwardly at first, not quite knowing what to do, following his instincts which were urging him to delay no longer and take her forcefully, penetrating her body and freeing them both of their virginity.

Unschooled with women, he hardly knew how to converse with them let alone engage in intimate acts. He felt her mouth soften deliciously under his and the press of her tongue engulfing him in sweet honey. His cock leapt and she slithered across his lap, legs wide open, the hair fringing her labial lips tickling his helm. He stifled a groan, emotion swelling in his chest, his heart pounding, his phallus throbbing with need.

She sat up and stared at him with her wide amber eyes. 'I've not done this with a man before,' she murmured. 'But there must be no secrets between us and I'll be frank with you. Phila and I have pleasured one another.'

'Women together? How can this be?' he asked, the thought sending a further jolt of excitement to his groin.

'We kissed, like this,' and her lips were on his, tasting and teasing, her tongue a darting point of fire. 'And we fingered our nipples, as I'm doing yours, Sandor, my love. I want you to do the same to mine.'

She took his hands and placed them flat on her wet breasts. He felt the nipples standing up against his palm, then caught them in his thumbs and forefingers, feeling the exquisite little pips hardening, seeing the pigmented areolae crimping and hearing Varna cry out with pleasure.

Gaining confidence he held her naked body against his chest, her head resting on his shoulder, and continued to pluck her nipples, following her instructions as she whimpered, 'Not too hard. They are very delicate. That's it, a feather-light touch. Oh, oh! That's so good. It makes my nubbin throb.'

'Your nubbin? And what's that?' he asked, striving to control the urge to rise from the bath and spread her out on the bed, then fling himself down on her, ravage her hymen and relieve the pulsing in his balls.

'You really don't know?' she asked, slanting him a mischievous glance.

'I know nothing about women,' he admitted, shamefacedly.

'I'm glad,' she said. 'Now I can teach you. And you must show me what pleases you, for a man's body is unknown territory to me. But first we must wash, make ourselves clean and sweet-smelling before we plumb the depths of sensation. We're like innocent babes. Isn't that wonderful? I always swore I'd give myself to a warrior, nothing less, and to find one who is as pure as myself is a dream come true.'

She took up a soft sponge and bathed his chest and back and though this exited him, it also made him feel cared-for, a sensation he'd never had before.

'Rion brought me up,' he said, almost purring like a big cat under her tender ministrations. 'I never knew a mother's love.'

'Neither did I,' she answered. 'But my father loved me, and devoted nurses looked after me in childhood. Now you must let me love you, be your mother, nurse, mistress and wife.'

'Gladly, sweetheart,' he said, hardly able to speak for the choking in his throat. 'Will you really be my princess-bride?'

'Yes,' she answered simply. 'When my duty has been done and my country freed, then I'll marry you, Sandor.'

He felt her hand slip down under the water, and the caressing of the sponge round his balls and bottom crack, and then he started as her fist encircled his shaft. It hardened further, the glans showing above the soapy surface, and her eyes were riveted on it as if, indeed, it was the first time she had examined the male organ.

It was almost too much to bear. He could feel his balls and cock pulsing, heading at full gallop towards release. He did not want this to happen yet. She was offering him the gift of her glorious body and he was honour-bound to express his love through the joining of their flesh. But it must be done correctly. He would never recover from the shame if he disappointed her.

He took the sponge from her and let warm droplets run down across her breasts and nipples, then bent his head and tongued each in turn, licking her clean. Her eyes were heavy, her arms resting on the rim of the bath, and he knew she was more than ready to go further. Very gently he trailed a hand down across her belly and touched the dark wet triangle, and the deep avenue between it.

He saw the shudder that passed through her, and ventured further in. She slid down a little to give him easier access to her secrets. Sandor leaned above her, trying to see through the soapsuds, wanting to learn everything about those slick-wet folds he was now exploring.

He kissed her breasts and the long line of her throat as she arched it for his mouth. Her lips, her eyelids – he wanted to taste and savour every inch of her.

'Is this what Phila did to you?' he asked.

She roused as if from a trance. 'Yes,' she said huskily. 'Come, I'll show you more.'

The water cascaded from her as she rose, holding out her hand to him. Laughing, they enveloped one another in fluffy white towels then, still partly wet, made for the bed.

'Lie down, my love,' she urged.

Sandor lay back on the silk sheet, amazed by the beauty of this woman who was giving herself to him. 'I love you,' he said, and the words tripped awkwardly on his tongue.

Her eyes blazed and her face was radiant. 'And I love you, too, Sandor. I don't know much about this emotion, but I guess that's what I'm feeling. I want to be with you every hour of the day and night, to share everything; hopes, dreams, ambitions. If this be love, then I can truly say it is what I feel for you.'

He looked up at her, framed as she was in her cloud of dusky hair, and thought that he might die of wanting. Lying beside him she carefully examined his body, fingers light as they explored his brown pubic fur, and ran up the length of his throbbing cock. Her long eyelashes flickered and he wound his fingers in her mane, seeking to drag her mouth down to his again. She resisted, but gently.

'I've seen your cock and balls, and understand that your helm will be sensitive, making you spill your seed when you enter me,' she said, and spread her legs apart.

'Now, I want to show you how I bring myself to crisis, and how Phila has sometimes done it to me. Lean over me, beloved. Watch closely. If you learn well, then this will make you a most amazing lover. If you don't heed this lesson, then I shan't be able to reach the heights of bliss with you.'

Sandor did as she told him, bending his head close to her pubis and watching as she parted her pink outer lips and displayed the deeper rose of the inner ones. He could smell her fragrance, and wanted to touch, to dabble his finger in the dew that wetted her cleft, seeping from the opening below. But, mindful of her words, he contented himself with rolling his thumb-pad over her nipples.

'That's right, oh yes,' Varna sighed, and her middle finger explored her slit, wetting the tip. 'Now, see. The little knob at the top of my crack is covered with a hood, just like your foreskin. If I push it up, like this, you'll see my clit emerge, like a pink pearl. Oh, the feeling is wonderful. Do you bring yourself to ecstasy, Sandor? Do you play with your cock until it spurts?'

He could feel heat rising into his face, but nodded, 'Yes. I do that most days, sometimes more than once.'

'Well then, this is what I feel when I rub my bud. It gets more and more intense until it explodes. This little gem is equivalent to your member. Watch carefully, for I'm going to bring myself off.'

'But I want to do it,' he said.

She laughed, low in her throat. 'So you shall. One climax is never enough for me.' Varna had never realised she could be so bold, wantonly displaying her secret parts for Sandor to view. But it was lovely, her arousal so strong that she could hardly bear to go on with her demonstration.

The closeness of his body, the unique smell of him, the scent of his wet hair, the sight and feel of his erection was enough to tip her over the edge. She slipped her fingers each side of her labial wings, keeping them still for a moment and avoiding her clitoris.

She wasn't afraid of his penetration, not as she had feared being raped by the Valdivians on the battlefield. She was looking forward to the act, yearning to feel the uniting of their flesh.

His eagerness was exciting. The way he was controlling it so that he might learn how to please her was heart-warming. She loved his boyish enthusiasm. He was about her age, still filled with the optimism of youth, without a trace of the cynicism warping the witch and Rion. Now was the time for love. In a few moments she would know what it was all about.

She moaned as her fingers started to move again, circling and petting her clit, avoiding the tip but tracing its stem back to where it rooted deep within her pubic mound. Sandor lipped her nipples and kissed her mouth, then she pushed his head down again, wanting him to watch her masturbating. Using her other hand she spread her flesh leaves wide.

'See how my nubbin sticks out?' she panted, and wetted her fingertip in her dew, spreading it up and over her thrumming bud.

'I see it,' he said and his warm breath tickled her, helping raise her to the heights.

Now she forgot him, where she was or what she was doing there. Completion filled her horizon. She *must* have it.

Her finger flew over her swollen flesh and the sensation pulsed and receded, pulsed and grew mighty, sweeping from her toes to her groin to her cortex. Sandor tried to touch her there but she pushed him away roughly. Nothing must interrupt this sure climb to pleasure. Waves washed over her, carrying her upwards and she peaked, bringing herself expertly to an overwhelming orgasm.

'Oh!' she gasped, her whole body shuddering, her

finger pressed to her throbbing clit.

'You've reached it?' Sandor sounded jubilant. 'Can I go into you now?'

'Yes, *yes*… now... do it now.'

She clawed at him, pulling him over her, frantic to have his strong cock inside her, vaginal muscles needing something around which to convulse. She was blind to everything save its generous size, rearing to touch his navel, twitching and bucking as if it had a life quite independent of his. She was a little worried lest he damage her, but he pushed between her widespread knees and rubbed his helm against her slippery virgin opening. The sight of him like that, almost exploding with need, roused her lust again. She felt the sensation of skin on skin, his unshaven jaw chafing her face, her breasts crushed to his, hungry flesh seeking hungry flesh.

She braced herself as that huge helm penetrated her narrow entrance, an inch, no more. The sweat was running off him, soaking her and the sheet beneath them. To help him Varna raised her legs and rested her ankles on his shoulders. He hoisted her up, hands cradling her buttocks, and thrust.

There was a moment's resistance, and then she felt him stab her to the heart. The stretching, sickening pain was atrocious and she screamed. Beyond the point of no return, Sandor grunted, moving his phallus in and out of her. The pain was replaced by a heat that grew and grew. With savage jolts her vagina responded to his strong weapon. She ground her body to his, cleaving to him, and the pulsing volley of his semen shot into her, cooling the ache, flooding the tight flesh, filling her with the ecstatic knowledge that she had given him unalloyed pleasure.

And Cragfor, watching them, felt the ice inside her melt as she came. She was so absorbed in this intercourse by proxy that she forgot the magical mask. Her face changed, the features distorted and coarse, with a low brow, a broad flat nose and crooked teeth. Her chin jutted, pendulous jowls drooping on each side like a barnyard fowl's wattles. Her hair stuck out, reddish and wiry. Her breasts became huge and saggy, her waist thickened, her legs bowed under so much weight of big bones and fat.

Yet even she, the odious brat of a mismatch between two monsters, softened and became radiant in the rainbow hued glow emanating from the powerful centre, the wellspring of hope and redemption, generated by the heroic lovers.

Chapter Five

'Welgard is hidden in the underworld of Quexol. Go and find Cym, Queen of Thieves. She stole it. She'll let you have it, if you offer her enough.'

Varna awoke with the words ringing in her head. Time was meaningless in the belly of the volcano, day and night as one. But outside it must be dawn, and Cragfor keeping her part of the bargain.

Sandor was asleep, stretched on his back at her side. They were pressed close from shoulder to thigh. He had an arm flung over his eyes. His breathing was deep and even, and she marvelled at the rush of love that flowed through her. This man, *her* man, forever now, it seemed. Had he, too, received Cragfor's message? Was it imprinted on his brain?

This thought fortified yet alarmed her. She didn't want him to risk his life for her. No one must suffer; not him, nor Phila, not even Merrisan, though she had a score to settle with Lagras on her own account.

Instinct told her she must keep her love for Sandor secret. For his sake and her own self-preservation it was essential that she was thought of as a pure virgin. This way she might survive the perils of the city and, if fate conspired against her and she fell into Lagras's hands, it just might persuade him to respect her. A forlorn hope, she knew, but safer than if he scorned her as an immoral slut who had given herself to a man without waiting for marriage vows.

The room was illumined by the soft glow of greenish-blue light from opalescent globes set in wall-brackets shaped like graceful feminine arms. It was opulent, steeped in luxury, and Cragfor had left no stone unturned in her effort to create a bridal chamber fit for the lovers. It was thickly carpeted and ornamented with arches and mosaics, arabesques and elaborately worked tapestries.

Varna sat up suddenly, galvanised by the thought that their crafty hostess had watched them making love. She had forgotten this in the heat and passion of the night. Cragfor had used alchemy in order to get under their skins and into their very souls, sharing their emotions, their sensual delight and carnal satisfaction. The whereabouts of Welgard had been their reward. The witch had kept her promise.

'You must find it yourself.' Another voice insinuated itself into her mind, one she recognised. 'This is the only way.'

'Asvald, is that you?' she whispered. 'What must I do?'

She thought she saw him from the corner of her eye, his armour flashing a heavenly azure blue, but when she looked again the room was empty. Her heart jumped with fear, but the voice had merely told her what she already knew. It would be dicing with death to go to Quexol alone, but Asvald's support would give her the courage to do so.

She slipped out of bed, wincing at the soreness between her thighs. It wasn't an unpleasant ache, and reminded her of the way Sandor had penetrated her. Oh, she'd enjoyed a plethora of sexual delight with Phila and pleasured herself with her own fingers, but this joining of a man's flesh with hers was so new and exciting.

After washing away their sticky mutual juices she padded to the armoire and found a simple travelling outfit; a halter top and knee-length skirt made of pale, greyish brown chamois leather. It was soft and supple, warm too, and there was a brief undergarment, cut high at the sides but providing a pouch to cover her pudendum.

At the bottom of the cupboard was a selection of footwear and she laced her feet and calves into a pair of doeskin boots finished with beaded fringes. A cloak of thick alpaca completed her attire and then she looked around for a weapon.

Her own had vanished, but a superb glittering sword was propped up near the stone fireplace. She drew it from its sheath, testing its balance, lunging and retreating, spinning the shining blade above her head. Then she slung the embroidered leather baldrick over her right shoulder and adjusted the three-strapped holder at her left hip so that it cradled the scabbard.

There was no more excuse to delay. Reluctantly she tiptoed to the bed and laid her lips gently on Sandor's. He stirred but did not wake. It was terribly hard to leave him when all she wanted to do was lie at his side and use her hands to rouse his cock. It was semi-hard already and she knew that within seconds she could be riding it again.

Sighing, she made her way to the central cavern. Phila and Merrisan were curled up together, spoon-fashion, on a couch. Slaves slept on the floor and Cragfor in her massive bed. Varna hardly recognised her, so ugly in slumber, and pity welled up. Not so for Rion, however, snoring on the breast of his dominatrix, one of her nipples between his lips.

'Asvald, why can't you show yourself?' she asked aloud. 'Do I have to do this alone?'

Alone, whispered the echoes. *Alone... alone*.

'So be it,' Varna said, and drew herself up, throwing her cloak around her as if it were a royal robe. She touched the great main doors and they parted like water to let her through. No one obstructed her passage up to the entrance of the cavern. She stepped out into the dawn.

The gale plucked at her with unseen fingers, nearly hurling her into the canyon. It tossed and buffeted her, forcing her across the unstable rope bridge. Huge forms reared up, tearing at her clothes, there one moment and gone the next, to be replaced by other dimly seen horrors. Shrill laughter and bellows rent the air. Whatever it was, the force was pushing her inexorably across the chasm, and she could not fight it.

The roughly plaited hemp seared her palms. Her arms and legs ached and the bridge swung crazily from side to side. She gritted her teeth and hung on, urged forward by solid yet invisible hands. Then her scrabbling feet met earth and she collapsed at the rim of the precipice, heart pounding, breath rasping in her throat.

A swirling black mass gathered above her and she heard the creatures snarling and spitting in harsh guttural tones, followed by chilling grunts and howls. She was being pursued by djinns!

She wrapped herself in the cloak and pulled the hood up over her head. The winds whipped at it, tearing it apart. She felt her legs being opened and her wrists held immobile in a giant paw. The air buzzed with the sound of a thousand flies hovering over a putrefying corpse. Varna yelled as something started to gnaw tantalisingly at her crotch. It penetrated the chamois leather, teasing her clitoris. The thin line between excruciating agony and complete pleasure blurred and she wasn't sure if she was dying slowly or climaxing in great waves that would last for eternity.

The thing dived between the lips of her cunt and pecked at the sensitive mouth of her bottom. Other foggy forms were swarming all over her, pinching her breasts, tormenting her navel, burrowing in her pubic floss. Her clothes formed no barrier against this invasion. She might as well have been naked. She was lifted, held high, arms twisted over her head, legs dangling, and every nerve in her body was roused to painful sensitivity and a sexual awareness more intense than anything she had ever known.

She clenched her teeth tightly together, helpless against the scaly fingers clawing at her nipples and a long tongue circling, rubbing, licking at and massaging her engorged nub. She heard herself screaming and laughing and begging it to go on – on – on! Orgasm wrenched through her, a tearing, blinding cataclysm. She was dropped like a sack of potatoes, unable to help herself or break her fall. Giving her no time to recover her tormentors drove her to her feet and along a path leading into a gloomy wood.

It was quiet as the tomb now. No bird sang or insect chirped. The fiends were still there. They were lashing at her. She yelped under the sting and smart of whips she couldn't see. She wept, missing her companions, realising how foolish she had been to think she could survive without them. Yet they would have been defeated by these devilish elementals. Even Sandor, strong and fearless as he was.

Oh, Sandor! How cruel of fate to bring us together only to tear us apart, she bewailed inwardly.

She could no longer see the mountain, greenery blocking her view. The devils were quiet but she had to keep running. Even so, she couldn't avoid the bite of their whips. The forest dripped. It seemed a dour, lifeless place and she was desperate to leave it. Surely this footpath must soon yield to a pass which, once crossed, would take her to Quexol?

She wasn't certain what she would do when she arrived there, or how to find the Queen of Thieves. It seemed she could trust no one. But surely, she thought frantically, once I have Welgard in my hand, I'll be able to carry out my plan and, eventually, meet up with Sandor.

The track widened. Panting and sweating she raced forward, blind to danger. A net landed over her. She was completely trapped. The mesh tangled her limbs and her struggles only served to draw the bonds tighter.

Faces peered at her as she was hoisted like a landed fish, swinging between the trees – soldiers' faces, men in armour with plumed helmets and black and crimson uniforms. The djinns had accomplished their task. Now they had been replaced by human devils.

One of them stepped closer, grabbing a handful of her hair through the netting, holding her head steady and saying, 'Stop threshing about, Princess Varna. It's no use. I'm Captain Cafless of the Cutha Lancers, and it is my duty to convey you to King Lagras.'

'Let me go. How dare you?' she spluttered, aware that her skirt had ridden high and her scantily covered hindquarters were exposed. The damp gusset of her thong had disappeared into her crack.

Cafless barked an order and she plummeted to the forest floor, the sharp stones and pine needles hurting her. The net was hauled away and she crouched there like a cornered beast, lips curled back and eyes flashing. Cafless's men circled her, each armed with a razor-tipped lance.

He paced round her slowly, tall, thin and elegant in his tight red breeches, leather boots and braided jacket. A loose, fur-lined cape hung from one shoulder. He was handsome in an effete, dandyish way. He removed his helmet and bowed. His hair was sandy, drawn back into a queue, apart from little plaits hanging over each ear.

A supercilious smile lifted his lips under the drooping reddish moustache as he said, 'Welcome, princess. Behave sensibly and no harm shall befall you.'

'Go to hell!' she snarled and leapt at him.

She succeeded in raking her nails down his cheek before brutal hands grabbed her and pulled her off. She could feel bruises forming on her upper arms yet still she writhed, spat and kicked.

Cafless drew out a white lace-edged kerchief and

dabbed at the bloody claw marks marring his face. His pale blue eyes glinted coldly as he said, 'Headstrong as well as beautiful. The king will enjoy making you submit. Rumour has it that you're a virgin. Is this true?'

'I'm saying nothing,' she replied defiantly.

Her sword was removed and she was frog-marched to where a large log lay on the ground. It was waist-high and the soldiers forced her to lie over it on her belly, her haunches raised, her legs splayed. Her wrists and ankles were roped to it securely. She was unable to move, but too full of rage to be frightened.

A whiff of perfume told her Cafless was behind her. She felt his hands lifting her skirt, and then the coldness of steel as his dagger sliced through the ties that held her thong in place. Now chilly air played around her bare and vulnerable fissure. She turned her head and saw the guards watching with lecherous eyes and grim smiles. Valdivians to a man, and in Lagras's pay. As for Cafless? She was given no time to wonder about him, her body bucking as he opened her labial lips and tried to slide a finger into her vagina.

She yelped, more with indignation at this outrage than pain. Her inner muscles went into spasm, resisting him. He paused, frowning a little and saying, 'You appear to be undefiled. You're certainly extremely tight.'

His men murmured excitedly, their faces flushed, their distended codpieces betraying their arousal.

'So she *is* a virgin,' one of them shouted, pulling out his prick and fondling it. 'Can we have a go at her, cap'n?'

'Certainly not, Olaf,' Cafless snapped, hand flying to his sword hilt. 'She is destined for the king and, till we deliver her to him, she'll be fully protected at all times. But there's no law against her being viewed, examined, finger-fucked even. But I shall give the order. And you know what happens when I'm disobeyed, don't you? My wrath is swift and very, very painful.'

'Has she been had up the bum?' Olaf insisted, and Varna trembled at the eager note in his gruff voice and the way he stood with his large cock in his hand, the purplish glans poking between his fingers.

'I'll find out,' Cafless said, and she could not restrain a shriek as his sinewy finger pushed against her most tender aperture that had never yet known penetration. She was cold and dry there, shrinking from contact.

Her sphincter resisted and pain seared her as his hand smacked down hard on her bottom. The flesh went numb, then rushed into life with a burning heat.

'Oh! No! You can't...' she yelled.

'Can't? To me?' he replied with deceptive blandness, and smacked her again on the other buttock.

'Stop!' Varna cried, sobbing and tugging at her bonds.

She felt his mouth at her anal opening, his tongue rimming and wetting it, and his finger going deeper into her innermost recess. He alternately struck her harder, then inserted his finger more strongly. It seemed as if every blow and every finger probe was lacerating her. She had lost all shame and modesty and could hear herself screeching like a madwoman.

Cafless redoubled his onslaught, her bottom jutting out more prominently, his hand hitting her haunches and the sensitive backs of her thighs, narrowly missing her delta but getting ever closer. His finger succeeded in breaching her rectum. She felt it enter till the second knuckle ground against her nether mouth.

'She's a virgin there, and in her cunt,' he announced. 'The king shall have the satisfaction of deflowering her in both places.'

'Have you humiliated me enough? Release me now,' she cried.

'You owe me, princess,' he said softly. 'I shall bear your claw marks for at least a week. You've quite spoiled my looks.'

His hard hand landed again, slapping her buttocks till they burned, the flesh covered in red blotches that bore the imprint of his palm. The heat seemed to spread to her vitals. Her vagina ached to feel Sandor's prick stretching her, her anus was in a state of tingling irritation and her clitoris pulsed. This new experience of pleasure brought on by pain confused her. To her shame she could feel fresh juice wetting her crack and was afraid Cafless would be aware of it.

He appeared in front of her. His fingers caressed her lips and she tasted her own salty dew on them. He stared deep into her eyes, and his were the colour of a frozen sea.

'You're very wet, princess,' he commented calmly.

'Are you happy now?' she grated.

'To know you're a maiden?' he whispered, and a strange intimacy existed between them. 'Oh, yes. I can tell my lord and master. This will please him.'

'He'll never possess me,' she declared. Whatever Cafless was – a pervert, a woman lover, or a man who preferred male apertures – she wanted to rile him, vicious though his response might be. 'I want to know love, Captain Cafless, and give myself freely to a man I desire. Whatever horrors you or Lagras inflict on me, nothing can take that away.'

He stood up and she could smell his own personal odour above that of highly perfumed hair pomade. 'We'll see, princess,' he replied, and signalled for her release. 'I fancy you'll change your tune once Queen Naram and her professional torturers get their hands on you.' He swung round on the scarlet heel of his boot and shouted to the guards, 'Put her in the cage.'

Sandor fought his way into consciousness. It was as if he'd been drugged, then enmeshed in the unbreakable web of a formidable giant spider. He could not move, and his mind was clouded by a sickly green fog.

One thing stuck out beacon clear. Varna was in danger.

Frustration nearly drove him mad. His head whirled. He couldn't even see properly. Everything degenerated into a murky blur. He tried to speak, but his tongue cleaved to his bone-dry mouth. Then something came to squat across his thighs. It was Cragfor. He heard her singing triumphantly; a high, weird, wailing sound. He watched as she opened her painted lips and took his cock in her mouth, greedily engulfing him.

His head told him he was being seduced by a vile succubus, a vampire intent on sucking out his vital fluids and life's blood. His rampant body said it didn't matter. She was taking every last inch of his swollen flesh into her mouth, and her fleshy tongue was divine.

He watched her, pushing his cock in and out of her mouth, and she looked unreal, but her cheeks hollowed as she worked expertly on his erection, her head rising and falling to meet his thrusts. He couldn't help himself. The feeling was exquisite. He speeded up, and so did the succubus. The room whirled and he didn't know which way was up or down. Voices rose deafeningly, chanting an eldrich litany of lust.

Sandor bucked and gasped. His balls boiled. His cock jerked. He climaxed, spurting down the witch's throat. Then he was falling, spiralling through space, lost in a black sea of nothingness.

Cragfor woke up, spitting and snarling, furious because she had been careless and allowed herself to be captured. It all came of getting soft over a man. When she should have been psychically alert she had been indulging herself, milking Sandor's cock.

She couldn't move a muscle, lifted high in an iron restraint. Her arms were stretched above her head, her body arched, her legs drawn up to her belly, her darkly fringed lips poking out between her thighs. She groaned, seeing her mottled skin and the vast areas of flabby flesh confined by chains. She was so fat in some places that they almost disappeared in the folds.

She recognised the place, had been there before in the old days before she fell out with Lagras and his sister. It was Naram's bedchamber, equipped not only with every possible decadent luxury, but with instruments of pain as well. Dull bronze hangings stirred in the breeze, letting in shafts of sunlight, incense billowed from gold dishes set before the goddess Izar. The onyx-coloured floor reflected every feature like water, and a great, shell-shaped bed occupied a central position. Naram's slaves watched from the shadows, their eyes gleaming, their bodies too, oiled and supple.

'Well, well,' said a silky-smooth voice in Cragfor's ear. 'I must say you're not wearing very well, my dear. Unlike myself, of course, who never puts on an inch.'

'Get away from me, Naram, you bitch,' she grated, angry beyond all reason because Lagras's queen was viewing her in all her unmitigated ugliness.

Naram raised an arm and Cragfor writhed as a many-tailed, lead-tipped lash struck her across one full moon of a breast. 'Not so clever now, Cragfor,' she mocked. 'And we've got your little protégéé. She's being paraded through the countryside in a cage like a wild beast heading for the circus, chained and helpless, mocked and ridiculed. By the time we've done with her she'll have forgotten her pride, her name, her status – everything.'

'You know you can't hold me. This is an illusion. I'm not really here,' Cragfor reminded, part of her revelling in this confrontation. What was the use of having dangerous enemies if you couldn't play them at their own game?

Though wearing the form she was born with, she felt

undeniably young and invigorated after allowing her spirit to possess Varna's body and Sandor's, too. She had enjoyed their sensations and shared their orgasms and had no intention of allowing this nasty vixen to deny her further access to them.

Astral sex had provided a most agreeable respite from the problems of being an enchantress. She had rioted her way through Varna's clitoral orgasms, and known the thrill as Sandor thrust himself inside her. She had played with them a little, refusing to let him climax more than once until he had given Varna a series of mini-explosions, making her wet and languorous. Then, taking possession of his virile body, Cragfor had let go, appreciating that male charge as his cock fired its creamy essence into the girl. She hadn't been able to resist when, Varna gone, she had roused him from sleep, taking her pleasure of him one more time.

'Illusion or not, I can make you suffer,' Naram threatened, applying the whip again. This time it struck the backs of Cragfor's bloated thighs, flicking the ripe fruit of her juicy sex and the stalk of her large clitoris, roused to iron hardness.

Cragfor chuckled. 'Do it again, slave. I nearly came that time.'

'Monstrosity!' Naram said, but lowered the whip and leaned over Cragfor's exposed genitals, breathing deeply of her sour-sweet odour.

'And you love it,' the witch scoffed. 'Go on. Touch it. Rub my gem and bring me off.'

'I'll make you suffer for that,' Naram cried, as if afraid she might yield to the witch's temptation. 'You'll never win against my king and me. We'll have Varna and Sandor. Oh yes, I've seen him in Izar's pool and I'll bed him soon. It was Lagras's hellish minions, the Were-demons, who delivered her to us, and Sandor will follow.'

'Were-demons! Those sad old things!' Cragfor retorted

scornfully. 'Couldn't he do better than that? They weren't able to invade my domain and had to hang about outside. You think you're very clever, but you know nothing.'

She laughed again, exerted herself and counteracted Naram's spell. There was a moment's tug, a flash, the sensation of rotating, a shape-shift and she arrived back at the Forbidden Mountain, intact and beautiful.

'Damn! She's slippery as an eel,' Naram exclaimed, staring angrily at the empty chains.

Varna gripped the bars to steady herself against the jolting. The road was uneven and full of potholes. The wooden wheels of the cart caught in the ruts. The cage was secured to the chassis by thick ropes, and the surly driver was mounted up front, a long whip to hand, a stubby clay pipe clenched between his blackened, broken teeth. The vehicle was drawn by a team of four heavy horses with noble heads and feathery forelocks.

Varna was chained so closely that she could do nothing but stand or crouch in the straw that littered the floor. They had been travelling for hours, crossing the border into Valdivia, and had reached the outskirts of a small town.

She was hungry and thirsty. The sun beat down mercilessly on the uncovered cage. The movement, the heat and the prospect of continued captivity made her head ache.

Soldiers rode each side of the cart and Captain Cafless was always there, his icy eyes resting on her. Though the cortège halted several times so that the troops might refresh themselves, she was offered nothing. She hung on as long as she could, but when desperate to pass water had no option but to squat and urinate on the straw, in front of them all. She dreaded the thought of voiding her bowels.

Her anger turned to bitterness. I'll make Lagras pay,

she vowed.

The procession entered by the South Gate, and as they passed through the streets with their half-timbered houses that blocked out the sky, people peered from their windows and doorways and started to gather on the cobblestones. Word spread like wildfire. This was Princess Varna of Trokles. She was now King Lagras's prisoner.

The guards kept them at bay and the crowd were obviously frightened of them, yet getting as close as they dared. Old men, young men, boys whose only experience of sex had been wet dreams, and women fat and thin, comely and plain, farm women in town for the market, goodwives with baskets over their arms, mothers with babies close to their breasts, tucked into a fold of their shawl.

There were slaves, too, wearing spiked collars and short chains, doing their owners' bidding. Varna burned with hatred of a system that allowed this traffic in human beings. Shopkeepers lounged against their doorjambs, arms folded over their chests, and hucksters stopped haggling with punters to stare. Everyone was speculating on the girl in the cage.

She felt their eyes on her, some mocking, some lustful, all curious. She longed to be able to stand straight instead of being hobbled. But she did what she could, throwing back her tangled locks, gripping the bars with her manacled hands and staring out across the heads of the bystanders. She had never felt more wretched, but pride would not let her weep or plead for mercy.

Even Cafless was impressed, flicking her with his riding crop as he steered his horse close and said, 'You're giving the populace a treat, princess. There's nothing they enjoy more than a spectacle. It provides them with an excuse to get drunk and behave lewdly.'

'Are we staying here tonight? What are you going to

do with me?' she asked, giving him a glance of withering contempt.

'You'll see,' he answered, and rode on ahead.

The cart rumbled over the cobbles and, with a great crowd following and others joining it en route, they arrived at the market square. Cafless was already there, leaning from his horse and engaged in conversation with a portly man wearing an apron over his homespun breeches and shirt. His bald head shone in the fading light. He stood under an inn sign and there was a buxom woman with him, her skirt hitched up at one side over a scarlet petticoat, her hair concealed under a white coif.

The cart came to a halt and Varna heard the man say, 'It will be an honour, my lord. Yes, my lord, by all means leave her there while you enjoy the comforts of my humble hostelry.'

'I'm glad you agree, for I should have taken it over anyway, and now you'll get paid for your services,' Cafless replied grimly, then turned in the saddle to issue orders.

The horses were released from the cart's shafts and led away. The wheels were lashed together and fastened to one side of a wooden structure that was used as a platform for public whippings. Varna, jolted and jarred by the movement of the cage, hung on to the bars to steady herself.

'Think yourself lucky that you're not up there, tied to the stake and waiting to be beaten,' Cafless remarked, reining in beside her.

'Am I not to come into the inn? Do you propose to leave me here all night?' she said levelly. There was no way she was going to give him the satisfaction of hearing her beg.

'You're a captive,' he reminded gravely. 'There are to be no privileges. I but carry out my king's commands.'

'You enjoy it,' she retorted pithily.

He smiled without mirth. 'Do I, Princess Varna? One thing is for sure, you won't enjoy your night in the cage.'

Leaving four hulking soldiers, including Olaf, to take first watch, he dismounted. An ostler ran to lead his horse to the stable, and he strode to the inn where the obsequious landlord bowed him through the door. Varna's arms had been tethered in such a way that she was forced to remain standing, facing the ever-thickening crowd. At first they whispered, but as the guards showed no inclination to be harsh with them, they gained courage and made loud comments about her. These became ever coarser.

In the background stood several young blades of the town, in fashionable clothing and with elaborate hairstyles. They were escorting ladies who giggled and chattered, flaunting themselves in silk dresses with exceedingly low necklines. They kept their distance, unwilling to rub shoulders with the mob, but their hot eyes were even more alarming than the ones closer to her. Varna looked above and beyond them, fixing her mind on Sandor. He would know by now that she was gone and might be in pursuit of her. At any moment he could come striding into the square, brushing aside all obstacles and rescuing his beloved.

This didn't happen, and she was left with the reality of being a side-show for a libidinous bunch of Valdivians.

At first no one attempted to touch her, satisfied by simply looking and commenting rudely. Then, 'She is beautiful,' said a corpulent, well-dressed merchant who had pushed his way to the front and was examining her from top to toe. 'I'd pay a fortune for her, if the king would allow.'

'She's not for sale,' said Olaf brusquely. 'Least ways, not yet awhile. But the cap'n says she can be touched though not penetrated. She's a virgin, and to be kept for the king.'

‘Really?’ the merchant’s face reddened, his fat cheeks wobbling. ‘I can really touch her?’

‘Not too much,’ Olaf warned, and Varna was sickened by the almost proprietorial way in which he was regarding her.

‘A little feel?’ the man insisted, keeping his voice down, and she saw him slip a purse into Olaf’s pocket.

‘All right,’ Olaf said and stood aside so the merchant could insert a hand between the bars. ‘Just a small one. And you’re not to make her come. Understand?’

Varna tried to squirm away but her shackles made it impossible to avoid his fingers. She glared down at him, insults forming on her lips, but Olaf was watching her and she feared what he might report to Cafless if she refused to co-operate. The mob were cheering, the sight of her enflaming them. Breasts were being bared for the pleasure of ogling men. Nipples were pinched and impudent, seeking hands pushed up skirts and landed between plump, willing thighs. Not only the men were behaving badly: more than one was having his breeches undone and a female hand slipped inside to fondle his parts.

The landlord was doing a roaring trade, tankards replenished with foaming ale, goblets brimming with the rough red wine of the country. They were losing control, staggering and shouting, roused to reckless wildness.

‘King Lagras knows how to please his people,’ said the merchant to Varna as he reached up to lift the brief bodice and cup one of her breasts in a sweaty hand.

‘This is no way to rule, by bribery and corruption and moral decay,’ she shouted back, and renewed her fight to protect her flesh from being defiled by his alien caresses.

‘Ha! There speaks one who still has principles,’ he said, and used his other hand to infiltrate her skirt, trailing a finger over her tightly clenched slit, tugging at her maidenhair and forcing his digit between the lips to prod her clitoris. 'You must get wise, princess, and use your assets to further yourself. Open up, sweetheart. Let me have a good feel of your puss.'

'Get away from me, you filthy old goat!' she cried, and something in her manner brought him up short.

'Have it your own way,' he said, offended. 'Ye gods, girl, but you've a lot to learn.'

He stood back. His place was immediately taken by one of the young bucks who had edged forward. 'I can understand you finding him repellent, princess,' he began. 'But you won't say no to me.'

'That's what you think,' she raged, tugging impotently at her chains. 'If I were only free, I'd make mincemeat of you, carve you up and use your balls as earrings.'

'But you're not free, are you?' dimpled his companion, a smug blonde woman who gave herself airs but acted like a harlot. 'Up with her skirt, Raoul, and let's see what she's got.'

Those nearest to them took this up, crying, 'Lift her skirt! Let's see her fanny! Is a princess made differently from ordinary tarts?'

The one called Raoul slid the supple leather up to her waist and tucked it in the band so that it would not slither down and cover her. Her belly was exposed, her navel and dark pubic wedge. The woman pushed her hands through the bars and opened the front of the halter, drawing its edges tight each side of Varna's breasts, making the globes stand out and teasing the nipples till they peaked, hard as nuts.

The audience applauded. Raoul smirked and bowed, then, with a foot on the wheel, lifted himself till he was the right height to press his face to the iron and stick out his tongue, flicking it over Varna's teats.

His female companion laughed, and said to Olaf, 'Can't you make her to open her legs? Adjust the chains.'

It was dusk now, and oil had been ignited in cressets hammered to the walls of the houses. The inn was particularly well lit. The diamond-paned windows glowed, though shadowed every so often as customers passed and re-passed. Varna longed to be within its shelter, enjoying a meal and anticipating a bath and a comfortable bed with a feather-filled mattress. But it was her lot to be reduced to the status of a freak, caged, humiliated, the plaything of anyone who felt like toying with her.

Olaf, accepting yet another bribe, unlocked the chain that linked the manacles round her ankles. He replaced it with one that was longer. She wasn't hobbled now, but this was even worse for it meant her legs could be forced apart and her most intimate places provide sport for whoever lusted to touch her there.

She was spread wide, skirt up, thighs taut, the night air cooling her lower lips. She could feel them opening, the hair-bordered outer pair swollen, the smooth inner petals damp and unprotected.

'Get her out of there and on to the block,' someone shouted. 'Strip her. Whip her. Lay the stripes on thick and fast till she bleeds!'

'That's it. Bare her body. Thrash her arse!'

'And her breasts!'

'And her cunt!'

Varna turned her head and buried her face in her arm, her long hair veiling it. These people were animals! No, that was an insult to the beasts who were never so cruel, killing to survive, not for fun, and mating to reproduce their kind. Humans were an abomination and should be destroyed by the gods!

'No, princess, don't hide your face,' said Olaf, and reached in to turn her chin. 'Captain Cafless's orders.'

'Help me,' Varna whispered, her eyes swimming with tears.

'What will you give me, if I do?' Olaf asked, his rugged face earnest as he watched Raoul lightly fingering Varna's exposed slit then smelling her scent that lingered on his hand.

'I have nothing, no money or jewels,' she gasped, wincing yet at the rush of longing in her loins as Raoul pushed back the hood of her clit and crooked his finger, stroking the ardent little organ.

'Promise that if I come to you by dead of night, loosen your bonds a bit and push my cock through the bars, you'll pleasure me with your hands and mouth,' he muttered, sweat beading his forehead under his helmet.

This was a foul option, yet Varna had no alternative but to agree. She nodded, murmuring, 'Yes, yes. Whatever you want. Just get these people away from me.'

Olaf leapt into action. 'All right, you horrible lot!' he shouted above the uproar. 'The show's over! Get back to your homes or I'll let my lads loose on you. Go on. Get you gone!' and he used the flat of his blade as an added incentive to shift fast. No one tangled voluntarily with the Cutha Lancers.

The crowd cleared. Soon the square was empty of all save Varna and the sentries. Bored, they settled down to roll dice. One of their friends brought over a tray of pies and flagons of small-beer from the inn. Olaf eased Varna's chains so she could sit down on the straw.

'Can't you get me something to eat? I'm starving,' she said, looking at him under her curling lashes and humiliating herself even more by pretending to be nice to him.

'Later,' he muttered. 'When they're asleep and before the next watch comes on duty, I'll be with you. I expect you to keep your word. My cock's all a-twitch, waiting for your lips, sweeting.'

Varna watched him go back to his mates, that hulking,

coarse-grained soldier who she had promised to please for the sake of peace and privacy – for the sake of a little food. She bowed her head in her arms and sobbed quietly.

Chapter Six

'So, you are Princess Varna.'

The voice was crisp and authoritative, its owner a large man seated on a throne and wearing a crown. Cafless prodded Varna in the back but she refused to heed this heavy hint that she kneel. If anything, Lagras should be kneeling to her and begging forgiveness for depriving her of father and country.

'I am,' she answered haughtily.

Inside she was trembling, weak with hunger, grimy from the journey, plagued by Olaf whenever they stopped. He offered her protection, but she paid dearly for it. Even now she could taste his sour semen.

Lagras left his chair and paced slowly down the carpeted steps from the dais. She stared at him as he came closer. Ice trickled down her spine. She had seen him before in her dreams. They had been in conflict then, as they were now. This man, this *murderer*, had her in his power. She loathed him, yet his striking, feral appearance made her tingle. He was handsome, olive-skinned and black-bearded, his oiled ebony ringlets falling about the shoulders of his purple robe. Every inch a king, and she couldn't deny it. Neither could she deny his hypnotic presence and charisma.

'On your knees, bitch!' he hissed, his dark eyes narrowing.

'No,' she returned, mentally throwing down the gauntlet. Let him know just exactly who she was and how impossible it would be to break her spirit.

A shocked murmur rippled through the throne room. The courtiers drew in sharp breaths, their eyes wide. No one dared move a muscle. Even the bodyguards stood rigid, waiting for the storm to break.

Lagras's sullen gaze focused on Varna. 'You dare defy me, even now?' he said. 'It's obvious that you've not been punished enough. Get down on the floor.'

'No!' she repeated, glaring at him.

He snapped his fingers and a large man stepped forward. His skin was dark brown. He was shaven-headed and ugly, his torso glistening, his biceps bulging. 'Yes, sire?' he said in a deep, gravely voice.

'Make her obey me, Aswad,' Lagras ordered, balancing his weight on spread legs, his thumbs hooked in his jewelled belt.

Varna was gripped from behind in Aswad's steely arms and flung down. Her head hit the floor. 'You have no right,' she spluttered.

'I have every right,' Lagras answered, and she saw the toe of his black leather boot appear on a line with her eyes. 'You're a prisoner of war. *My* prisoner and I'll do what I like with you. Prostrate yourself.'

Aswad yanked her knees from under her so she was forced to lay flat with her arms and legs open wide. Her cheeks flamed and her mind was in turmoil. There was no more servile position than this one.

She saw a small bare female foot with gilded toenails appear next to Lagras's, and heard a woman say, 'She needs to be chastised, your majesty. Look at her bottom. Totally unblemished. I can honestly say I've never seen one so ready for the whip. Have you ever been thrashed, princess?'

'Never,' she replied, her voice muffled.

'I found it necessary to smack her, sire,' she heard Cafless say. 'She was rebellious on capture, and attacked me. But to the best of my knowledge she is a virgin who has never enjoyed a man, or felt the kiss of the lash.'

'Thank you, Captain Cafless,' Lagras said, a thread of

amusement in his voice. 'This is splendid news indeed, and both conditions need to be rectified. Don't you agree, Naram, my queen?'

Perfume drifted above Varna and she felt a hand laying back her torn and filthy skirt, then fingers running lightly between her anal crease like little mice. But strong, too, and unrelenting, exploring and delving, finding her clitoris and lingering there.

'I do, sire. She's ripe for it.'

'I'll administer it myself,' he said.

The courtiers rustled and shifted closer. Varna glanced up, but could see nothing except the hems of robes and the tips of toes. She had known when she was captured that her first meeting with Lagras would be bad, but had not realised the extent of it.

The tiles were cold and of unmitigated hardness. They ground into her cheek, her breasts, and the tender tops of her thighs. The courtiers were whispering among themselves. Queen Naram, who she could not yet see, had already humiliated her in front of them by probing at her sex. The sun had gone out in her life and all that was left was darkness. No father. No Sandor. Only these enemies who were without pity or mercy or honour.

She dared to move, lifting her head in time to see Lagras grab a whip from Aswad. With his long robe flowing around him and his hair swinging forward under the coronet, his intention was so fiercely expressed that dread shot through her heart.

He stalked back to her and the atmosphere could have been cut with a knife. 'You'll soon beg to be my concubine,' he said, and dangled the thin lash over her hinds, then added, 'As this is your first time, I choose to be lenient. This is a single thong, and you may lick my foot in gratitude.'

Her face was thrust against the leather. She rested her cheek on his arch, horrified to discover the first stirrings of submission within her. This was Sandor's doing, this new melting sensation that made her forget her warrior training, turning her soft and womanish. She fought it, quickly withdrawing her lips from Lagras's boot.

'What's this?' he grated. 'Still disobedient?'

Without warning he flung back his arm and brought down the whip with a vicious snap, a blow calculated to cut into both cheeks where it would sting the most. Varna grunted at the impact, stunned and numb. Giving her no time to recover, he struck again. This time she shrieked, agony rushing through her. What she had endured at Cafless's hand had been as nothing compared to this.

'Be quiet, or I'll have you gagged!' Lagras shouted, and trailed the whip across her buttocks so that those watching could see the red weals forming against her pale skin.

'A pretty sight,' Naram agreed, and Varna felt her cool fingers tracing the path of fiery heat searing her tortured rump.

'You wish to take part?' Lagras asked magnanimously.

'No, my king, watching you do it is rousing me,' she replied and clapped her hands. 'Rana! Fetch Jat. It's time that boy earned his keep. He can fuck me while the punishment continues.'

Jat. The name drifted somewhere amidst the pain. Then Varna remembered. Merrisan had said her young brother was the queen's slave, and that he was called Jat.

Then all thought was driven from her as Lagras lay on the whip with deft precision so that it kissed both her bottom cheeks and the side of her hip. This was followed by a period of quiet. Varna strained her ears but she couldn't hear him. Terror swamped her. It was far worse than knowing the whip would fall in a regular rhythm. The anticipation was awful. Had he left her to suffer there? Would others – even more of strangers than him – seek to whip and use her?

Then she caught a small sound. A woman was gasping in ecstasy. Her voice rose to a wail and Varna recognised it as belonging to Naram. Jat was doing his duty. Her labia ached, her nipples, too. She wanted Sandor, but remembered to blank out thoughts of him. She was at a sorcerer's mercy and they must not read her mind.

Testing her captors, she moved slightly. At once a heavy foot came down on the back of her neck. 'Did I say you could rise?' Lagras asked, and pressed harder till she thought she might suffocate.

He left her, but she dared not try this again. She waited. Time ticked by. She had no recollection of its duration. It could have been a minute or an hour. She tried to hide inside herself, to escape the smart of her damaged derrière. The floor was brutally hard, but when she made tentative motions with her hips a pulse throbbed deep in her pubis. Her exposed crotch was ultra sensitive. She was aware of every breeze or movement of air. She felt wet and aroused there. It was as if Lagras, radiating demonic energy, had ignited a raging fire in her loins.

She whimpered softly, wishing for water, for a finger on her nubbin, even contact with the lash. Stealthily she slipped a hand underneath her and massaged her bud. The spasms mounted as she worked her thumb against the pulsating tip. Climax was near and she could not repress a moan as she rose towards the peak.

Abruptly, a bolt of pain stung her thighs. Six blows were delivered one after the other with no pause between them. She was almost unconscious, yet sensed Lagras's nearness even when he stopped whipping her. But, in the surrounding silence when all she could hear was her own breathing, the pain came again. This time she knew the warning signs – the air whistling as the lash passed through it – the vibrations of Lagras's sexual energy – the agony that leapt up and possessed her, body and soul.

She was reduced to a cringing, shuddering creature,

devoid of dignity. This was slavery indeed, this submission to another's will. He focused on her arse, larding it with stripes, and Varna was in a trance-like state. The sound of leather meeting bare flesh was muffled and she began to absorb the fire. The tingling rush of pain was transformed into arousal. She wasn't angry any more. She wanted him to complete her degradation by taking her, filling her, ravaging her.

As if he sensed the change in her, he eased off. Blessed peace descended on her and she hoped they would let her lie there forever. Death would have been a relief from the anguish of body and mind, for shame burned as keenly as the welts. What was happening to her? Where was her pride now?

She moaned in protest when Aswad dragged her up from the floor. She staggered and would have fallen had not his arms upheld her. The slave-master turned her to face Lagras.

'Are you ready to kiss my feet, or do you need another beating?' he said.

Aswad used the flat of his massive hand to make her crawl across to where the king stood. She wanted so much to refuse him, but placed her lips on his instep and kissed it abjectly.

The fringing of his robe brushed her face and his legs rose above her, his bare thighs disappearing into the mauve shadows of his belted tunic. She looked up, trying to discern the solid mass of his testicles and cock. Aswad raised her to her knees and just for an instant she saw the extravagantly attired sycophantic courtiers, and the Cutha Lancers, all flash and braid, and the slaves cowering under the whips of Aswad's assistants, and the stern-featured, sombrely-clad woman who was Naram's servant. The ostentatious throne room with its frescoes, gold ornaments, crimson drapes and basalt pillars inspired her with awe.

The queen's violet eyes met hers from where she bent over one of the arms of the throne. Her sequinned skirt was pulled up to her waist, her naked posterior presented to a slim youth who very much resembled Merrisan. His body was constricted by leather straps and pierced with metal rings, and he was thrusting his penis into Naram, his hands cupping her breasts, the nipples protruding between his fingers.

'You see what you're missing, princess?' Naram shouted gleefully. 'Do as Lagras commands, and all this shall be yours, and more.'

Why fight them? Why not surrender? Varna's body ached, every inch awash with pain, yet the blood coursed hotly through her veins and the sight of Jat shafting the queen made her long for some of the same.

Unable to resist, she sat back on her heels and ran her hands up Lagras's hairy thighs. Her fingers met the spongy firmness of his balls. She was aware that his cock was erect, tenting his tunic. She touched it and gasped. So did he.

'Well, well, not such a shrinking violet after all?' he murmured, with a sardonic smile.

'I've never shrunk from anyone,' she rapped out, and dropped her hand, the moment of madness passing. 'I'm a warrior and now a queen, inheriting my father's realm.'

He looked at her with the blackest scowl she had ever seen on a man's face. 'Still arrogant!' he shouted. 'You have no realm. It belongs to me.'

'It will never be yours and you can't break me,' she said, still on her knees but not humble.

'You say you're a virgin,' he snapped, brooding on her.

'I said it, majesty,' put in Cafless. 'When I tested her, she was tight as a drum in both orifices.'

'Examine her, Naram,' Lagras ordered.

She wriggled out from under Jat and aimed a slap at

his bottom. 'Come along, Rana,' she called imperiously. 'You, too, Aswad. We'll soon find out the truth. Will you take her then, brother?'

Lagras chewed his thumbnail, not a happy man. Varna, who had fully expected to have to fight him off, was puzzled. Though he had whipped her, he'd made no attempt to rape her. What was it he wanted of her?

She found her answer when he said, 'I don't know. She has eluded me, and continues to defy me. A woman of such courage deserves more than a rape.' Then his eyes fixed Varna's and she could feel herself drowning in the inky pupils when he added, 'You'll come to me willingly, princess. I *will* subdue you. I swear it by Izar!'

It cost her in pain, but Varna weaved to her feet and held her head high, meeting that intimidating gaze and declaring, 'And I vow by my god, Udin, that I shall never, never yield to you. Do your worst, Lagras.'

At his nod, Aswad propelled her to a pillar in the centre of the room, bound her hands together with rope and strung them to a hook above her head. Her ankles were fastened to the base, legs splayed, and then Naram and Rana approached her.

The courtiers were watching, as lustful as the commoners in the villages. They wanted to please their king and queen, but were enjoying seeing Varna's downfall, especially as she laid claim to being pure and of royal birth.

She slumped in her bonds, the rope scoring her flesh. Naram smiled her feline smile, that gorgeous, flame-haired woman with the violet eyes. Her companion was thin as a beanpole, such leanness exaggerated by her black attire and tall, birdlike head-dress.

'Begin,' Naram said.

Stern and hatchet-faced, Rana started to stroke Varna's inner thighs, the pressure becoming heavier as she inched towards her bushy mound. Then she imprisoned Varna's labia between her fingers and teased the unfurling inner flesh. Her middle finger slipped along the crack, seeking the vulva.

Varna doubted she would be so lucky as when Cafless attempted to invade her. Rana and Naram were experienced in such matters and it wouldn't be easy to deceive them. Rana inserted the finger in the tight mouth and waggled it experimentally. Despite the fear of discovery and the stiffness of her bruised body, Varna felt a tingling thrill. She wanted more, her sex suffused with warmth. The whole of her seemed to light up.

'Well?' Naram said impatiently.

'I can't feel her hymen, but her passage is very narrow,' Rana answered, withdrawing her finger and licking it. 'I don't think she's ever been penetrated.'

'What have you to say about this?' Naram questioned, gripping Varna's face and turning it towards her.

'I'm an athlete, a warrior. I've spent most of my life on horseback or running, jumping, working out with sword, javelin and spear. It would have been a miracle if my hymen hadn't been broken,' Varna said, looking Naram squarely in the eye.

'I suppose so,' the queen replied slowly. 'Indeed you have a frigid air about you, too dedicated by far. You like making love to women, though, don't you?'

'Do I?' Varna was hot all over and surprised to find that her fear had gone. She wanted more of Rana's fingers, ached to feel them on her clit – soothing, enticing.

'I've seen you.'

'When? How?' Then Varna remembered those nights back in Ciophos, when she could have sworn Phila and she were being watched. Realisation dawned and, 'You spied on me, using sorcery,' she accused.

Naram gave a slow, ironic hand-clap. 'Well done that girl. Someone give her a medal for intelligence and observation.'

'I saw you, too. That's when I determined to have you,' Lagras added, leaning against the pillar and looking at her with that same expression of bafflement, but whether at her or his own reaction to her it was impossible to gauge.

'He's such a romantic,' Naram said acerbically, and Varna guessed she was jealous.

'Romance be damned,' he returned gruffly. 'What about her arsehole?'

Varna let out a jarring cry when Naram poked into her anus. It burned unpleasantly, her ring taking the queen's finger no more readily than it had Cafless's. Naram pushed firmly, then shook her head and said, 'She needs serious attention there before she can pleasure you, my lord king. Shall I apply a balm containing an aphrodisiac?'

'It won't make any difference. I'll resist you all the way,' Varna said. She was shaking, appalled by her feelings when Rana touched her lightly again. The whole of her awareness was heightened, her sex on edge. Waiting, aroused, strung out as if on a rack.

'You're obstinate, Varna. I'll leave you here to mull over my proposal,' Lagras said with a shrug and turned away. A copper-skinned slave-girl answered his summons, kneeling in front of him, lifting his tunic and taking his prick into her mouth.

'My lords, ladies and gentlemen,' Naram's voice echoed under the high ceiling. 'It is the king's wish that you avail yourselves of this stubborn princess, but no one is to despoil her. She is his prize, his to own and possess.'

There were cheers, and the crowd surged towards the pillar. Varna closed her eyes to blot out those sneering faces, just as she had done when in the cage, but she could not escape the hands that roamed her with gross familiarity, fingering her pussy and anus and toying with her breasts. They brought whips and switches and belaboured her hips and thighs, adding fresh pain to her scorched and agonised rump.

She hung limply in her bonds, dazed by their treatment and berating the gods who had brought her to this terrible hour. It dragged on for what seemed an eternity. Then they grew bored and wandered off to seek other diversions. Varna rested exhaustedly against the pillar. Every muscle in her body ached, but she knew she'd have to remain there until Lagras ordered her to be freed.

At that point of the night when the world seems suspended in space awaiting the arrival of the sun, she felt a hand on her leg and heard him whispering, 'Have you had enough? Come with me and I'll see that slaves bathe you, anoint your sores, feed you with delicacies and dress you in silk. Then you can share my bed. What d'you say?'

'No,' she repeated dully.

He snorted in exasperation, 'You really are pig-headed! Why, Varna? Why go on with this charade? You know you'll be mine in the end.'

'I shan't.'

He seized her, shook her, dug his nails into the bruises and welts, then captured her lips with his and ground them against her clenched teeth. 'Don't you understand?' he muttered. 'I'm offering you the highest honour in the land. You can be my second wife, almost as powerful as Naram. We'll teach you the secrets of magic, give you life everlasting. Everything you desire shall be yours.'

He shot out an arm. Flames blazed from his fingertips and set fire to the drapes. He lowered his hand and they vanished, the curtains undamaged. At a snap of finger and thumb a diamond necklace appeared out of thin air. He pushed back the hair from her nape and fastened the jewels round her neck.

'Is this supposed to impress me?' she asked coldly.

'Conjuring tricks unworthy of a king?'

The necklace disappeared and he glowered at her. 'I can do much, much more. You want me to raise a storm? Have the city destroyed by a tornado? Show you my Were-demons, perhaps?'

'I've seen them, been subjected to their disgusting abuse,' she answered and turned her head away.

The light in the throne room was ethereal, a greyish smudge growing steadily, turning the candles wan. Outside a bird gave full-throated song. Soon it would be morning. A natural morning organised by nature, not a magician.

'I'm so tired,' she said.

'Then let me take you to where you can sleep for hours, if you want,' he insisted.

She smiled at him wearily. 'You're a wizard. You can do anything,' she reminded. 'You can have anyone, except me. I shall always hate and despise you. You can force me to marry you, but I warn you that at the earliest opportunity I'll kill myself.'

'Damn bitch!' he said, and hit her across the face.

She could feel her mouth filling up with blood, the lips already puffing. She did not even try to answer.

'Aswad!' Lagras shouted, so loudly that slaves dozing on the floor jumped up in alarm.

'Yes, sire,' the man said, materialising from the gloom.

'Take Princess Varna to the dungeons.'

'Where is she? Tell me or I'll throttle the life out of you!' Sandor roared.

He had woken not long before and found that Varna had gone. Striding into the great cavern, he now glared at Cragfor who, as dainty as a water-nymph, was allowing her women to dress her hair. Pearls were being woven amidst the emerald green tresses, adding to the illusion that she was some kind of sea-sprite, a mermaid perhaps.

'Oh, calm down do, you great galoot,' she chided briskly. 'She'll be all right.'

'How can you know that?' He towered over her, a barbarian in his skins and furs, his brown hair mussed, his chin unshaven. It made him look rough and dangerous and thoroughly desirable.

She batted her eyelashes at him. 'I've told you. I know everything. Now why are you bothering about her? Stay here with me. I'm experiencing one of those rare moments when I almost wish I was mortal.'

He shook his head, buckled on his broadsword and slung on his wolf-pelt cloak. 'I'm off. Thanks for telling us where Welgard is. At least, I suppose it was you as I woke up with the information in my head. I assume Varna knows as well.'

'She does, and that's where she's gone. To Quexol. Unfortunately, she was captured on the way and taken to Lagras's palace.'

'What about me? You haven't forgotten your old benefactor, have you?' Rion whined. 'You're going to kill Firestorm, aren't you?'

Sandor's frustration found an outlet. He lifted the dwarf by the scruff of the neck and shook him like a dog shakes a rat. 'I have more important things on my mind,' he roared.

'But the treasure,' Rion wailed, struggling feebly.

'To hell with it! Later, much, much later, I may turn my attention to it, but for myself, not you,' and Sandor threw him aside. Cragfor's laughter echoed through the cavern.

'What's going on?' Phila asked, already equipped for action.

'You're going to Quexol?' added Merrisan, taking up a stance close by, breastplate gleaming, helmet part covering her sun-streaked hair. Armbands, greaves, kilt with metal strips for added protection, all proclaimed her to be a fighter.

'That's right. Welgard is owned by Cym, Queen of Thieves, who runs a very successful operation in the vice-ridden slums of the city. You'll get on well with her. She's tough as old boots,' Cragfor said with a grin.

'What are we waiting for?' Sandor cried, already halfway to the door.

'Ah, the impetuosity of youth,' the witch exclaimed. No one saw her move, but she was at his side, undulating her sinuous body against him. 'Don't you want directions how to find Cym? You think it will be easy and that you can just walk in and demand she see you? Oh, no, my dear. You're likely to end up garrotted,' and she clasped a hand round her neck and pulled a ghastly face.

'Then tell me,' he bellowed, exasperated.

'There are codes, secret signs and passwords,' she said, yellow eyes twinkling. 'The thieves are close as clams. Listen carefully...'

He tried to commit everything to memory, but her instructions were numerous. He was thankful that Phila and Merrisan were taking it in, brows drawn together, faces intent. As they had said once before, three would be better than one on an expedition such as this.

'First you have to get into the city,' Cragfor went on. 'You'll stand out like sore thumbs. What you need are pilgrims' robes, sober grey and hooded. Let me see what I can do.' At once Sandor found himself enveloped in coarse wool. It was stiflingly hot on top of his cloak.

'Remember, heads bowed, a meek attitude,' Cragfor instructed, tweaking Merrisan's hood over her bright hair. 'You, too, Phila. No strutting and war cries. It won't do you any harm to practise humility for once. Now, off with you.'

'Lagras will use magic to obstruct us, won't he?' Sandor asked, still bemused by events he could barely recall. Varna and he making love then, later, a succubus...

or was it Cragfor?

'He used demons to trap Varna, but he couldn't penetrate my mountain so knows nothing of your affair with her.'

'You mean that was real?' he said, a sudden burst of happiness exploding in his chest. 'I wasn't sure if I'd dreamed it.'

'It was real. She loves you and you her,' Cragfor explained slowly, as if teaching a dimwit.

He struck himself on the forehead, eyes shining. 'That's right. I remember now. Varna, my beloved. I want her back. Let's get going.'

'Take care, my hero,' Cragfor said and reached up and kissed him, thrusting her tongue into his mouth.

And Rion watched, crouching at the feet of Leila, an expensive mistress who was demanding much. He needed Firestorm's hoard more than ever now. His bloodshot eyes fastened malevolently on Sandor's indifferent back as he went out of the great door.

Darkness, dampness, a heap of mouldy straw thrown down in a corner. The slimy walls shone green as Aswad's lamp swung backwards and forwards.

'What have I done to deserve this?' Varna cried in despair.

Aswad looked at her without compassion. 'You've brought it on yourself. Anyone who speaks to the king like you've done is a fool,' he scolded, snapping metal cuffs round her wrists and looping their chains over an iron ring set in the wall.

This was hateful. For a few hours she had been free of shackles. Now they weighed her down again, restricting movement, making her constantly aware that she was a prisoner.

'Why do I have to wear these?' she asked, trying to kick out. He hit her, stars dancing across her vision. Then he gripped her ankles and closed the leg-irons. 'I can't run away. I've no idea where I am, only that it's somewhere underground. You'll lock me in, so why can't you at least give me the freedom to walk around?'

'You can have as much freedom as you want, if you do as he wants,' Aswad said, testing the links. He turned his attention to her body, thumbing her nipples, exploring her belly and dragging thick fingers along her delta.

She winced, but couldn't move. 'Who are you that you take such liberties?' she shouted.

The whites of Aswad's eyes and his perfect teeth gleamed as he grinned genially. 'Me? Why, I'm the king's right-hand man. I go to the auctions and buy slaves for him, and take care of those he brings back from battle. He trusts me, lady. I keep his harem in order and find him the prettiest boys. Rana is the queen's creature, but I'm loyal to King Lagras.'

He was strong and he had principles and she did not want to be left alone in the darkness, almost wishing Olaf would appear. After assuring himself that she was securely bound, Aswad went out. She heard the key turning in the lock and bolts being thrown. At first she could see nothing, but as her eyes became accustomed to the darkness she saw a ray of light filtering down from an aperture high up in the uneven ceiling. At least this would give her some idea of the time of day.

Aswad had left her a crust of bread and a pitcher of water. She was so hungry and thirsty that this went down as sweetly as the richest feast and vintage wine. She dragged herself to the straw, tried to shake it out and make it more comfortable, then gave up. She was too bruised and battered, her body and mind screaming for rest.

'Asvald, protect me,' she whispered, sinking back on this harsh bed that gave no respite to her soreness.

No answer came, no messenger of the gods in shining

armour appeared. She was too worn out to care, curling up as best she could and sinking into a fitful, troubled sleep.

In the heart of Quexol, miles from the main gate, stood an inn. At least, the creaking sign over the door proclaimed it as such – *The Three Doves.* A harmless enough sobriquet, deceptively so, as this was the headquarters of one of the most lawless, hedonistic, and downright wicked gangs in the whole of Valdivia. Situated as it was in a disreputable area known as The Rookery, it offered sanctuary to every kind of miscreant. Even the Cutha Lancers refused to enter its murky, twisted alleys, overshadowed by dilapidated houses.

Cym owned *The Three Doves.* She was the most influential person in this stronghold of thieves. Not only influential: she was bold, beautiful and bi-sexual. She had reached the zenith of power. Only one person had more than her, and that was the king. Now she was bored, sitting in her parlour at the back of the taproom, playing cards with her latest lover who was boyishly handsome, and rather drunk.

She hadn't had him yet, and was still trying to make up her mind whether she really wanted to be bothered. He'd only go and fall in love with her, and this was tedious.

It was high time she took part in an adventure. Once she had been a pickpocket, a burglar, a footpad. Now, because of her organising abilities, she received stolen goods and got rid of them, taking a substantial percentage of the profit. She sighed impatiently: the thief had become a bookkeeper and it was impossibly dull.

The young man placed a hand on her knee. It felt hot through her long straight skirt. This was slit at one side for ease of movement and access to her sex, if she felt inclined. She never wore anything underneath. She leaned an elbow on the table, cupped her chin in her hand and stared at him.

'I thought we were playing cards,' she said sternly.

'Look here... I don't care about the money you've won from me. Take it. Have it all. Let me go to bed with you.'

'Tut, tut!' she scolded, his impetuosity sending chills through her. Maybe he would do to wile away an hour after all. 'But you're nothing but a baby. Does your mother know you're here?'

He blushed, the colour rising to meet the errant lock of hair that tumbled over his forehead. 'My mother is at the palace. She's got friends in high places,' he answered.

'Well, she would have, being a notorious courtesan.' Cym knew the woman, had lent her money more than once, with a high rate of interest. Whores were some of her best customers, especially those scrabbling to climb the ladder of success.

'Everyone who is anyone is there these days, trying to catch a glimpse of Princess Varna.'

'The king's latest captive. I've heard about her,' Cym said thoughtfully, but did not stop him as his fingers found her smooth thigh beneath the skirt and advanced towards her crotch.

Cym deliberately dropped a card. As she leaned forward to retrieve it from the floor the deep neckline of her blouse parted, showing the valley between her breasts. The boy goggled, moistened his lips, then took a swig at his flagon of beer, but did not relinquish his grip on her thigh.

'You want to see her?' he offered. 'She's exhibited daily in the dungeon. Mother could get you in. People are paying to look at her.'

'Why? What's so important about her?' Cym was getting irritated by his caresses. It was like being touched by a fumbling schoolboy.

'I don't know exactly. Seems she was hard to capture and now refuses the king.'

'And he tolerates this?' She wriggled her hips, trying to make him understand that she wanted his fingers on her clit, not way off beam at her cunny entrance. 'She sounds a spirited woman. I'd like to meet her,' she went on, then pushed back her skirt and opened her legs. 'That's where I want you to touch me.' She pushed him away and massaged the red-pink folds surrounding her stiff nubbin, then used the dew to wet the head and massage it eagerly.

His eyes followed the path of her fingers and his hand dropped between his legs, rubbing his erection. Cym lifted one leg and placed her foot on the bench where they sat. She pushed a finger inside herself, going as deeply as she could. It wasn't far enough, and she yearned for a collection of men to service her. She'd have one in her cunt, one in her arse, another in her mouth, and one each side of her, their cocks in her hands. When they'd spurted their places would immediately be taken by a fresh batch.

The young man took out his cock and lovingly smoothed his jism over the helm. Why didn't he put two and two together and come up with the answer that this was precisely what she required? The clit and the glans were twins and responded to the same stimulation, a fact of which many men were ignorant, as she had proved through lengthy and varied experience.

Female lovers, however, never disappointed.

Even so, she enjoyed a virile stud, one with a big prick who'd use her as a stallion uses a mare. Her hand moved faster and she moaned gently, her clitoris throbbing with excitement. Totally absorbed in the mounting pleasure she growled with anger when one of her bullies appeared in the doorway.

She paused in her labours, though not altering her pose.

Her thug had seen her like it before, and had even joined in, a broken-nosed, ugly-handsome bruiser that men avoided and women went mad over. He grinned across at her, lounged against the doorframe and said, 'There's someone asking for you.'

Missing her orgasm by a heartbeat, no more, Cym took her hand from her pussy. 'Who?' she rapped out.

'Pilgrims,' he answered, giving a belly laugh.

'A likely story. Who is it really?'

'He says he knows Cragfor. He's dressed as a pilgrim but someone had taught him the jargon. He got through to here without having his throat cut.'

'A man, you say?' Cym's ears pricked up.

'Aye, a great hulking fellow, and he has two companions with him. They're wearing habits, but have got armour on underneath, and I'll stake my oath that they're doxies. I took the precaution of disarming all three.'

'Well done, Wicus. Let's see who dares enter my patch. Show them in,' Cym said, and dismissed the young man.

She ran a hand through her crinkly black hair and smoothed down her skirt. It was early yet, and the nightly crowd had not yet begun to gather. The pot-boy had scrubbed the bar and the round wooden tables. Fresh straw had been spread on the flagstones. A new bevy of whores had replaced the daytime ones, and all was ready for an evening's carousel. Not only this: Cym was expecting a haul from a pirate ship that had weighed anchor in the bay. She wasn't fussy where the loot came from, and never asked questions.

She waited, drumming her fingers on the table's polished surface, her spine chilled by a frisson of anticipation. One never knew what was round the corner. This is what made her life so rewarding: it wasn't simply that she was one of the richest women in Quexol.

The door was flung back, the aperture filled by a

stranger. He strode in. Two other grey-shrouded figures followed.

'Hold it there!' Cym commanded, rising to her feet, a cudgel to hand. 'Don't come any closer till you've told me your reason for being here.'

The man threw back his hood and tossed the folds of the cloak over his wide shoulders. He was tall and muscular, in the prime of his manhood. Even the roughness of his clothing could not disguise his princely bearing. His hair fell loosely down his back and his eyes were as green as the sea.

Ah ha! Cym thought, her vagina convulsing. This one is for me!

'I'm Sandor Deva, a Durani Knight, and I've come for Welgard,' he announced.

She was taken aback. The sword had come into her hands years ago. She had brazenly stolen it from a connoisseur of ancient weaponry who'd had it in his collection. She didn't believe it had magic properties, dismissing this as a fable.

'Have you, by the gods?' Cym answered steadily, but she couldn't stop feasting her eyes on this extraordinarily handsome young warrior. Her nipples were so hard they showed as sharp points under her white blouse. She had already forgotten the man she'd been seducing earlier. 'And why should I even consider letting you have it?'

'To save Princess Varna and free Trokles,' he replied, and he wasn't asking for the sword, he was demanding it as his right. He seemed to think it a forgone conclusion that she would give it to him.

'And why in the world should I put myself out for her? I don't even know her.' Cym was shocked by such effrontery.

'You'll do it because you love adventure and adventurers,' said one of the women with him, discarding the shapeless robe and showing herself as a slender-limbed, vitally attractive woman. 'I'm Merrisan, and I can tell that you thrill at the clarion call of the trumpet.'

'You look like a fighter. No one has got the better of you for years, have they? My name is Phila, and Varna is not only my princess but my dearest friend,' said the other one, equally lithe and beautiful.

Cym did not know who to look at first – Sandor or the two lovely women. A sword, no matter if it was reputed to be a magical one, was nothing compared to the joys of making love to all three.

Chapter Seven

'Leave this to me,' Merrisan whispered to Sandor, and got rid of the itchy pilgrims' mantle.

She faced Cym confidently, her thrusting bosom filling the moulded metal cups added to her leather armour for greater protection of the vital heart area. Her skirt reached halfway down her thighs, and she was holding her helmet by its chinstraps.

She was aware of Phila, that staunch ally who had also become her lover. Both of them were hell-bent on rescuing Varna, though each had a slightly different agenda: Phila was doing it out of loyalty, while Merrisan intended to release her brother. But there was this first obstacle to overcome – the iron-willed Cym.

Merrisan had picked up on her preference for women. Sandor might appeal with his mighty frame and height, but when it came to the final choice, she knew instinctively that she and Phila would win, hands down. Added to this was curiosity and sexual heat. Cym was a voluptuously sensual woman.

'I didn't believe it when Cragfor said you owned half of Quexol, but it seems I was wrong,' Merrisan began, closing the space between them in a couple of strides.

Cym preened herself. 'The witch exaggerates. This was ever her way. Suffice to say the underworld respects me.'

'Who wouldn't?' Merrisan murmured, her heat increasing. She could feel perspiration gathering in the deep cleavage that separated her breasts.

Phila gaped, clearly annoyed, but Merrisan winked at her without Cym seeing. Sandor was glowering, brows drawn together. He was taut as a coiled spring.

Cym was not easily deceived, too shrewd to be taken in by flattery. 'Sit down,' she said, and indicated the bench on the other side of the table. 'We should discuss this in detail. If I give you the sword, and I'm not saying I shall, what do I get in exchange?'

'A night to remember?' Phila said with a laugh as she slid along the bench by Merrisan.

'You think you're that good? Don't forget I can have almost anyone in the land,' Cym said cynically.

'But we're unique. In one, you can have a hero and two she-soldiers who are also titled in their own right.'

Cym pushed the wine bottle towards her and said, 'Have a drink on the house.'

Phila poured wine into goblets, while Merrisan extended her leg under the table and lifted her sandalled foot. She found the seat opposite and worked her way up Cym's thigh, parted the skirt and arrived at the furry fork at her apex. Cym gave a short gasp and looked directly at her, but made no attempt to move. Merrisan wriggled her big toe till it parted Cym's damp cleft and landed on her nubbin. Cym's eyes took on a glazed look.

Merrisan lowered her leg and Cym recovered her wits. 'What else do I get besides you?' she asked huskily.

'With the help of Welgard, I shall conquer Firestorm,' Sandor put in, big hands clenched on the boards. 'You can have whatever you want from the dragon's hoard.'

'Can I trust you? I've learned that all men are venal, women, too,' Cym said, but she relaxed against the back of the seat, her own toes contacting Merrisan and running the length of her muscled leg.

Sandor smashed his fist on the table, making the goblets rattle. 'I always keep my word!' he thundered.

'All right, I believe you,' Cym said, her eyes shiny with mirth. 'I suggest we all retire somewhere more private.'

'I'm not interested in sleeping with you,' Sandor

exclaimed bluntly. 'I'm in love with Varna and want no woman but her.'

'Very noble,' Cym commented with heavy irony. 'Do you think she'll feel the same?'

'I do,' he averred, his handsome face glowing with sincerity.

Cym placed a hand over his bunched fist and said, kindly, 'She's Lagras's prisoner. He'll make it nigh impossible for her to remain faithful. He's a master of sensuality, and so is Queen Naram. Varna will be subjected to pain and pleasure and he won't stop till he has her.'

'She'll be true to me,' Sandor declared vehemently. 'I know it.'

'So I can't persuade you to join us in the bedroom?'

He shook his head. 'Show me a place where I can keep watch. This is a wild and lawless city and I fear treachery.'

'Few dare to invade my territory,' Cym assured him, rising and looping an arm over Merrisan's shoulders and holding her other hand out to Phila. 'But sit here by the fire, if you must. My henchmen will be on the prowl outside. Goodnight, Sandor.'

'Can we have our weapons back?'

'Not till we've struck a deal.'

'Haven't we already?'

'This is only part of the bargain.'

Merrisan cast her eye over Cym's private domain. The room was darkly panelled and filled with costly objects that the Queen of Thieves had filched. One of the perks of the trade was that she keep the best for herself. There were fabrics made from the mulberry-eating silkworms of far away islands, artefacts fashioned by the mysterious Ka tribe of the Rile Desert regions, gold, silver and precious stones hacked from deep under ground by the dwarfs who mined the foothills of the Forbidden Mountain.

Tossing her helmet aside, Merrisan unlaced her tunic and eased out of it. Now she was naked to the waist, her magnificent breasts standing proud and high, the darkly circled nipples stiff. Cym pressed against her, raising her mouth to hers. Merrisan drank deeply of the honeyed sweetness, her tongue flickering and dancing over Cym's eager one.

Merrisan could feel the sap of arousal spilling from her cunt, wetting the thong she wore. Cym left her to lie down on the wide bed and Merrisan moved to join her, making room for Phila. She sat down as her companion's hands explored her breasts. Then Cym lifted Merrisan's skirt and touched her crotch, pushing aside the tiny strip of leather. Cym gasped softly and took off her clothes, sprawling on her back, legs apart.

'You're lovely,' Merrisan complimented. 'Isn't she beautiful, Phila?'

'Oh, yes,' Phila agreed, staring with admiration at Cym's generous breasts, wide hips and rounded belly.

Cym smiled at her, shaking her head in mock denial. Merrisan reached out and touched her breasts, then lowered her head to suck them. Her own swelled in response, cradled by Phila who was behind her, sliding her hands under her armpits.

Cym's lower lips parted like petals as Merrisan explored them. The sensation in her fingers was similar to when she masturbated – delicate wet tissue, satiny skin.

'It's true that men don't know how to treat women,' Cym sighed, lifting her pelvis high, chasing the sensation. 'They're clumsy oafs when it comes to giving pleasure. Too concerned about their own.'

Merrisan was slipping away into that wonderful trance of perfect lovemaking that could only result in orgasm. Phila was tweaking her nipples, caressing them, varying the touch, and Merrisan left Cym's lips, going lower so that she could latch on to the woman's teat and suck it. The skin tasted nutty, the nipples enlarging as she sucked. At the same time hers swelled, too, stimulated by Phila.

She found Cym's clit and caressed it as if it were her own, the swift passage of her fingers making Cym claw at her back, nails digging in painfully as she came to a rapid climax. Then Merrisan was swamped with passion as the three of them made love slowly. She found herself lying between Phila's thighs, mouthing her nubbin and cunt. And Cym had positioned herself so that she could reach Merrisan's cleft, finding her fat bud, her tongue flicking over it.

Without once abandoning Phila, Merrisan pressed her pubis to Cym's face, feeling Phila convulse as she came. The girl's frantic excitement added to hers, and she strained to reach her apogee, hands clenched in Cym's hair, dragging her closer to her pubis. It was almost too intense. Merrisan was stranded on the plateau, unable to peak. Phila reached down and pinched her clit, her fingers joining Cym's tongue. Together they coaxed Merrisan up and over. She achieved the acme of bliss, giving an animal cry.

Now their caresses became light slaps. Buttocks turned pink and the heated skin fused with the heated genitals, adding to the arousal. Merrisan joined in eagerly as they scooped at each other's inlets, nibbled at breasts and clits. Cym's and Phila's scents and tastes entranced and intoxicated Merrisan till, exhausted, she rested and watched as they used a double dildo.

'I've never had a man,' Phila warned when Cym produced this object which looked like two phalli stuck together at their bases.

'Never fear, this is even better,' Cym answered. 'It will be tight at first if you're a virgin, but trust me.'

Both smiling into each other's eyes, they succeeded in inserting the carved lingams into their vaginas. Cym helped Phila and, after a moment's struggle, they were linked, communicating happily, moving sinuously, causing deeper penetration. They advanced and retreated but carefully, so as not to dislodge their plaything. They kissed, fondled their breasts, fingered their buds that pressed against the slippery wood.

Merrisan wanted to feel one inside her, ready for another climax. She could see they were approaching the heights, the twin-headed serpent thrusting in and out rhythmically. Cym's face wore a tortured expression. Phila's was rapt, her eyes tight shut.

'Now!' Cym gasped. 'Now! Now!' and she stiffened, then sank back among the pillows as Phila writhed, then lay still.

And Merrisan came against her own finger, massaging herself briskly, fiercely, almost painfully. The smart of her buttocks added to her intense pleasure and she wanted Cym to spank her again.

Morning was well advanced when Sandor tapped on the door.

'Come in,' Cym murmured sleepily.

'We should be leaving,' he said, glancing at the tumbled bed and its occupants. 'Give me Welgard and I can go to the palace and demand that Lagras free Varna.'

'It won't be that easy, my young friend,' she warned, disentangling herself from her lovers. 'Maybe we can cook up a plan which will be less dangerous and more likely to succeed.'

'I can't delay any longer,' he said urgently. 'I know she's in peril. I feel it in my heart, blood and guts.'

'Don't forget your promise to me,' she snapped, shrugging on a robe and going across to the fireplace. 'Firestorm's nest contains the most valuable jewel in the world, a marvellous ruby called The Passion Stone. Not only is it the fabled colour of lust, it imbues its owner with an appetite that can't be appeased. I want it.'

'You shall have it,' he said, and she did not doubt his word.

She pressed a carved leaf on the fireplace surround and, with a low grinding sound, a panel slid back. 'Come,' she urged, and disappeared through the aperture carrying a lighted candle.

The air was damp and fetid, and he followed her down a set of winding stone steps. When they reached the bottom he found himself in a large cellar built into the foundations. The roof was so low that he banged his head before remembering to crouch. The place was clean and absolutely empty. Cym walked to a far wall and the stones pivoted at her touch, revealing another vault beyond.

'This is my strongroom. No one knows how to get into it but me, so it would be a waste of time for you to try and rob me,' she said, her face illumined from below, planed with shadows, the lashes spiky against her eye-sockets.

'I wouldn't do that.'

'I don't think you would. You're perhaps the only honest man in Valdivia.'

They stood close as if banding together against the gloom. Sandor's nostrils were pervaded by the scent of this woman, redolent of sex, of the hours she had just spent with Merrisan and Phila, of the orgasms she had enjoyed. He could feel his cock swelling, lying diagonally across his belly, the tip rubbing against the inside of his trousers. He knew he should step back when Cym's hand curved round his erection, but he couldn't.

'I don't think you'll be able to keep your oath,' she whispered, a silken presence in the dimness. 'Not a man like you with such passion and need.'

'I'm used to being without a woman,' he said solemnly. 'Varna is my first and it only happened lately, while we were staying with Cragfor. I've always lived wild, and women were anathema to me. Fascinating, foreign beings. I dreamed of possessing them, but my hand was my mistress. It can be so again.'

'Won't you let mine perform the service?' she asked softly.

He felt her fumbling with his front lacing. He closed his eyes and visualised Varna while Cym's wily fingers found their way into his trousers and closed round his throbbing appendage, which needed relief most desperately. She lifted it through the gap, rubbed the stem firmly and agitated the ridge of his foreskin. It was stretched so tightly back from his helm that he thought he might burst at any moment, loosing it prematurely.

'Don't think of anything save the pleasure,' Cym whispered, and used regular strokes on him.

Sandor groaned and rested his palms flat against the wall, supporting his weight and boxing her in. Her hands moved expertly, sliding up and down his shaft, lingering on the sensitive underside, then giving him the ultimate thrill – dabbling in the clear pre-come wetting his single eye and coating the glans. His balls contracted, hard fruits of desire, and he could feel the rush as he spent into her hand copiously.

'That's better, isn't it?' she cooed, lifting her fingers to her mouth and licking them clean of his fluid with evident relish.

'It is. Thank you.'

'And technically, you haven't been untrue to Varna,' she added slyly.

'I suppose you're right,' he said doubtfully. Now that his testicles had been relieved of seed he was beginning to regret what had happened.

'I'll fetch the sword,' Cym said, and crossed between several iron-bound, heavily padlocked chests. She stopped when she reached a smaller one, covered in dusty blue velvet.

Sandor's heart had slowed after his climax, but now it started to pound again. She undid the catch and lifted the lid of the casket. The candlelight was reflected a hundred times over in the gems that studded Welgard's hilt.

'May I touch it?' Sandor asked. She nodded and he lifted it reverently from its resting place. At once he felt power tingling through his hands, up his arms and spine and settling at the top of his head.

'What d'you think?' Cym asked.

'I think it's everything Cragfor said, and more. A magic weapon which makes its owner invincible.'

'Good. Then you'll get The Passion Stone for me?'

'I promise, but Varna is my first priority.'

'I understand.'

'How is it that Lagras, with all his sorcery, hasn't found out you had it hidden here? He'd want to get his hands on it, wouldn't he?'

'I have my eccentric friend, Cragfor, to thank for that. We go back a long way and she owes me a favour or two. In return, she casts her spells around me. Lagras can't penetrate them. Keep Welgard wrapped in this cloth. It makes it invisible. As for you and your girls? You are safe here, but I can't protect you once you leave the inn.'

He carried the sword carefully upstairs. Merrisan and Phila were dressed, armed once more, and eating breakfast. He was hungry, the smell of food making him almost forget that he was now the guardian of the precious weapon. After he had eaten he wiped round his platter with a hunk of bread, sat back and gave in to their demands that he show them Welgard.

Each handled it with care, the warrior in them appreciating its superb balance and the steely strength of the blade which had been wrought by a master smith. 'It's made up of hundreds of layers of the finest ore, hammered and heated and folded and hammered again,' he explained, replacing it in its scabbard.

'It was destined for a hero,' Cym put in, smiling at him. 'I shall see you again when you bring me The Passion Stone.'

Sandor's last view of her was standing at the door of the inn, watching them go down the alley that would eventually lead them to Lagras's palace. The sword was still shrouded in its wrapping, carried over Sandor's back, along with his cloak.

They were hardly a quarter mile from The Rookery when horses came charging down the street, ridden by hard-featured, uniformed men. The three drew their swords, but Sandor could not get Welgard out in time. The fight was short and savage. Taken off guard they were outnumbered and Sandor found himself driven into a cul-de-sac. The soldiers poured in after him. He lost sight of Merrisan and Phila. He fought like a trapped lion, his flashing blade wreaking havoc among the troopers, but more and more streamed in, their horses' hooves pounding close, their endless array of broadswords and spears everywhere at once.

'Sandor!' He glanced up at the sound of Merrisan's voice. She was leaning from the top of the wall. 'Give me Welgard!'

He had no time to think, snatching it from his back and throwing it up to her. She caught it deftly and disappeared from sight. In the next moment he received a blow on the head that knocked him into unconsciousness.

Varna sat in a corner of her cell brooding on her situation. Despite everything, she had not yet given up seeking a means of escape. According to her reckoning she had been imprisoned for several days.

The monotony had been tempered only by the arrival of Aswad with her meagre diet of bread and water, and the occasions when he opened the grill in the heavy oaken door and let strangers peer in at her. She was once more reduced to the position of a circus freak.

She was young and resilient, and the bruises and welts of her cruel beating were healing. The bread sustained her, but she was lean as a greyhound now. Had it not been for her shackles she could have exercised, keeping her body supple and fighting fit. But Aswad had chained her cunningly, so she was only able to reach the bucket placed there for the relief of nature. She was glad that she was naked under her skirt or this task would have been made difficult. Her hands were fastened in a way that prevented her from touching herself below the waist.

He had smiled widely as he did this, saying, 'No way are you going to be able to play with yourself, princess. This will make you hot as fire, and after a day or two you'll be gagging for the king to take you.'

He was right. As her body healed so her desires awoke to torment her. She moved her torso from side to side so that her nipples chafed against the halter-top, but this aggravated the need in her clit. In vain she rubbed her thighs together, but this simply agitated her bud more without bringing it satisfaction. They knew what they were doing, these royal seducers, well versed in every sexual subtlety. Now the afternoon was drawing on, the sliver of light fading. She was condemned to another night of loneliness, frustration and despair.

She heard someone at the cell door, and automatically braced her limbs into a fighter's crouch. Aswad entered. He had a lighted lantern in one hand and a wooden bucket in the other. Water slopped over the rim.

'Hello, princess,' he said with his jovial chuckle, fixing the lamp to a bracket. 'I've orders to clean you up.'

'Why?' she asked.

'You're to be taken to the king's apartment. If you want my advice, you'll be nice to him, do everything he desires.'

While he took off her manacles she considered making a run for it, but he had locked the door behind him and the large iron key hung from his belt, along with several others. The cuffs had dug into her wrists, and she rubbed at the marks.

'That's right,' Aswad said, beaming his approval. 'Make yourself attractive for him. Take off your clothes.'

She hunched her shoulders and covered her breasts with her hands. 'Do I have to?'

'You stink, girl,' he vouchsafed.

She pulled the top over her head and then slid down the skirt, kicking it to one side. She wasn't embarrassed in front of the slave-master for he treated her impersonally, as if she was a prize heifer. But she wasn't prepared for his next action.

With a whoosh and a slosh he flung the contents of the bucket over her. 'Ah! Oh! That's freezing!' she exclaimed, her teeth chattering as she bent double in an attempt to shield herself.

'Better than dirt and smell,' he said. 'You'll be bathed thoroughly when you get to the harem.'

She reached for her old clothes, but he slapped her hand away. 'What am I to wear now?' she cried.

'Nothing,' he said, and pushed her out of the door.

The passage was lit by flares set at intervals along the walls. Steps, green with damp, led upwards. Varna, one arm over her breasts, the other hand hiding her mons, heard male voices ahead and was led through a guardroom. Soldiers with their armour loosened and tunics open over hirsute chests were dicing on the knife-dented boards of a trestle table.

She recognised Olaf, and would have spoken but Aswad used his short whip to prod her. The other men wolf-whistled and weaved curvaceous shapes in the air with their hands. One raised his clenched fist and made an obscene gesture, moving his forearm up and down from the elbow. As Varna passed by them they touched her bare bottom or grabbed at a breast or tried to pull her down on a burly knee.

'Leave her be, gentlemen. She's for the king,' Aswad reminded sternly.

She kept her head up, wet hair streaming, droplets clinging to nipples that crimped with cold. Her arm offered a little protection for her breasts, and her wide-spread fingers stopped the crude soldiers from staring at her bush. Aswad was like a great bull-mastiff shepherding her along and they left the guardroom and proceeded through ever widening, well-lit galleries till they came to the king's living quarters.

Soft music caressed the ear: stringed instruments and flutes played by concealed virtuosos. Varna was surrounded on every side by evidence of Lagras's wealth. As they went further into his apartment so the decor became more sybaritic and decadent. Her nakedness no longer seemed important as every mural, each painting or lifelike stature depicted nude couples straining in ecstasy and performing libidinous acts. Not only men with women, but men with men and women with women, threesomes, foursomes, a free-for-all of lewd activity. And when she arrived in the spacious room where Lagras slept, it was to find that the paintings had become reality.

Slaves fornicated where he could view them from the bed, and Naram was with him, her slender beringed fingers with their long oval nails clutching the lead attached to Jat's collar. A catamite wearing face-paint and a woman's skirt, his phallus sticking out through the folds, took the felt-headed mallet to a suspended brass gong. It boomed through the room. During the following silence Varna was pushed forward.

'More beautiful than ever,' Lagras purred. 'Solitary confinement suits you, my dear. You're most deliciously slim, with hollows at your hips, just like a boy's. Are you breasts still full? Remove your hands. Let me see.'

She let both arms hang at her sides, taking her weight on one leg, the other hip slack in an unconsciously classic pose. The slaves had stopped in the midst of their coupling. Cocks were still implanted in mouths, cunts or rectums, and hands rested on breasts and clits and phalli. But their eyes were riveted on Lagras. One women, reaching her peak, let out a cry. Aswad sliced her across her breasts with his whip. Her ecstatic wail turned to a sob.

Lagras swung his legs over the mattress and stood to his full height. He was not as tall as Sandor, but even so the crown of Varna's head did not quite reach the pit of his throat.

'You're magnificent,' he murmured, coming closer so that she could feel the top of his erect cock prodding her belly and leaving a wet trail behind it. 'I want to see you fight.'

This stunned her. It was the last thing she expected. 'You do?' she stammered.

'They tell me you're a formidable warrior. Prove it,' he challenged. 'I'll pit you against my own champion, the renowned Tigress. She's never yet been beaten, but I'll wager my money on you. What say you, Naram? Will you bet against me?'

'Yes, my lord. I've seen Tigress beat opponents from all over the empire. I think you'll lose. Jat, run and fetch my purse. What shall the stake be, Lagras?'

'Two thousand gold rohats,' he answered decisively.

She gulped, but refused to back down, adding crossly, 'You must be very confident in this captive, my lord.'

'Oh, I am,' he said softly, and reached between Varna's legs and stroked a finger across her labial wings, making her clitoris thrum.

She stood rigidly to attention, refusing to acknowledge

the desire that was making her wet. He was her enemy. She would keep her word and not give in to base lust, but it was becoming increasingly hard. Sandor had awakened her to the feel of a thick prick stretching her tunnel and jabbing against her cervix, and the sensation of a pair of weighty balls tapping against her perineum with each virile thrust. Lagras was so confident, exuding aristocracy and power. What better mate could she wish for?

Then she froze as she caught sight of a statue standing in an alcove near the bed. Ice gripped her heart at the deity's vicious appearance: the four snakelike arms, the weapons, the grimacing mouth and pointed tongue, and the hair made up of writhing snakes.

Lagras whispered in her ear, 'That's Izar, the goddess of the Valdivians. She thrives on sex. I sacrifice hymens to her, and blood. In return she grants me boons.'

'She's horrible!' Varna declared forcefully.

'Not so,' he reproved with deceptive mildness. 'You will soon come to appreciate her beauty, once you are my queen.'

'Dream on, Lagras!'

'Oh dear, that's no way to address your sovereign lord,' said a thin, ancient-sounding voice from somewhere near the bed-drapes, and a man stepped into view. He was indeed extremely old, wrinkles seaming his face, white hair straggling down from the bald dome of his head.

'And who are you to tell me how I must speak to the man who slew my father?' she demanded.

He gave a wheezy laugh, his eyes bright under bushy white brows. 'I'm Chedon, the court astrologer.'

'The court wizard, soothsayer and poisoner,' put in Naram in her customary spiteful fashion. She teased the old man, bending towards him and kissing his withered cheek with her crimson lips.

'I foretold your coming, Princess Varna, saw it in the

stars,' he went on, putting a hand up to where Naram's mouth had been.

'And what outcome is predicted?' she demanded eagerly. 'Shall I conquer?'

Chedon cast a sideways glance at Lagras and mumbled, 'How could such as you, a weak woman without an army, hope to prevail against his might?'

She heard his words, but read a different message in his eyes. Was he a friend or a foe?

'Enough of this,' Lagras said impatiently. 'You shall hold the stakes, Chedon. Aswad, prepare the princess.'

He took her to a robing room. There, Rana was putting the finishing touches to Tigress's costume. She was naked apart from a short transparent kilt, shin-guards and sandal-boots. Cornsilk-coloured hair flowed freely over her shoulders and undulated whenever she moved. She approximated Varna in height and muscular development.

Varna met her hard blue eyes, and Tigress's upper lip curled.

Aswad dropped a white chiton over Varna's head. It was diaphanous and brief, and moulded itself to her body. It slipped from her shoulders and bared the top curves of her breasts. He passed a gold girdle round the back of her neck, crossed it over her chest and beneath her breasts in front, then tied it tightly round her waist. The flimsy material hugged her curves and her nipples came erect, lifting into sharp points, their darkness showing through.

She, too, was given greaves and buskins, but when she expected to be handed a sword or stave she was marched back to the main chamber. Wide-eyed and apprehensive, she watched as Aswad beckoned a brawny slave who carried an armful of terribly supple four feet long whips.

The atmosphere was electric. Lagras lounged in a chair made of dark carved wood, and Naram occupied its twin, her turquoise gown parting over her legs, giving an uninterrupted view of her shaven pubis and bejewelled labia.

'Choose your weapons,' Lagras ordered, and Naram giggled and rested her fingers on his crotch.

'You might as well simply hand the money over to me,' she said, subjecting Varna to a scathing glance.

Varna looked the whips over. Their handles were bound in multi-coloured ribbons. They suggested carnival batons, till she noticed that at the tip of each dangled a bunch of thrice-knotted thongs, whose sinister outlines failed to be disguised by a coating of gilt paint.

She selected one and swished it in the same way as she would have tested the temper of a sword before engaging. She ended by swinging it about her head in hissing arcs, thankful that her training had included the use of the whip. Yet she had not quite recovered from the shock of finding that Lagras had ordained she should fight Tigress in such a manner.

'Look and tremble!' she taunted, knowing the value of intimidating a rival. 'You'll not like the taste of this!'

'It's you who'd better watch out, you soft-arsed bitch,' Tigress retorted.

Aswad and Rana marked out a circle on the floor and the contestants were told to stand within it. Both crouched, waiting, the whips' shanks held vertically before them in an on-guard position.

Lagras kept them in suspense. Then his handkerchief fluttered and Varna uttered a war cry and leapt forward. She lashed out with such vigour that Tigress spat an oath as the whip caught her across the upper arm. Varna followed up this advantage, aiming accurately at her hips and thighs. But Tigress recovered quickly, and Varna felt the agonising sting as her rival's whip struck her, coiling round her buttocks, then drawing red parallel streaks across her breasts, belly and legs.

Varna staggered but kept control, aiming such a vicious

swipe across Tigress's rump that she uttered a scream and part sank to her knees.

'Get up! Strike harder, damn you!' yelled Naram, on her feet, face flushed with excitement. 'If you lose I'll have you flogged.'

Tigress heard, dashed drops of sweat from her face and, eyes blazing, breasts heaving, leapt to the centre of the ring, panting, 'Come on, you Trokles whore!'

Whips whistled violently, the triple tips tearing at fabric and skin till their garments were in tatters and their flesh vividly patterned with scarlet streaks. Varna was blind to everything, possessed of that savage, battlefield instinct. She was immune to pain, her arm rising and falling as if it didn't belong to her.

Tigress was bleeding from her cheek, her fury intensified by this threat to her good looks. She reversed her whip and used the butt to swing at Varna's head. The blow knocked her to the floor. Her nose started to pour blood. It spattered her sweaty breasts and the remnants of her chiton.

Giving her no time to recover, Tigress landed on her, legs straddled each side of her torso, winding her. She drove the butt under Varna's chin, ready to strangle her. 'Do you yield?' she roared.

Varna brought up her knee and jabbed Tigress. She jerked back and dropped the whip. Varna seized the moment, rolling out from under her and grabbing her round the throat. Tigress clawed at her breast and squeezed. Varna grunted with pain but did not let go. They heaved and broke free, then used their fists and feet to finish the fight.

Varna could dimly hear Lagras exclaiming and Naram urging Tigress on.

'Bitch!' snarled Tigress as they went into a clinch. 'I'd like to fuck you raw.'

Varna's loins clenched. The smell of female sweat and

the slippery feel of her opponent's splendid body made her hot inside. Tigress thrust a thigh between hers and rubbed her naked cleft against Varna's skin. It was wet and warm, making her want to frig her rival's clitoris and stick her fingers into her cunt. Bloodlust was turning into something else. She couldn't find it in her heart to hate Tigress. She was a sister warrior, like Merrisan and Phila.

'Get on with it!' Naram shouted, coming closer. 'You're not here to give each other pleasure.'

They broke apart, dishevelled, wild-eyed, bloody and naked, circling about but obviously tiring. Suddenly Varna bent, snatched up her whip, reversed it and drove its butt upwards into the base of Tigress's belly. She doubled over, clutching her pubis. Varna hit her again, the stock of the whip landing on her forehead. She dropped to the floor.

Varna, crimson streaks slowing running down her body, planted the sole of her buskin on her adversary's neck and pointed her whip at Lagras, using the gladiator's gesture for a signal to indicate that the defeated should be spared.

Lagras smiled, and held his thumb upwards.

But Naram shrieked at Rana, 'Flay that wretched creature! I want Tigress thrashed. I want her birched, whipped and caned. And stretch her on the cross while you do it. I want her to be sorry she was ever born!'

Chapter Eight

Tigress was punished, and Varna, too. Both of them were dragged to a crosspiece within sight of Lagras's bed and chained either side of it, arms stretched high, legs spread and fastened tightly.

'This isn't fair,' Varna protested, tears blurring her vision. 'I won the wager for you, Lagras.'

She tried to ease her lacerated back against the wooden struts, her fingers spread, seeking support, straining on tiptoe to relieve the drag on her manacled wrists.

He strolled over, handling her breasts familiarly, taking one teat into his mouth and palpating it with his tongue, causing mayhem in her loins. Then he released it, regarding her with smouldering dark eyes as he said, 'And so you should, my dear. I told you to. This is just a little sample of what happens to slaves who persist in rebellion. I'll ask you once more. Are you willing to be my bride?'

'No, I'm not,' she hissed, but was filled with a longing to give in, craving his tongue on her bud and his large prick in her vagina.

He sighed and lifted his shoulders under the lavishly embroidered toga. 'Then you must suffer with the defeated one. Aswad, begin.'

The mechanism of the cross was such that a slave leaning his weight on a lever could turn it. The harder he worked, the faster the cross revolved, the chosen implement of pain landing indiscriminately. Tigress was facing the centre post, and Varna gazed outwards, unable to avoid seeing those who were witnessing her humiliation.

Aswad's tawse slashed down on her thighs at the first revolution. The leather strap, cut into strips at the end, sent a torrent of appalling agony through her. She yelled, fruitlessly bucking against her bonds. Lagras laughed and insinuated a hand between her legs and cupped her delta, his forefinger bent so he could massage her clitoris.

'Stop! Please stop!' she wailed as her bud throbbed in response to his deft stroking.

'As you wish,' he said, and stood back.

The slave sweated at the lever, the cross creaked and spun, and she heard the tawse land amidst a stream of violent oaths from Tigress. Round they went, and round again, and each time one of them was lashed. Varna hung there, head bowed towards her breasts, her arms wrenched in their sockets, muscles screaming in protest, every inch of her having its own particular centre of agony. She drifted in and out of consciousness.

Suddenly Lagras barked, 'Enough! Take the princess down.'

She groaned at the smallest movement, but the shackles were unlocked and Aswad lifted her in his arms. The next thing she knew was softness beneath her and hands working balm into her wounds. Opening her eyes she stared up dizzily into the silken tenting of Lagras's bed. Incense swirled in clouds from elaborate burners upheld by tripods, and shadows danced fantastically over the orgiastic scene. Lagras, in a wide-legged stance, arms folded across his chest, a smile on his saturnine features, had given the slaves free rein.

The males grabbed at any available female, burying their cocks to the hilt. Others gained access to the nether holes of men, and those already shafting women took no exception to being entered from the rear. Naram was eyeing them, playing with Jat's erection and at the same time keeping a close watch on what her brother was doing with Varna.

'Careful with her,' Varna heard him say, and she felt the touch of his lubricated fingertips skimming her ribcage, her navel and, finally, her mound.

One of the women brought a cup brimming with nectar and Varna supped it thirstily. It slipped down her throat and warmed her belly but she was aware of a bitter aftertaste. Too late she realised they had laced it with a herb that would make her more malleable. She had difficulty focusing, everything changing size, shrinking or becoming impossibly large. Lagras's eyes burned into hers and his hands plucked at her nipples. They were greasy with heavily scented lotion. Her body was covered in it, the salve soothing her hurts. The bed was heavenly, far removed from the dirty straw of a damp cell.

The drugged drink made her head spin and she was losing her grip. What price honour and sacred vows and a love she'd sworn never to betray?

All that remained was Lagras, his hand on his cock, fingers fondling its length and thickness. She wanted to have him thrust it into her, filling her to capacity. Everyone should go away, leaving them alone on the wide bed, then she would coil her legs round his waist and pull him into her female depths. The aphrodisiac was rousing her beyond endurance and pleasure stabbed her as he found her clitoris, drew back the hood and rubbed his thumb over the tip.

Varna sobbed and tears ran from the corners of her eyes, streaking across her temples. 'Why do you torture me? I've never done anything to hurt you.'

'I don't need to explain myself. How dare you even ask? I'm the king, and my word is law.'

'I'll never love you. You know that, don't you?'

For answer, he bent and took one of her swollen nipples into his mouth, sucking strongly, then letting his tongue idle over it. Varna shuddered, the drink and the magical balm making her forget the scarlet welts and purplish bruises that scored her skin.

'I could change your mind,' he murmured. 'I've a potion which would make you forget life before me. I would become the centre of your existence.'

His voice was seductive, softly invasive, penetrating her to the core as surely as if he had taken her physically. A tingle of fear ran down her spine. His black eyes bored into hers but she managed to drag her gaze away lest he hypnotise her.

'It would be false... a spell,' she reminded.

'Why fight me?' he whispered.

'Because I must,' she insisted. 'I loathe and detest you. You can use your enchantments and your drugs to master me, but I'll never be truly yours. Never, never!'

'She-devil!' he shouted, beside himself. He hit her, open-handed, across the face. 'Forget any ideas you may have about getting Trokles back. I've placed a governor in Ciophos. The country exists under martial law.'

'Oh, my poor land! You're an evil, wicked man!'

He hit her again and with stars whirling madly against the blackness of her eyelids, she felt him flip her over, facedown amongst the pillows. He pushed a hand under her hips, grabbing her by the pubis, forcing her to her knees, her rump raised, every one of her secrets on show; the damp delta, the rose-red stalk of her clit, the entrance to her vagina, the crinkled amber mouth of her anus. She could do nothing but submit, his nails digging excruciatingly into the zigzag laddering of her stripes. He spread her buttocks wide, his thumbs gouging the soft inner sides. He was strong, his legs straddling her, the weight of him keeping her immobile.

'I won't take your virginity... not yet,' he said triumphantly. 'But you'll pleasure me, none the less.'

She felt the wetness as his saliva dripped on to her most private portal, then his finger sliding into the eye of her arse. She yelped as slowly, painfully, he forced the tight ring open, and then it was something larger than a finger seeking entrance.

'No! Please! Don't!' she pleaded, incensed at this invasion, striving to clench her muscles, closing herself against him. It was useless. He pushed harder and she could feel his phallus entering her an inch at a time. The sweat of exertion was running off him in rivulets, soaking her skin.

'Izar! She's tight!' he complained loudly.

'She needs training, my lord,' Naram answered, coiled near the bedhead, her legs tucked under her, her rings flashing between them as she worked enthusiastically, rousing her clitoris. 'Send her to the High Priestess for a while. Let Izar's votaries purge and stretch her.'

'You're right,' he gasped, and withdrew his member. But instead of leaving Varna he took it in one hand and rubbed it up and down her crease, pumping himself to a climax, his buttocks clenching as his semen shot out.

It fell like warm rain on her rump, dripping between her legs and wetting the silken coverlet beneath her. 'You disgust me,' she cried.

He laughed, wiped his limp organ dry, and accepted a goblet of wine from Naram. 'By the time the priestess and her handmaidens are done with you, you'll be begging to come back to me,' he said, lounging beside her, heedless of her spitfire fury.

'Who is this woman and where am I being taken?' she demanded, thankful to have escaped being sodomised, her anus stinging and sore from his attempt.

'You'll find out all too soon,' he replied grimly.

There was a commotion at the door and Captain Cafless burst into the room. 'I'm sorry to interrupt you, majesty,' he said, bowing so low that the feathers on his crested helmet brushed the floor. 'But we've caught the man Queen Naram wanted.'

She stopped tantalising Jat's balls, clasped her hands

together and beamed at Cafless. 'You've got him! Capital! Was he where I told you to look?'

'He was, my lady.'

'Excellent! My crystal skull is working again. And he's unharmed?'

'Yes, my lady.'

'What's this, Naram? Giving my bodyguards orders?' Lagras said, frowning.

'Bring him in. At once!' Naram cried, then linked her arms round her husband's neck and kissed him fondly. 'It's to your advantage, beloved. He's the man who helped Varna reach Cragfor's lair. I swore he would be mine, but you can have sport with him, too.'

Sandor? There? Varna kept her eyes on the door, hoping, praying, fearing it was he. If he'd been captured their cause was doomed. She might as well surrender her body to Lagras without further ado. This could mean that Phila and Merrisan were slain, and any hope of possessing Welgard gone forever.

Her heart did a somersault in her breast when Sandor walked in. His feet were shackled and his hands chained in front of him. His lip was cut, his hair clotted with dried blood. His muscles strained against the torn hide jerkin, and she could see Naram licking her lips like a cat with a bowl of cream when she looked at his impressive build, and the bulge filling his codpiece.

'What do you mean by this outrage?' Sandor said crisply as he halted in front of the king and queen. 'Is this how you treat strangers in Quexol?'

'We have reason to believe that you're a traitor, and aided the fugitive, Princess Varna,' Naram answered, and took up a seductive pose on the bed, her breasts escaping from the flimsy silk bodice, her skirt thrown back, exposing her thighs and a flash of silken smooth pudenda.

Jealousy gnawed at Varna's gut as she saw how Sandor was looking at the queen, staring as if mesmerised at her depilated mons and the deep furrow dividing it. Was he so weak that the sight of Naram's cunt drove all other thought from his mind? Did he want to play with the rings in her labia and suck the little diamond in her clit?

Then his gaze switched to her and she withered at the condemnation in his eyes. She was on the bed with Lagras. Her welts were plain to see, and the wetness of the king's juice glistening on her body. Sandor must be under the impression that she had embraced the decadent life of the court. And, the most horrible thing of all: there was nothing she could say or do just then to defend herself. Lagras must not suspect that Sandor had been her lover and taken that precious commodity – her much-prized virginity.

'Princess Varna, I'm surprised to find you taking part in their depravity,' he said in his deep, accented voice.

'I was given no option,' she managed to croak in reply, pain as sharp as a knife inside her. He was looking at her as if she was a stranger. Was this the man who had sworn his eternal love?

'And she's about to go to the convent of Izar where she'll undergo further indoctrination,' Naram said and reached for Jat, tweaking the wine-red nipples that marked his pectorals like pennies. 'You, Sandor, are to remain here with me. I have plans for you.' Her eyes narrowed to violet slits and her red lips shone as she added, 'I want to see you wearing my uniform. A gold spiked collar round that strong neck and damascened bracelets on your wrists. I'll have them pierce your nipples and foreskin. I think a haematite ring would look delightful in your cock.'

'I'm to be your plaything, is that it, lady?' Sandor said, a derisive smile curving his full lips. He loomed over her, dominating the room with his great height.

'The alternative would hardly be worth considering, too painful by far,' she answered, running her hand between Jat's legs and jiggling the full globes of his balls.

'I might consider it preferable to becoming your slave.'

'You might, but I doubt it. D'you fancy being put on display in the market place? You'd be tied to the whipping post and flogged, excited at the same time, till you couldn't stop coming, spurting in front of the jeering spectators,' she said airily. 'You'll have to tell him what it's like, Jat.'

'Aswad, take the princess away,' Lagras commanded. 'Order a carriage and see to it that she reaches the convent without mishap. Fail me in this and I'll have you castrated.' He turned his attention to Sandor. 'As for you, young man, I'll turn you over to my trainer when Naram has amused herself with you. Your physique is superb. You'll become my champion in the next games.'

'I won't have him killed or even maimed,' Naram pouted, and rose to glide across to where Sandor stood, weaving her arms round him and snaking a leg up his thigh.

'We'll see. I make no promises,' Lagras answered with his dark smile.

Before she knew what was happening, Varna was raised, draped in a plain white robe and swung high over Aswad's shoulder. She screamed in fury, hanging head down, her long hair streaming. In a kind of frenzy she hammered at his naked black back, twisting wildly. But it was useless, and she gave up the struggle, flopping limply.

Her last glimpse of Sandor was of him gazing down into the queen's face with an inscrutable expression.

She was carried to the courtyard and bundled into a box-shaped carriage with bars at the windows and leather curtains blanking out the view. Once inside the stuffy gloom Aswad dumped her on one of the padded seats and seated himself opposite. He thumped on the roof with his fist and the vehicle jerked into motion. She was on her way to Izar's temple-convent, and the High Priestess.

'They've got him? Damn!' Cym exclaimed. 'What about my ruby?'

After Sandor had been captured in the alley Merrisan and Phila had hared back to *The Three Doves.* Cym wasn't pleased at their news.

'We still have Welgard,' Phila said, easing off her helmet and shaking out her blonde hair.

'Yes, but who is going to face Firestorm?'

'We'll do it,' Phila answered, and rested her hand on the back of Merrisan's. 'Where can we find the dragon?'

'Its den is many miles from here, through perilous country. It hasn't shown itself for years, sated from its last bout of destruction when it swept through the land setting all alight and gorging itself on flesh. Once a year the people from the villages around tie a maiden to a rock at the mouth of Firestorm's cave. Then the earth shakes and the dragon rumbles as it wakes. Next day, the girl is gone.'

Cym's face was solemn, and Merrisan's fingers itched to drive Welgard through the mean old dragon's brain. 'Tell us how to get there,' she urged.

'But what of Sandor?' Cym reminded, though her eyes sparkled at the bravery of the girl warriors. 'Aren't you going to rescue him first? Isn't it traditional that a dragon is slain by a man... a hero?'

'Stuff tradition!' they cried in unison.

'We can do it,' Merrisan averred.

'Of course we can,' put in Phila.

'All right. This is the route to the highlands and Bald Spur, that's Firestorm's mountain fastness,' and Cym picked up a quill-pen, dipped it in a squat brass inkwell and started to draw a map on a piece of vellum. When she had finished she dusted it all over with a pepper pot shaped sander, folded it and handed it to Merrisan. 'May the gods go with you.'

The temple was large and grim. Resembling the main architecture Varna had glimpsed as she was dragged by cart through the streets of Quexol, it was like a square pyramid, with steps all round its massive sides.

The carriage stopped in an enclosed court. Aswad used his whip when he forced her out, for she was still in a fighting mood. The courtyard was lined with cloisters supported on arches and there were women in plain blue robes going about their duties, some drawing water from the well, others bringing trugs of vegetables and foodstuffs from the storehouses. No one looked up as Aswad hurried across the paving stones and into the cool shadows of the cloister. There he paused before a large wooden door and knocked gently with his knuckles.

'Enter,' said a female voice.

Aswad lifted the latch and, pushing Varna before him, crossed into the room. More height of ceiling, bare walls and long narrow windows. The light fell on the head of the woman bending over a book on a table. It gave her an undeserved halo, illumining the white veil that covered her hair and folded under her chin. Her form was indistinguishable, shrouded in a black habit, girded by a length of gilded rope. When at last she condescended to glance up the piercing blue of her beautiful, black-lashed eyes transfixed Varna.

'The king has sent her,' Aswad said, jerking a thumb at Varna.

'Welcome, child. I am Laudine, High Priestess of the Order of Izar,' the woman said and stood, a regal figure. 'And what is it his majesty requires, Aswad?'

'That her nether hole be opened to accommodate him. You may treat her as you will, use any methods to curb her disobedience, but no one must penetrate her vagina.

She is a virgin and you are to ensure she remains so or it will be the worse for you.'

'I understand,' Laudine said calmly, and approached Varna. 'Take off your clothes.'

Varna was by now resigned to obeying this command. It seemed that, wherever she went, all wanted to view her nakedness. She undid the buttons that ran down the front of the garment and it dropped to the floor, forming a puddle round her bare feet. She stood defiantly, blushing as those experienced blue eyes assessed her attributes.

'She's been chastised recently – the welts are fresh,' Laudine observed, pacing slowly round her, the rustle of her black skirts betraying their silken weave. This was no sackcloth and ashes penitent who served her deity humbly and without reward.

'She has, milady,' Aswad replied with a touch of pride. 'I performed the duty myself.'

'They are well laid on. I've seen samples of your skill before. The laymen don't realise just how much concentration and effort goes into administering a thorough beating. It's almost an art.'

'Thank you, milady. Mine are the even stripes. The others were inflicted by a warrior-woman called Tigress, a common slut the queen pitted against the woman you see here, Princess Varna. His majesty decided to wager on the outcome of a whip fight between them.'

'Crudely done,' Laudine agreed. 'And who won?'

'The princess.'

'Proud, eh?' Laudine laid a firm finger under Varna's chin and lifted it. Their eyes locked and Varna out-stared her, refusing to back down.

'I won't yield to the king. He's a tyrant who overran my country and slew my father.'

'Harsh words indeed to spring from such luscious lips,' Laudine chided, and her slender white hand reached out and lifted Varna's right breast. The nipples puckered instantly, large and rosy, and Varna could feel herself heating, lubricating, wanting. The blue eyes sharpened. 'You've experienced pleasure, haven't you, princess?'

'I can't deny it,' Varna said, holding herself taut.

'But not with a man. Women have been your chosen sex.'

Varna looked down and could clearly see Laudine's nipples rising hard against her habit. She must be naked beneath it. The neckline plunged into a deep V, and resting in the valley between those gently rising and falling breasts was a pendant on a chain. It depicted Izar.

'We specialise in pleasure here, and pain, too,' Laudine said. 'I guarantee you'll be a changed woman by the time you leave, and will acquiesce to everything King Lagras wants.'

'I very much doubt it,' Varna stated stubbornly with a toss of her dark curls. 'I refuse to be coerced.'

'Hoity-toity,' Laudine mocked. 'You were sent to me to have your arse trained in submission. There are far worse fates than that. Be a good girl and I'll be gentle with you. Make me angry and I'll have you tied to the crosspiece with the largest plug in my collection shoved up your rectum, one that will remain there for hours.'

'The notion warms me to the cods,' Aswad purred, rubbing a hand over the massive tool hanging down the inside of his left thigh.

Laudine smiled and sank to her knees, his penis swelling as she burrowed into his pantaloons, freeing the huge dark-skinned organ. She took it in her hand, though unable to close her fist round its girth, then her mouth moved up his erection to where the glans glowed a deep purple.

It seemed they had forgotten Varna, and she could feel herself melting and becoming lubricious as she watched them. The priestess's tongue flicked its way delicately under Aswad's glans. He grunted and pressed into her deeply and she opened wide. Now her face was against his wiry black belly-hair and Varna's hand strayed to her own pubis and parted her feather-fringed labia. Her nubbin was engorged and she stroked it rapidly, rousing her passions so that she might climax before anyone stopped her.

But Laudine and Aswad were totally absorbed. Her mouth worked his cock, sucking avidly. Her hand joined in, rubbing his stem vigorously. Aswad drove his fingers into her veil. It fell back, revealing a mass of autumnal hued hair. He grabbed at it, and with his other hand, administered sharp slaps to her body. She moved her head up and down faster, determined to milk him, and he came into her mouth, holding nothing back, the sound of his pleasure bouncing off the convent walls.

Varna came too, her whole body bounding towards orgasm. She squeezed out the final spasm, her finger pressed hard to her clitoris. It gave a last throb and she glided back to earth from a lofty pinnacle.

Laudine staggered to her feet, Aswad's emission bubbling from her lips and smearing her chin. She dabbed at it with her veil. The glance she gave Varna left her in no doubt that she had seen her masturbating.

'A wanton as well as a princess,' she said crisply. 'Who gave you permission to pleasure yourself?'

'No one,' Varna shot back, suddenly ashamed of her action.

'In future you'll not touch yourself unless I say you can. Is that understood?'

'I suppose so,' Varna brought out uncertainly. 'But I don't see why.'

'Yours not to ask. I give the orders round here.' Laudine picked up a cane and whacked it down on Varna's haunches. It cut into her, augmenting the marks of the whip. She jolted forward, reaching blindly for support.

At Laudine's command two beefy-looking women

wearing blue robes and veils entered and stood on either side of Varna, looking to Laudine for instructions.

'Take her away and purge her,' she said. 'Then bring her to the inner sanctum.'

The flagstones were icy under Varna's bare soles, the air chilly on her naked body, the grip of iron fingers on her arms painfully tight. The massive women did not spare her, hurrying her along, almost dragging her. The door slammed on Laudine's chamber, and a long grey-stoned passage yawned ahead.

She could hear noises from other parts of this weird nunnery; women talking, laughing, the sound of flutes and drums, the ordinary domestic clashes brought about in the kitchen. It seemed that a large number of people lived there.

'Are there only women here?' she asked the large lady on her right.

'Mostly, but we do get visits from the priests who live in that building over the way,' she answered gruffly. She was exceedingly plain, with heavy brows, a big nose and a shadowy line of moustache on her upper lip. 'Why d'you ask? Can't you live without cock?'

'She's a virgin, Winola. Or hadn't you heard?' said the other, a rotund figure of some twenty stone, but with a smiling, far more open face.

'I heard, Otka, but I don't believe it,' grunted Winola, and kicked open a door at the far end of the corridor.

Varna was propelled inside. It was a bare chamber resembling a sluice-room, with plenty of running water and several deep baths set at floor level. There were marble slabs, too, with smooth white surfaces, shelves containing jars and pots and bottles of perfumed oils. Varna could only hazard a guess at their purpose.

There were half a dozen other women there attired, like Winola and Otka, in blue robes and with white veils draped round their heads. They stood in a line awaiting orders, and the monumental Winola said briskly to Varna, 'Right then, princess, on your knees by that slab over there.'

'What are you going to do?' she snapped, pulling back in their arms.

'You need to be thoroughly cleansed inside before we take you to Laudine in the sanctum,' Otka answered. 'It will be less painful for you this way. We know best, and so does our High Priestess.'

Varna was led to the slab and knelt beside it, the top half of her body lying across it and her arms folded under her head. 'Not like that,' said Winola, and placed cuffs round her wrists and attached them to rings set in the sides of the slab.

The coldness of its smooth surface bit into her breasts and belly, and someone parted her knees so that she found her posterior jutting high, the cheeks spread wide. Otka picked up a tall vessel with a metal tube protruding from its base and carried it to the slab. Varna could see that it contained a milky liquid with steamy haze wafting from the surface. At first she thought it was another drug, but its true purpose was quickly revealed in all its horror when Otka hoisted the pitcher and Winola fed the tip of the tube into Varna's anus.

'No!' she yelled, and kicked out, but two of the women flung themselves on her legs, holding them still and stretching them wider.

The tube slid in, deeper and deeper, till Varna felt as if it had entered her very guts. The sensation was strange and she cried out in dismay. The women laughed at her and one of them patted her buttocks. Then Winola tilted the vessel and the warm liquid gushed down the spigot and into Varna's rectum.

'Ooh...' she groaned, finding the fullness entirely disagreeable.

Otka slipped a hand under Varna, supporting her

swollen belly and rubbing across her clit. It seemed that her bowels were capable of holding an astonishing amount of fluid, and when at last Winola drew out the tube Varna felt she was on the point of exploding.

'Hold on,' Otka instructed.

'I can't,' Varna groaned in great distress.

They untied her arms and lifted her to her feet, then took her into the garderobe. She made the stone seat just in time to empty the contents of her bowels into the privy, reeling from the force of the purge. Shaking, sweating, she slumped there for a moment, drained of all strength.

'Finished?' enquired Otka.

'I think so.'

'Come then. Time to be bathed, then you'll be refreshed inside and out.'

When she had been thoroughly soaped and washed, hair too, now fragrant and piled on top of her head, Varna was told to lie on a padded couch and then Otka massaged her. Now the use of the jars and pots became apparent; they all contained scented oils, each with its own purpose – to soothe or arouse. It seemed that Otka used both.

Surrounded by women's gentle voices and the tinkle of water, Varna relaxed, Otka's capable hands soothing the abrasions left by her whippings. She moaned in need as the fingers drifted up her back, finding that sensitive point where the spine joins the base of the skull. Visions of Sandor floated across her mind and she wanted to weep. He was lost to her. He'd never believe that she had been unwilling to succumb to Lagras's seduction.

Massaged till she was limp and pliable, Varna was at last encouraged to stand, a clean robe slipped over her head and tweaked into place. The material was like a cloud of white mist, her nipples thrown into prominence, the darker shadow of her pubis only partly hidden by its fragile folds. She was given no choice but to go to the sanctum. It was awesome. Even she lost heart when she saw another statue representing Izar, though this time she was not so much hideous as lustfully seductive. Her arched torso was wreathed in the smoke of incense, her great breasts jutting, the nipples huge, and her sex lips open displaying a clitoris almost the size of its male counterpart – the penis.

The interior was brilliantly lit with hundreds of candles, and the walls decorated with splendidly executed murals. Each one contained the painting of a saturnalia, with couples disporting themselves in a multitude of sexual postures. The sound of chanting sent shivers down Varna's spine and as she walked towards the altar where Laudine waited, she saw that she was surrounded on both sides by blue-clad priestesses. Not only them: there were taller figures among the acolytes, hooded, robed in black, undoubtedly male. Hands touched her as she passed, fondling her through the gauzy gown. She trembled and tried to withdraw, but if she moved to one side it was to find other sets of fingers waiting for her.

Laudine watched her progress from her place in front of Izar's plinth. She had changed into a shimmering gown through which her body gleamed. Her face was free of veils and she was stunningly beautiful, with sculptured cheekbones and that glorious fall of chestnut hair.

The chanting rose and Varna reached the High Priestess. The congregation gathered round, buzzing with suppressed excitement. Laudine nodded, and Winola and Otka guided Varna to the altar of black basalt. They lifted her, rolled up the chiton and chained her arms, then made her raise and open her knees, her sexual avenue completely exposed.

Laudine faced the goddess. 'Help us to prepare this woman for your loyal servant, King Lagras,' she intoned, then bent, scooped a handful of pungently aromatic oil from a soapstone basin and spread it over the ivory phallus she held reverently in her hands.

Varna's eyes bulged. The thing was huge! They couldn't possibly be intending to feed that into her poor bottom, could they? But she had a horrible feeling that this was precisely what they were about to do. This was why they had purged and prepared her.

Udin! she breathed, clenching her bottom.

Laudine smiled dreamily and advanced towards the foot of the altar, standing between Varna's outspread feet. She held the phallus high and the worshippers gasped. Varna's eyes widened with mounting unease. The dildo was nine inches long with a circumference of four. It glistened wickedly in the candlelight.

'Don't tighten up,' Laudine advised, and signalled to her handmaidens to jack Varna's hips high and hold her there firmly.

Then she positioned the phallus between Varna's avenue and teased the anal opening. Fingers slipped round the puckered mouth, then pushed inside, easing the way for the mighty tool. She felt it slide in, well-greased but agonisingly large. She winced and gasped as Laudine pressed it in further. Varna felt the shock as her muscles gave and it shot into her like a battering ram. Her rectum ached and smarted. She had the urge to expel the thing, but Laudine held it firmly in place.

'This is the first size, princess,' she said, and slid a slippery finger over Varna's cleft and engorged bud. 'You'll keep it in for several hours. Even when you rise I shall ensure it can't be dislodged.'

The dildo was kept in place by a harness that fitted Varna's lower body closely. Straps passed between her crack, with a special metal cup to stop her stimulating her clit and a leather pad to keep the ivory plug securely buried within. No matter how she wriggled and strove she could not rid herself of this invasive object. She cursed Lagras when she was at last alone, locked in a cheerless cell with a hard board bed and a single scratchy blanket. The morning promised scant relief as Laudine had promised that the present dildo would be replaced with an even larger one, a foot long and with a five inch girth.

It was a relief to get out in the sun. A week of close confinement in the temple had been too much for Varna; a strange passage of days spent in being alternately stretched with increasingly large phalli or flogged with a variety of implements – whips, flails, paddles, rods and birches.

Worst of all was the frustration of never being allowed satisfaction. The inmates of the convent used her for their own pleasure, men and women demanding that she handle their sex organs or bring them to orgasm with her mouth. If she refused she was told she was disobedient and must adhere to the rules pertaining in the temple. She soon learned to give in to their demands. The only one she enjoyed serving in this way was Laudine.

Stretched within and sore without, she was learning submission, despite herself. That morning Laudine had smiled at her and said, 'Today I shall allow you a treat. You may go with Otka and gather the herbs that grow wild on the cliffs bounding the seashore. You've been an apt pupil and I'm pleased with you, Varna, and the king will be too, when I return you to him soon.'

Now she and Otka climbed the steep incline that led to the cliff tops. Each carried a basket and Varna straightened her back and shaded her eyes, looking out at the wide expanse of blue sea. White spume ran up the beach below, and she longed to go down there.

'Can we bathe?' she asked.

Otka was panting, the ascent too much for her. 'Not allowed,' she puffed.

'Oh, please,' Varna pleaded, knowing the fat woman fancied her and playing on this. 'We could lie on the sand afterwards and...'

'And?' Otka perked up, her red face glistening with little beads of sweat.

'Maybe, make love?'

'What about your belt and plug?' Otka said dubiously, but Varna could see she was relishing the possibility of having her all to herself.

'Take it off for me and release me from this awful dildo. It's the biggest one so far and most uncomfortable. You can put it back in place before we return.'

'Oh, all right, just this once,' Otka relented and, baskets abandoned, they took the winding path that brought them to the beach.

The sea hissed and pounded, the breakers running up the sand. The sun was hot and the air like wine. The cove was small and secluded, and Otka undressed first, her large body emerging from her robe. Varna slipped out of hers and stood fidgeting impatiently while Otka unlocked the belt and released her sex. She gave a long-drawn groan of relief as the carved wooden dildo slipped out of her bottom.

She ran to the water's edge, was aware of Otka plodding behind her and then the beach seemed to explode. Men were running round from the next cove, wild-haired, wild-eyed, dressed in brilliant velvets, in head-scarves, in sea-boots, and they were heading directly towards her.

Their leader was a tall lean man, a handsome swashbuckler. His eyes feasted on Varna's curves and he shouted to his subordinates, 'Hey! Here's a piece of luck! We dropped into the bay to fill our water kegs and have found ourselves a couple of doxies.'

He stalked towards Varna, moving like a sleek panther, his hair in disarray, a hand resting on his sword-hilt. She came to life as he hauled her against his body, deliberately flaunting the hardness of his cock. She didn't struggle, simply freed herself with an agile twist and fell into a forward stance.

Her blow was blocked by his arm, a seemingly effortless deflection. She shouted in order to focus her energy, accepting his challenge, but he merely smiled tigerishly, defending himself against her swirling kick, her lunging punch. He hardly moved, but she knew she was tangling with an expert in unarmed combat. No doubt he would be equally proficient with a sword.

Losing concentration for a fraction of a second she found herself on the sand, with him kneeling over her, his hands clenched round her wrists.

'You fight well,' he said. 'Who are you?'

'Princess Varna of Trokles,' she answered, glaring up into his swarthy face.

'Then let me introduce myself,' he said, grinning. 'I'm Kron, pirate and slave-trader.'

While his men were amusing themselves with Otka, who seemed not in the least concerned, he snapped a rope round Varna's hands and drew it tight, then stood up, the loose end of it in his hand. He tugged her to her feet.

'Where are you taking me?' she cried, not sure whether to be pleased or sorry by this turn of events.

'To my ship, and then we'll head for Eblon. It's a rich island with one of the most prosperous slave-markets in the world, and a king who has an insatiable appetite for beauty. You'll earn me a small fortune, princess, and provide me with entertainment on the journey. I think we have unfinished business between us, don't you?'

Chapter Nine

The jolly-boat bobbed over the waves, speeding towards the galleon rocking at anchor in the bay. Varna sat in the prow, staring at the rapidly diminishing shoreline. Kron was beside her, the tail of the rope binding her wrists held in his sinewy brown fingers. He gave it a yank now and again to remind her that she was his prisoner – more than that perhaps – his property.

His hand shot out, closing on her right breast and dragging her closer. The oarsmen grinned at him, cracked obscene jokes and eyed Otka's sumptuous body lecherously, assuming that she was fair game for all.

The big woman quivered, tears streaking her face, but at the same time her nipples had stiffened and her thighs parted, displaying her nude sex and coarse bush glistening in the harsh sunshine. Varna struggled in Kron's grip, but could not help being aware of his flagrant masculinity. He was a tough freebooter, a reckless laughing rogue. Gold earrings gleamed against his olive cheeks and the rat-tails of his unkempt hair, and there was a savage strength about him, the undeniable power of command.

Determined to display his dominance over her, he ravaged her lips, his unshaven chin prickling her skin, his tongue forcing its way into her mouth. Heat shot from her nipples to her clit and she purred deep in her throat like a lusting lioness, unable to help herself. She had been tormented and roused in the convent, but denied the force of a prick plunging into her and the bounteous flood of male semen. Sandor had opened her to the need for union and, now fearing that she'd never see him again, her flesh was urging her to yield to this vagabond and dealer in slaves.

Shame tortured her as Kron smiled into her eyes triumphantly and rubbed his erection against her. He had felt her response, knew her carnal desires, and intended to fulfil them.

'A hot piece of arse, eh?' he murmured, and slid his hand across her crack, then brought it up, the fingers shiny with her dew. 'Wet, too,' he went on, and touched it to his lips.

'Leave me be,' she cried, yet was filled with longing.

'You don't mean that, princess,' he said smoothly. 'You'll be sold as a slave, but not until I've sampled your wares.'

He laughed loudly and the rowers joined in as they bent their backs to the oars, the boat skimming over the water. The steep wooden hull of *The Raven* loomed above them. Treating her with no more respect than if she was a sack of potatoes, Kron hauled Varna over one broad shoulder and, balancing himself adroitly against the swell, climbed the rope ladder. Upside down, his arm locked under her bottom, she could not even cling on with her bound hands. Feeling sick, she took one dizzying glance back at the heaving boat below and the foaming sea, then screwed her eyes tight shut.

Hands seized her and she was dumped unceremoniously on the deck. Never once did Kron release his hold on her. When she'd recovered her power of speech, she said, 'Let's make a deal. I'm the heir to Trokles and if you help me fight King Lagras I'll see you're pardoned and handsomely rewarded, your men, too.'

Kron spread his booted feet and stared at her, arms akimbo. His eyes crinkled up with mirth. 'I admire your nerve. Spirited wenches are more fun than passive ones. But treat with you? Why should I? You're intended for King Rashad's seraglio. He pays generously for beautiful slaves.'

In the background she could hear Otka protesting loudly as she was brought aboard. Kron's hellions were gathering around her, a motley collection, their skins varying from white to glistening black, their clothing equally diverse. Some wore shabby velvets or sober wool, jelly-bag hats or turbans, others calico breeches and tarred pigtails. All were excited, mouths agape, saliva running as they slobbered over Otka. Cocks were lifted from pantaloons and rubbed to full erection. Others had their hands deep inside, fondling their balls. All were driven almost insane with lust.

They bent Otka over a cannon, her generous white buttocks spread, ankles tethered wide apart. Two men held her wrists outstretched and the rest queued, jostling and eager to be the first to mount her. Rank counted here and the boatswain eased between her legs and worked the blunt snout of his prick into her wet pink opening. Otka shrieked once, but the sound contained pleasure, not protest.

Varna was astonished by her own reaction to this scene. It wasn't anger or indignation or downright horror. These emotions she had experienced on the battlefield, but much had happened since then and what she felt now was unadulterated passion. *She* wanted to be the one undergoing ravishment.

Kron lifted her up till her breasts were crushed against his chest. The buckles of his leather baldrick ground into her nipples and the mighty swell of his cock pressed its length along her belly. She drew in a sobbing breath as he tied her to a bulwark and unbuckled his belt, then fed it through the loops of his breeches.

'You've known the caress of the whip, and lately, too, by the state of your arse,' he commented, eyes glowing like hot coals. 'And who did this to you, princess?'

'Izar's priestesses,' she answered.

'And who before that?'

'King Lagras. I was his captive.'

'Now you'll have me as your master,' he promised darkly.

She jerked as he pressed the end of the flexible belt between her labia. They parted, wet with juice, as he worked towards the stiffening bud at the apex. She writhed and thrust up against it, trying to take control of the rising pleasure, but he snatched it away, mocking her. He spun her round to face the bulwark and stepped back a pace. The air cracked as the lash cut through it. She felt its vibrations and then pain shot through her rump. Blow after blow fell on her agonised flesh, on thighs and back and buttocks.

She could hear Otka's cries of pleasure as she was brought to climax by her crude lovers, could see the blue sky, the white sails belling out as *The Raven* was prepared to weigh anchor, could smell Kron and her own sweat and love-juice. She wanted to weep with shame, but even in the midst of this acute distress, was aware of the dark heat in her loins filling her with devilish pleasure.

Kron barked brisk orders to his crew, then took her down a companionway and into his cabin. He locked the door behind him. There were sounds of activity from overhead, the thump of bare feet, the squealing of winches, and a vibration that thrummed through the entire ship. The gentle rise and fall of the cabin became livelier. They were on their way to Eblon.

She backed away as Kron unfastened his breeches and released his serpent. It was immense, a rigid bar of flesh with a veined shaft and rounded red head bedewed with a pearly tear. Her blind panic had brought her up against the bed. Her knees caught on the edge and she fell back across it. Instantly he was on her, his hands gripping her breasts, his body pinning her down. His cock lay against her belly, searing hot. His eyes held hers, inky-dark and compelling and he reached down, finding her cleft and swollen bud.

Varna moaned, coming to instant climax. Kron raised himself on his knees between her thighs, then entered her in one powerful lunge. Passion engulfed her, a lust that had nothing to do with love. She kicked up her legs and rested her ankles on his shoulders so he might penetrate deeper. Her channel expanded to take all of him till his knob butted her womb.

She clung to him on an emotional high, feeling a queer kind of affection and kinship for him as he ground his way towards his own apogee. She thrilled when he barked his release, his balls rapping against her anus as he thrust frenziedly, his spunk gushing into her.

She sank back, Kron slumped in her arms, his face buried in her loosened hair splayed across the pillow. She didn't hate him. This hadn't been rape. He wasn't evil like Lagras. All he wanted was her body, not her soul. She was soothed by the motion of the ship and the heavy breathing of the man she held.

He stirred, rolled off her, raised himself on one elbow and played with her nipples, teasing them into points. 'Perhaps I won't sell you after all,' he said, lazy and relaxed as men are after loving women.

'Oh, and what would happen?' she asked, pulse running away with itself as her desire was renewed.

'You'd stay with me,' he said, and bent to suck her breasts, his tongue flicking over the nipples. 'We'd fight side by side, live together, fuck each other legless! My men would accept you as their leader, second-in-command to me. I'm rich, princess. You'd want for nothing.'

He released her and left the bed, naked and muscular, his shoulders tapering to a narrow waist and lean hips. She watched him, aching to have him plunge his long prick into her again.

He paused at a brass-bound chest, took a key, stooped and inserted it in the lock. Curious, Varna joined him, the silken coverlet dragged over her body. He flung back the lid and she was dazzled by the mass of gems within, jumbled carelessly together; diamonds, rubies, emeralds and sapphires. There were bracelets, necklaces, strings of pearls, tiaras and coronets, gold and silver chains, a fabulously valuable haul.

He pushed a hand among the jewels and let them run through his fingers like shimmering rain as he said, 'Women like gems, don't they? In my experience their virtue counts for nothing against possessing some of these.'

'Not I,' she replied, and she let them trickle through her palm as he had done but came away empty.

He selected a rope of flawless pearls and dropped it over her head. 'Didn't I make myself clear? You can have the lot. Say yes, Varna. You'd rather have me than some fat, overindulged potentate, wouldn't you? For I swear, that will be your fate if you refuse me.'

It wasn't the jewels, or the prospect of being a pirate queen that was so tempting. She couldn't help thinking how simple it would be were she to stay with him, forgetting her vows, her country and her people. All her life she had been taught that duty was paramount. She could leave this behind, leading a roving existence, free from responsibility.

Torches flared along the walls of the great reception hall. A banquet was in progress. It wasn't a special occasion, just Lagras's need to be surrounded by admirers. He cynically recognised that such adulation would be short-lived should he show the smallest sign of weakness or if Chedon stopped supplying the magical formula that kept them in an euphoric state.

The finest delicacies and choicest cuts were reserved

for the king's table, and he lay back in his carved chair and observed the array of dishes and pyramids of fruit stretching into infinity, lost in the shadows beyond the light of the candelabrum. Scintillating facets of cut glass reflected the colours of the rainbow, and the shining gold platters contained roast venison, a saddle of beef, a boar's head complete with apple-stuffed mouth, and glazed pheasants in a gamy sauce. There were trout and salmon from the great River Akkad, entrées of squid and other seafood that testified to the skill of Valdivian fishermen. The dairy products and vegetables were a tribute to the farming communities, albeit squeezed from the serfs as part of crippling taxation.

'Some may label me a despot, but this country has prospered under my rule,' Lagras said to Naram who shared his wide chair, her left thigh and breast pressed into his side.

'Who dares call you that?' she flared up, hair teased high about her head in a fiery cloud.

'Varna would, for a start,' he growled.

'Have you decided how you'll punish Laudine for her negligence?'

'Not yet. Perhaps I won't, but I'll keep her in suspense. She'll never know when the blow will fall. Damned woman! I had faith in her and she let Varna be abducted.'

'Are you sure this is what happened? She wasn't rescued by any chance, and is even now plotting against you? I've tried to find her in my crystal skull, but there's interference.'

He shook his head, the gems in his coronet flashing, and his face was grim as he said, 'A ship was seen flying the flag of a sea-wolf. A slave-trader, I shouldn't wonder, who carried her off. Even now she may be standing at the auction block, her virginity already wrested from her by some filthy, black-hearted villain.'

When he had first heard the news of Varna's

disappearance he had fallen into such a violent rage that he'd had the unfortunate messenger flogged to the point of death. He resisted the urge to send soldiers to the convent with orders to rape and kill every living being there, then raze it to the ground. He feared the wrath of Izar. It was dedicated to her, and the priestesses were her Chosen Ones. It would be unwise to anger the vengeful goddess. He had enough trouble on his hands as it was.

Varna was gone. The loss of her left a gaping wound in his heart that nothing would fill. After all these years and a multitude of lovers, he had lost the only woman he had ever really wanted, a woman who fought and defied him, such indomitable spirit making her doubly desirable.

He'd gathered courtiers round him that night in an effort to console himself, but nothing could change the evil mood that possessed him. He raised a glass of blood-warming wine to his lips and cast a glum eye over his guests, seeking diversion. It was all there for the taking; the noblemen, their wives and daughters, their slaves and servants. Jewels sparkled on arms, necks and in ears, and the bodices of the women were cut indecently low, showing rouged nipples. Others wore delicately woven silver mesh over their alabaster or dusky skins. A few were modest, but most flirted brazenly with their foppishly dressed escorts, red lips inviting, slender hands caressing intimately.

Lagras yawned, bored to distraction. At a gesture his musicians changed their tune for something more exotic. He glanced at his personal slaves chained arms over heads to the pillars. The females wore scanty tops that accentuated their breasts and their little skirts opened over shapely thighs and showed snatches that had been depilated or had retained their crisply curling pubic hair. The men, each an example of physical perfection, were banded by chains and leather thonging. They had been ordered to keep their cocks constantly erect. Aswad strolled round them, his eagle eye fixed on their crotches and, at the smallest indication of drooping, he applied a short cane to the offending member.

Lagras felt not the slightest stirring in his own usually rampant shaft. He scowled. Varna had unmanned him. It was unforgivable.

Someone had to pay – and pay *now*!

'Aswad, fetch in the gladiators,' he shouted.

Sandor was in the armoury when the call came. He had been practising swordplay with the trainer, Nelek, a wiry battle-scarred soldier. Renowned in his day, he could still show the younger ones a thing or two. In the week he'd been there Sandor had learned a lot from him.

He needed to, for Lagras was determined to have him fight his most able man, Zoltar, the darling of the arena. The king was infuriated both by Naram's interest in Sandor, and the fact that he had assisted Varna.

Knowing that the summons was imminent, Nelek had massaged and groomed the contestants. Sandor did not want to fight the bulky Zoltar. Not because he was afraid, but he had no quarrel with the man and a bout to the death seemed pointless. Also, he suspected that the outcome might be rigged in his favour if that sly-boots, Naram, had anything to do with it.

For days she had plagued him to shaft her, using every sensual device at her command. Her sulks and threats had been to no avail. Though his heart had grown cold when he saw Varna on the king's bed, and her banishment to Izar's temple for further training in debauchery had cut him to the quick, he distrusted the queen and his pride would not allow him to yield. He was a Durani Knight with high standards. He must not mate with an enchantress.

So, in a spitting rage, Naram had told her husband to do his worst. Whipping was too good for this stupid barbarian. Let him be cut to ribbons by Zoltar.

Sandor had heard about Varna being kidnapped. Now it seemed more hopeless than ever. They'd never be together again. His anger and pain had given his arm extra strength and his brain a lightning reaction. He was determined to escape and, if nothing else, keep his promise to Cym. Maybe, once away from the corruption of the court, he would regain his faith in Varna and go searching for her. But this was in the future. Now he must focus on winning the fight.

Aswad stood at the door, full of self-importance in his role as Master of Ceremonies. Sandor wanted to punch him. This was the cur who'd officiated when Varna was whipped. It was he, the king's lick-spittle, who had borne her off to the convent. Sandor felt he had just cause to hate him.

The centre of the hall had been cleared for this event. The courtiers were imbibing deeply and filling themselves with food, but a gasp rippled round the tables as Aswad led the fighters in. They were followed by Nelek, a surgeon and stretcher-bearers. This was to be no pretty mock fight. Lagras meant business.

Sandor was wearing a leather jerkin under a shining breastplate, and leather breeks. Metal leg-protectors reached his knees, and calfskin boots were laced around his ankles. More metal and leather spanned his arms from wrist to elbow, and a gorget guarded his throat. He wore a pot-helmet and carried a broadsword, so did his similarly attired opponent.

Lagras was not satisfied with this, however. He left his chair, paced round the ring and said to Nelek, 'Let them put away their cleavers. I fancy the trident and net tonight.'

Nelek did not bat an eyelid. 'Very well, sire,' he said, and sent one of his apprentices to the armoury to fetch them.

Sandor alerted and flexed his muscles. He had not actually fought with these weapons, though had come across them when practising. They were unusual and somewhat crude, consisting of a net in which one could tangle one's enemy and bring him down, and a three-pronged spear with dagger-sharp tines to finish him off. Netting required some skill, but brute force was the only attribute needed by the trident user.

Nelek handed him both objects and Zoltar stopped preening himself in front of his fans and grabbed a set for himself. The two men stood on either side of the makeshift arena and scowled at each other. Zoltar was out to kill, and Sandor knew he could expect no mercy unless Naram intervened, and then the price would be him servicing her to exhaustion.

The crowd was in an uproar. Money changed hands rapidly as bets were placed, jewels, purses of gold rohats and even slaves as earnest for their wagers. Zoltar was the favourite. Then an expectant hush fell as Lagras signalled to begin.

Sandor side-stepped neatly as Zoltar lumbered down on him. Sandor turned on his heel and flung the net. It missed Zoltar by a fraction, the man dodging it with incredible speed for one so large. He struck out with his spear and the outer tine sliced across Sandor's upper arm.

'First blood to Zoltar,' Nelek shouted, acting as umpire.

Sandor caught a glimpse of Naram. She was leaning forward in the great double chair, and her glowing violet eyes were on him. Was she casting a spell? He had no time to wonder, seizing a chance to trap Zoltar, his net flying out and landing on the big man's left arm.

'Free yourself!' yelled his supporters. 'Don't let the barbarian best you! Zoltar! Zoltar! Our champion!'

He grinned at them cockily and slashed at the net with his spear, cutting through a portion and shaking himself free. Sandor gripped it and pulled back. Without his net his chances of survival were minimal. They circled again warily, arms spread, knees bent, crouching low. Blood seeped into Sandor's armband.

Zoltar's eyes burned with a murderous fire and he bunched his massive shoulders and arms, his muscles writhing as they tensed and relaxed. Then without warning he launched himself on Sandor like a charging rhinoceros. His net rose, hovered, but Sandor's hand locked on Zoltar's wrist and the two struggled together, swaying backwards and forwards, close as lovers and pouring sweat.

The audience howled with excitement.

Suddenly Sandor released his grip, planted his palm flat on Zoltar's chest and pushed. His muscles stood out in relief under the bronzed skin of his arm. Zoltar's face registered amazement as, despite the power of his own grip, he was thrust slowly away. Sandor grabbed him by the wrists again, bent, and threw him over his shoulder. Zoltar hit the ground with a force that shook the hall. He dropped his trident. His helmet fell off and his bald bullet head gleamed under the light of the flares.

Sandor twisted agilely and flung his net over his antagonist fair and square, then brought one balled fist down into his face. There was the crunch of broken bone as his nose shattered. Zoltar lay there, flopping like a stranded fish. Sandor knelt over him, forcing his knees open, spear poised above his cock and testicles, ready to plunge downwards in an emasculating stroke.

'Cut off his balls!' Naram shrieked, jumping up and down, her breasts bouncing. 'Kill him! Finish him off!'

'Be quiet, woman!' Lagras stormed, furious because Sandor still lived.

The onlookers fell silent, the atmosphere fraught.

Naram ignored the king, leaping into the ring and crying, 'Go on, Sandor. What are you waiting for? I want to see his cods burst like overripe plums.'

Lagras grabbed Aswad's whip and, rearing back, brought the long thong down across her buttocks with a vicious snap. She screamed, her body doubled up as pain ripped through her.

'You grow presumptuous, madam,' he snarled savagely, and dug his fingers in her hair, yanking at the thick red mass.

Nelek stepped forward, asking, 'Do you want Zoltar killed, my lord?'

Lagras paused, stared into his impertinent queen's eyes, and said, 'Is this your wish? For if it is *I* shall give the order to see that it's done, not you.'

Sandor kept the tines aimed at Zoltar's private parts and the man no longer thrashed, resigned yet full of stubborn pride. He'd never plead for mercy.

'I won't slay him, not for you King Lagras, or for anyone. We have no quarrel, both victims of your diabolical slave system,' Sandor grated, but did not release Zoltar, having no faith he'd view the matter in the same light if he should gain the upper hand.

'Then you'll die in his stead,' Lagras pronounced, releasing Naram with another slashing cut of the whip.

'I'm willing to do so, if that's the only alternative,' Sandor answered. He got to his feet and, after untangling the net, held out his hand to Zoltar and helped him up.

The onlookers booed their once favourite, and he hung his head, his nose pulped into a red smear, one of his eyes closed by a rapidly purpling bruise. Now they were cheering for Sandor.

'There is an alternative,' Naram said, sidling up to Sandor and catching his blood on an extended fingertip. She raised it to her lips and sucked. 'Lagras will spare you, won't you, my king?'

'Will I?' Lagras cocked a questioning eyebrow at her.

'I know you will, dearest. It's my birthday soon, and

haven't you promised me anything I desire?' she simpered, smearing her fingers with more of Sandor's blood and drawing them across her face.

'That was rash of me,' he sighed wearily. 'What is it you want?'

'Sandor's life, and that of Zoltar. You know you don't really want to see your champion killed. Make me a present of Sandor.'

'As you wish,' he said resignedly. 'I suppose you'll give me no peace till I agree.'

'Don't worry, brother,' she murmured seductively. 'I'll wear him out and age him prematurely. There'll be nothing left of Sandor Devi, Durani Knight, once I've sapped him of his vital juices.'

'Leave me alone,' Sandor shouted, but he could feel the strength oozing out of him, the blood pumping from his wound with every pulse beat. He staggered, only his willpower keeping him standing.

Naram approached him with a goblet. 'Drink, my hero,' she breathed, and the combined scent of her body, her hair and the sickly-sweet effluvium rising from the wine, made him feel light-headed. 'Drink,' she insisted, holding it up to his lips. 'Drink and all pain will vanish. Chedon will suture your wound. Let me take care of you.'

Sandor drank.

Now he was in a glade surrounded by hawthorn trees, their leaves dried up and autumnal. A maiden was walking towards him, leading a pure white unicorn by its scarlet reins. Where the leaves had hung, withered and brown, fat green buds were forming, their leaves unfurling as he watched, translucent in the warmth of the afternoon sun. Flowers rioted among the long grass, meadow-sweet and campion and blood-red poppies, and larks were ascending with their distant, trilling calls.

The maiden was fair, blue-eyed and innocent-looking. Her hair tumbled down her back to below her waist and she was crowned with a wild-flower wreath. The aura of youthful vulnerability that hung around her touched Sandor to the quick. The dappled sunlight played over the pale skin of her bosom. The white gown she wore was exceedingly low and the material so fine that her nipples lifted the fabric. He could see the division of her legs and the blonde floss that glistened there.

'It's an illusion – she isn't real,' whispered Chedon in his ear as his gnarled fingers worked away diligently, repairing the gash in Sandor's flesh.

'That can't be so,' he objected, and next minute he was back in the glade and the maiden was so close to him that he could feel her scented breath on his face.

Her guileless eyes met his, their colour celestial under thick lashes that were dark at the base and gold at the tips. Dog-roses sprang into being among the trees, their perfume heavy on the warm air.

'What is your desire?' she said, low and clear, and dispatched the unicorn to graze on the lush grass.

'I'd like to see you naked, but this is too much for a virgin to perform,' he stammered, and his cock stiffened inside his hide trousers.

'Someone has to be the first, and I want it to be you,' she replied, her words and the gentle timbre of her voice turning Sandor to jelly inside, but making his prick stand to full erection.

With a shy smile the maiden slipped her dress over her shoulders and down, until she stood before him, naked. Her breasts were lifted proudly, her nipples perking up. Sandor had the ignoble longing to despoil her, to bend her flesh to his will, to thrust his cock into her and hear her cries as he took his pleasure of that virginal hole.

For a flash he remembered his vows – a knight dedicated to protecting the weak – and he saw the love on Varna's face as they had lain together – then he forgot. Nothing mattered but the woman he was with.

Acting totally out of character, he took out his dagger and cut a hazel switch, flexing it between his fingers. It was supple and wiry. Excitement made his cock jerk. Pre-come juice wetted its tip. He envisaged the maiden's white bottom disfigured by angry red welts. He'd never hurt a woman before, but something told him this one would enjoy it. He brought the switch down on her rump and her howl told him it had bitten home.

He struck her again, this time across the breasts and looked down at the marks scoring her alabaster skin. Her nipples flushed darker and she groaned and leaned towards him, sinking to her knees. Her nimble fingers found the lacing of his breeches, pulled open the front and released his cock. Amidst that unnatural burgeoning of nature, Sandor's sight was blinded by a strange and secret light, and his thoughts were tumbling madly in his head.

He placed his glans against the maiden's lips and it slid inside her mouth. She made no attempt to resist him, sucking strongly. He could feel his crisis would soon be on him and that if he didn't stop her his seed would pour in a hot tide down her throat. He held her head steady.

'No,' he said on a gasp. 'Not like this.'

He laid her on the grass, then went down on her, burying his face in the perfumed garden between her thighs. Then he began to lap at her wetness. She groaned as his tongue found the knot of her clitoris and licked it slowly and gently, and then harder and harder.

'Yes! Oh, yes!' she shouted, flinging back her hair and closing her eyes, the sunshine pouring over her upturned face.

Sandor felt her quivering and went on licking her till she screamed out, reaching the ultimate bliss. Before she could recover her senses he pushed her back and guided his hot and starving cock to her slippery wet opening. He thrust, plunging into her without difficulty, though her avenue was tight and slippery smooth within. He could feel the semen gathering at the base of his cock and knew he couldn't last long. With a satisfied sigh the maiden accepted his impaling spike. His thick, curving shaft stretched her, filled her, drove against her cervix. He could feel her flexing her hips beneath him, releasing him for an inch or two, then swallowing him up again.

Sandor responded to this blend of passion and pain, her hands under his tunic, her nails rending at his back and clawing his nipples. All thought had vanished from him now in the immediacy of the moment.

'I shall come again,' she said, and the quality of her lovemaking had become ferocious.

They rolled on the grass; sometimes she was on top, sometimes him, and he was astonished that one so innocent could be possessed of such wild sensuality.

Orgasm was roaring through him, his buttocks twitching as he emptied his seed into her and felt her convulse beneath him.

He opened his eyes wide, horror suffusing him. The scene was wintry, the trees bare, an icy wind presaging snow. The woman in his arms changed, too. Just for a moment he glimpsed Naram, then she was gone. So was the glade. He was lying on a couch and Chedon was with him.

'Ah, recovered consciousness?' the warlock said.

'Have I been asleep?' Sandor pressed the heels of his palms into his eyes, trying to clear his head. He felt dizzy and his arm throbbed abominably.

'Not exactly. I administered a narcotic so you wouldn't feel the passage of my needle and catgut through your wound. But it was all part of the queen's enchantment, too.'

'I was in the forest. It was summer. There was a virgin and a unicorn.'

'Naram, I fear. She was quite determined to have you,

by fair means or foul… preferably foul.'

Sandor cursed and struck his fist into his opened hand. 'Damn the witch and her spells. Am I never to be free of them? Where am I now, and is this real?'

'You're in my tower. The queen had me mend you and then fulfilled her base appetites with you, giving you a splendid dream so you'd not reject her again. Now I've been instructed to tend you and make sure you recover from the fight. If not, she swears she'll have my guts for garters,' Chedon said with a hoarse chuckle.

'Do you always obey her?' Sandor asked, feeling discouraged and ashamed. How could he have allowed himself to be carried away?

'Oh, no, my dear. I frustrate her when I can, as she has always frustrated me. She'll take her pick among the young stallions, but I'm never allowed a slice of her delicious pie or a peep at her treasures. So, although she and Lagras despise me as an old idiot, practically senile, I play my own games with them. I've drawn a veil over her scrying-glass, but know everything that goes on with the help of my own.'

Sandor sat up, gripping Chedon by the lapels of his cassock and demanding, 'Help me to escape.'

'There's no need for aggression,' the wizard said, his rheumy eyes twinkling. 'Why d'you think I'm lingering here now that the bitch-queen and her husband have retired to sleep? I'm pledged to aid Varna. Don't ask me to explain. It's far too complicated. However, I know the prophecy and have sworn to see it reach fruition. You are part of the grand plan.'

'Me?' Sandor thumped himself in the middle of the chest.

'Yes. It was preordained before you were born.'

'I don't understand.'

'First of all I get you out of here, then you find Welgard and slay Firestorm and find the next piece of the puzzle.'

'Where is the sword now?'

'Merrisan has it and she's journeying with Phila, looking for the dragon's lair. But if you hurry you'll catch them up.'

'How can I do that?' Sandor said abruptly, wondering if Naram was right and the elderly warlock had taken leave of his senses. 'This place is guarded on every side. There's no possible means of escape.'

Chedon smirked and put away his medical paraphernalia. 'That's what you think. The city is honeycombed with secret passages, and the palace no exception. I can get you out of here in a trice. Cym is an ally, and I know all the haunts of her gangs, and those who meet to stir up rebellion against Lagras. Oh yes, there are many who would overthrow him.'

'And you would see this done?' Sandor was reluctant to trust him.

'It is time,' Chedon replied seriously.

'Won't they know it was you who let me go?'

'They think I'm beyond it, a daft old dodderer. Sometimes their arrogance gets in the way of common sense. Besides, I'm the only one who knows the recipe for the brews that bring forgetfulness to the people. They can't do without me. Come now. Are you strong enough to walk?'

Sandor felt giddy, the drugged potion too strong for even his large frame and strong constitution, but he made himself stand upright. Slipping in front of him, Chedon led him down into the foundations of the tower, and there opened a door so cleverly disguised as a bit of wall that no one could have found it. A figure stirred in the gloom beyond and Sandor's hand flew to the hilt of the sword Chedon had given him, then he recognised Wicus.

'It's all right,' the wizard assured him. 'He's loyal to Cym. He'll take you to her and she will do the rest. Farewell. The next time we meet it will be when Varna is triumphant.'

'And this will happen? How can you be so sure?' Sandor said, stepping into the dark recess, his feet encountering a steep staircase that wound down even further.

'I know,' Chedon answered, and tapped the side of his nose mysteriously, then closed the secret door, plunging Sandor into gloom.

Chapter Ten

Varna stood on the deck of *The Raven*, the wind lifting her hair. She stared at the shoreline advancing towards her at speed. The sun was hot, beating down as the ship skimmed over the waves, sails taut and rigging creaking.

Kron had told her that Eblon was a large island, ruled by an emperor, and occupying an almost impregnable position in the Margos Sea. It had a strong naval force, and even Lagras had not yet decided to pit his army against these experienced mariners in an attempt to add it to his empire.

Now they approached the half-moon shaped harbour. It was a hive of activity, the craft as varied as the men who sailed them – dhows, full-bottomed barges, and a few snakelike galliots bristling with banks of oars. Straggling along the water's edge were wharves and warehouses. Beyond on higher ground lay temples and palaces, their domes glittering in white and gold.

Kron came to stand behind her. He slipped his hands under her armpits and held her breasts. His body warmed her from bottom to shoulders, and his erection moved like a serpent between her buttocks.

'You won't change your mind and stay with me?' he whispered, his breath tickling her ear.

'No, I'll take my chance here,' she replied, knowing that if she yielded to his request and joined the pirates she would quickly become as they, greedy for the easy pickings of the 'sweet trade', drinking too much, fighting too much, fornicating too much and, at the end of the day, filled with bitter regret because she had betrayed her vows.

'And nothing I can say or do will make you change your mind?'

'No. But what will happened to Otka?'

'She'll be sold with you.'

'I'm glad of that. We'll be able to support one another in adversity.'

'You may rue your decision.'

'So be it.'

But even as Varna spoke, her backside pressed against him, the heat of desire making her wet between the legs. He was so impressive a lover and she knew that she had to get away from him at once. Leave it even a day longer and it would be too late.

Now they were heading into the harbour and other ships sounded their horns in welcome. Fleets of ferries plied their trade, dodging caiques heavy with their cargoes of fruit and vegetables. Fishermen in bobbing boats were frying their catch and offering it to passers-by. The air was filled with heavy odours – spices and citrus and heat – palm and cypress trees, all blended into a potently heady brew.

As soon as they landed Kron sent a messenger to the emperor's palace. Then he handed Varna and Otka enveloping garments, saying, 'Keep a fold over your face. Women are not to be seen by anyone save their husbands or masters. It's the custom here.'

He hired horses and they finally arrived at a caravanserai crowded with muleteers, camel-drivers and a group of fierce-eyed desert nomads. The innkeeper came across to greet Kron. A weedy man, he wore a yellow tunic and red conical hat with a tassel dangling from the crown.

'Welcome! May the gods smile on you!' he cried, stamping on the packed earth floor and clapping his hands. Slaves appeared to lead the horses away, and he ushered his guests to his apartment.

'I'm expecting King Rashad's servants to arrive, Sinan,' Kron informed him, settling down and accepting a goblet of wine.

Soon there was a commotion at the entrance and a litter appeared, borne on poles by four sweating slaves and flanked by several uniformed soldiers armed with scimitars. Sinan scurried out to welcome the stately figure who stepped from the conveyance.

With fingertips pressed to his brow and then his heart, he bowed the newcomer through the door, crying, 'Will you deign to accept my unworthy hospitality? May I offer you a glass of wine?'

His visitor waved a hand pettishly, an obese person almost as broad as he was tall. 'Nothing, nothing. Out of my way. Where's Kron?'

'Here,' the pirate answered, a sneer curling his upper lip, his hand resting on his sword-guard. 'And you'll be courteous, Nadir, or your tongue will go the same way as your balls.'

The eunuch shot him a nervous glance and lost some of his bombast. 'You've brought the woman?' he asked.

Kron nodded to where Varna stood like a stone image, with Otka beside her. '*Women*,' he corrected. 'I'm feeling generous and you can have two for the price of one. The other female is a servant.'

Nadir nodded. 'I'm assistant to the chief eunuch. You're to come with me.'

Varna was thankful that her royal education had included languages. This had been invaluable during the past weeks. Now she looked from him to Kron and back again, and doubted the wisdom of her decision to leave him. Nadir was elaborately dressed, but carried a whip in his podgy hands, running the thong through his fingers, his piggy eyes shining viciously in his dark-skinned face.

'D'you want to see her unveiled?' Kron asked laconically.

'That won't be necessary. I trust your judgement. You've served us well in the past. Here's your payment.' Nadir tossed over a moneybag.

Kron caught it, checked the contents then spoke to Varna, his voice a touch regretful, 'Don't be afraid. You're so lovely that you're bound to capture Rashad's heart.'

'I'm not frightened,' she lied, a sinking sense of loss making her cling to his hand.

He accompanied her to the litter where Nadir waited impatiently. She was hustled inside and the hangings closed, trapping her in blue-tinted twilight with the eunuch. The conveyance was raised and she felt it moving. The rolling motion soon made Nadir's head nod, though he came awake smartly to slash her across the face when he found her trying to peep through the curtains.

'That's not allowed,' he grumbled.

'Where's the other woman, Otka?' she demanded, hand to her stinging cheek.

'She's following on an ass. Now be silent.'

Varna sank back, hearing the noises of the port and smelling its smells that penetrated the drapes. At last the litter stopped and Nadir alighted, dragging her with him. She was given no time to absorb the splendour of the pillared courtyard, for he struck her with the butt of his whip and herded her through an arched doorway into an antechamber.

Her heart was hammering. Was she about to meet the emperor? Would he try to take her? Oh, for a weapon, she thought, longing for a deadly sharp dagger with which to defend herself.

Otka was brought in, protesting loudly till Nadir took the whip to her, having her stripped so that he might watch the scarlet stripes blossoming on her plump white buttocks, back and thighs. Her moans and screams filled the room. Nadir ignored her pleas, having her bend over, hands clasping her ankles, huge hindquarters raised to give his whip greater access. She howled and urine trickled down the insides of her thighs, forming a pool between her feet. Nadir beat her even harder.

Then a lilting, musical voice from beyond a further door called them to enter. Nadir coiled his whip and stuck it into the belt girding his paunch, then beckoned to Varna. When they reached the inner room she was suddenly hurled to the floor.

'Kneel, woman!' Nadir hissed. 'Make obeisance to the chief eunuch!'

Outraged, she wriggled under the weight of his huge hand, shouting, 'I'm a princess. I kneel to no one, you turd-coloured dog!'

She heard someone laughing and looked up. Seated on a divan piled with embroidered cushions was a most extraordinary person. She blushed as she was scrutinised by sparkling brown eyes set in a delicate, sensitive face with high cheekbones, a narrow nose and rouged lips.

He sat with his legs crossed under him, extravagantly dressed in a rose-hued robe with blue-lined sleeves. His skin was pale and flawless, and one carefully manicured hand fondled the spotted coat of a leopard. It stretched lazily, displaying its pointed fangs in a wide pink yawn, then regarded Varna with slanting gold-green eyes.

'You show spirit. But in due course you'll learn to be submissive. I am Fareshah, and I shall train you,' he said, and dismissed Nadir with a languid gesture. 'Go away, fat one. Make sure the preparation room is unoccupied.'

'What of the woman outside? She's called Otka.'

'Yes, yes, I'll attend to her,' Fareshah said impatiently. 'Now, remove yourself from my sight.'

When Nadir had backed out of the door Varna rose and stepped closer to the beautiful eunuch, saying urgently, 'Let me see your king. Now. At once. I'm

Princess Varna. King Lagras invaded my country and killed my father. I need warriors to help me win it back. If I can speak to your ruler I know I could persuade him to aid me.'

'My dear lady, there's nothing new in this tale of yours,' Fareshah replied gently, and then addressed the leopard, saying, 'Isn't that so, Johor, my jewel?' and he scratched it in that delicate feline place under the chin. It purred its appreciation.

'But surely, you don't have many princesses turn up on your doorstep?' she insisted.

'You'd be surprised. Most women arrive under mysterious circumstances, sometimes abducted or sent as a bribe, offered by ambitious parents or husbands who've grown weary of them.'

'That's shocking!' Varna exclaimed. 'They're treated like chattels.'

'Yes,' he agreed calmly. 'And you, too, will learn to obey, haughty Princess Varna. Now, let's to business. I can see you have fine eyes and a pleasant voice, even though it is so angry, but...'

'You want me to undress, I suppose,' she said scornfully.

'I do, as a matter of fact. You're already learning.'

Feigning indifference, Varna raised a hand and unfastened the cloak. It fell to the floor. The garments she wore beneath were made of flimsy chiffon and patterned with spangles. Kron had unearthed them from among his loot. Without waiting to be told she unbuttoned the silk chemise and slim-fitting skirt and let them drop. Then, with a toss of her abundant hair, she stood erect, facing the eunuch.

'Are you satisfied?' she asked grittily.

He stood up, taller than she had thought, and placed his tapering fingers on her breasts, lifted and squeezed them, testing the nipple response. Then his hand cruised past the dip of her navel and parted her bush, sliding across her cleft and finding her clit with amazing accuracy. He teased it into fullness, smiling as her juices started to flow, spreading the cream over her bud and almost bringing her to completion.

'Good, very good,' he murmured, withdrawing his hand and washing his fingers in a bowl of rose water presented by a kneeling slave. 'You have the grace of a gazelle and are as ripely desirable as a pomegranate. I think you will enchant the emperor. But first, I must prepare you.'

'And my companion, Otka?' Varna asked, wary and apprehensive.

'I'll examine her later. I may allow you to have her as a servant. Now, come with me.'

She wondered if she should dress, but he handed Johor over to a naked male slave, opened a little door and led her along a corridor connecting with the women's quarters. A turquoise-blue bathing pool lay in the centre of an open terrace surrounded by shady colonnades. Clipped trees stood in terracotta pots and flowers cascaded from overhanging baskets. The air was cooled by fountains in marble basins, and there were domes in the distance, twinkling against a deep azure sky. Everywhere was evidence of indulgence and luxury. There was no need for Varna to feel so apprehensive, but she couldn't shake off this feeling of dread.

The white tiled cubicle into which Fareshah took her seemed to be nothing more than a massage room. A stern-faced woman stood there with her arms folded. She wore a black linen kirtle and headscarf, but was bare to the waist, with pendulous breasts and muscular arms.

'This is the Keeper of the Bath,' Fareshah said. 'She will attend you, but under my direction.' He nodded to the woman and she stepped forward to spread a white sheet over a high couch. He gestured again and she fetched a basin of hot water, a pile of neatly folded towels and a tray of implements, then he said, 'On the bed if you please, Princess Varna.'

'What are you going to do?' Despite his gentle mien, she found this situation even worse than when she'd fought the trolls, entered Cragfor's mountain retreat, or faced Lagras and Naram.

His soft hands were surprisingly strong as he gently but inexorably pressed her back till she lay flat. 'King Rashad dislikes hair on a woman's parts,' he said. 'I am about to shave you. Lie quite still and you'll feel nothing. It will soon be over, leaving your delta satin smooth.'

'But I don't want this done,' she cried, horrified that the last bastion of privacy was being snatched from her.

'The first lesson in humility,' he said calmly, stropping the blade of the cut-throat razor and running his thumb over the edge.

'The first? What are the others?'

'You'll see,' he replied and, drawing up a stool, positioned himself at the foot of the couch.

When Varna tried to close her legs and press her knees together the woman dragged them apart and secured her ankles. Then she stood at the head, her beefy hands clamped down on Varna's. Yet still she squirmed and struggled till Fareshah slapped her across her naked breasts, so hard that his fingers left crimson imprints.

Bending over her he stroked the thick curls that sprang from her mound and thrust one slim finger into her. 'You're not a virgin,' he said conversationally.

'Does this mean the emperor won't want me?' she asked.

'Not at all. He finds virgins hard work and usually orders one of his aides to break them in. Not myself, of course,' he answered with a smile. 'I take my pleasures in another fashion. I was castrated long ago, swept entirely clean of masculine appendages.'

'They cut off your penis? How could you have

survived?'

He shrugged and spoke as if it was of no significance. 'Not all live, of course, but the slavers know their jobs and their knifers are experts. They use ligatures to prevent excessive bleeding and, to tell the truth, setting aside the pain and risk, I was glad. I'd always longed to be a woman. Men find me attractive. It's said that once they have bedded me they never want a female hole again. Now, stop chattering. We must get on.'

The bathhouse-keeper rotated the brush in the shaving bowl, then handed it to him, and Fareshah applied it to Varna's pussy. She shivered at the unusual feel of bristles and soap laving her pubis and labial wings. Her clitoris seemed to leap at the tantalising friction and Fareshah soaped it lavishly until she sighed.

'Not yet,' he chided. 'Your orgasm is to be dictated by others... the king mostly. His will is our will, here on Eblon. Give me the razor,' he added sharply to his assistant.

Humming under his breath, he held Varna's slit together with one hand to avoid damage, and stretched it downwards, the sharp steel gliding in long strokes over her mound and lower belly. The heel of his hand pressed on her bud, squashing it between its protective fleshy folds. Varna sighed, filling up with want, her juices mingling with the soapy water trickling into her crack. She wanted to beg him to tickle her nubbin till she came. She was so aroused it would only take a second.

But staring down at him, angled as he was between her thighs, she could see that he was treating her impersonally, absorbed in his task. Her female treasures so wantonly displayed meant nothing to him. He was bereft of cock and balls, existing in limbo, neither male nor female, a member of the third gender.

Not a creature to be pitied, however. He was happy with his lot.

She lay there limp, knees bent, legs dangling over the end of the couch. She could smell the soap and her own female essences. The razor felt cool and she could hear the crisp sound as the hair was shaved away. When Fareshah lifted the blade to rinse it she saw her dark curls mingled with the white suds.

He ordered her to raise her legs and fold them back against her chest. Now she was completely exposed – clit, labia and nether hole. She flinched, then relaxed as she felt his blade searching out and removing any tiny hairs that clung to her bottom crack. 'You can put your legs down now,' he said.

Laying aside the razor, he scooped out a generous amount of cream from a porcelain jar and applied it to her depilated mound. Her skin stung, but only for a moment, then the smooth flesh warmed under the delight of his caressing fingers as he massaged the balm in. Her smooth pubis, the inside of her groin, the double lips that divided her, the swollen button at their crest, all needed him to rub faster, harder, until she exploded into climax.

Fareshah withdrew his hand, looked down at her with a shrewd smile and said, 'First we shall bathe you, then you'll be massaged, but not to orgasm I might add. This is the emperor's prerogative.'

Varna was still wary, unable to believe there wasn't a catch somewhere.

True to his word, Fareshah devoted himself to her, working with an artist's skill, subjecting her to the steam room, the pool and the massage slab till she felt boneless. When she moved the perfume of roses wafted from her as if she had been steeped in them, and her hair had never been more soft and silky. Her cheeks were rouged, her eyes outlined with black and her lips painted poppy-red. She felt as if she was a sacrificial victim being carefully prepared for a rite. It was unnerving.

Ready at last, she was taken from the women's quarters to a magnificent pavilion. The walls glittered with gold leaf and semi-precious jewels. There were divans and low tables, brass and marble ornaments, silk drapes and tapestries, and the light poured down from a stained glass cupola.

But Varna's eyes were riveted on an object in the centre of the tessellated paving. It was like a crosspiece but with a difference. Planted firmly on a low platform, it resembled a picture frame.

She tugged at her arm, but Fareshah held her in such a way that she couldn't break free. The great room was empty. She was alone with him, Nadir and the bath-mistress. 'What is this?' she demanded.

'Move,' he ordered, and walked her to the platform and made her mount the step, striking her rear with a white leather paddle. The frame loomed large above her head and on either side.

She measured the distance to the nearest door. If she took off now, running like the wind, she might just make it. But what then? The place was bound to be crawling with guards. She was naked and unarmed. Her chances of escape were slim indeed. Her only hope lay in trying to persuade the emperor to assist her.

'Don't even think about it,' Fareshah advised. 'You'd not get far and we'd have to turn you over to the soldiers who stopped you. They're a rough bunch.'

She knew enough about rough soldiers to drop the idea, but when he and Nadir steered her to the middle of the frame she couldn't help fighting them.

'What are you going to do?' she shouted, too angry to be frightened.

Before she knew what was happening Fareshah had hold of her left arm and she saw the gleam of gold as a bracelet was opened, then brought together with a snap, circling her wrist. He locked it, then said, 'You'll wear this forever, lady. It's a slave bangle and carries King Rashad's crest. You're his now, to do with as he wills.'

'Take it off! At once!' she shouted imperiously, but Fareshah merely laughed and slipped a chain through a ring on the bracelet, then hauled her arm up and out, linking it to a hook at the top left hand corner of the frame.

Varna raised a leg and kicked him where, had he not been emasculated, it would have hurt more. He stepped aside and then both he and Nadir completed the task of stringing her up by arms and legs, forcing a plank between her knees to hold them open.

Fareshah stood back, admiring his handiwork and saying, 'You're a sight to behold, princess. A lovely picture that will entertain the king hugely. But I've not quite finished.'

Hanging there helpless, her toes scrabbling for a purchase, she watched him as he came closer. He tweaked one of her nipples into a sharp point, then clamped it, cruel metal teeth digging in, turning the teat fiery red. Varna gasped. The pain was appalling, pinching her tender tip. He seized the other one and repeated this agonising operation. Her breasts ached, her nipples throbbed and her bare cunt was sensitive to every change of atmosphere, the twin lips mercilessly exposed.

'These next, I think,' Fareshah said, and Nadir's thick fingers were at her cunt, holding her outer labia open.

She screamed as another set of clamps were fastened there. When the fangs bit into the pink lips it felt as if they were being pulled to the floor. 'Oh, take them off! Please, please!' Varna had never thought she'd stoop so low as to beg mercy from an enemy, but she was beyond caring.

The pavilion was filling up with a rustling, perfumed collection of veiled women who walked round her, whispering among themselves. They were guarded by eunuchs wearing bright green trousers and short coats, heavily armed and alert for the smallest threat to King Rashad's wives and concubines.

'Be brave, princess,' Fareshah said, leaning towards her and slipping little silver bells on the nipple clamps. They tinkled at her every movement. 'The women have come to see how the latest favourite will react.'

'To hell with them, and with you!' she snarled through gritted teeth.

'Hush, he's coming,' Fareshah warned, and the women fell flat on their faces. Varna stared at the door, however, as the king entered with his entourage.

He was cloaked splendidly in a mantle of brilliant feathers that covered him from shoulders to feet. Black-maned and heavily built, tall and middle-aged, he was still handsome. His weight added to his dignity, making him seem more than a mortal man. As he paced towards Varna his cloak parted and she could see he was naked underneath, his dusky skin gleaming, a gnarled erection springing from the base of his belly.

She wanted to cry out in protest at this cavalier treatment, but his dark eyes went over her, undiluted lust etched on his face. His escort stood back and he mounted the step till he was beside her. He flicked at the bells on her, then tugged at those torturing her labia. Pain fired into her womb.

'Majesty... sire,' she faltered. 'We need to speak.'

'You have the temerity to address me without asking permission?' he growled and pulled harder, the metal teeth gnawing at the blood-engorged tissue.

'I'm a princess… your equal,' she insisted, though gasping with pain.

'She's a magnificent specimen, but insolent. Beat her,' Rashad commanded.

Fareshah bowed and then Nadir handed him a light, pliable whip. Varna opened her mouth to argue but was cut short as Fareshah flexed his arm and the lash landed on her bottom. The grovelling women moaned in sympathy and Nadir strode among them, lifting their robes waist-high and lashing their naked rumps till the flesh marbled, deep rose against white.

Varna twisted and writhed under the punishing force of Fareshah's whip, but she could not escape. The frame enabled him to attack her on all sides. The more she struggled and gyrated the harder he laid on the stripes. Every movement cost her dear, the clamps torturing her teats and lower lips.

The king watched, and she could not help focusing on his huge erection. He was a virile man, and the agony of her punishment was now blending with the heat of desire. The more the lash scorched her the more her loins throbbed, the shiny pink pearl of her nubbin protruding from the naked folds.

'Enough!' Rashad shouted and leapt to the platform, and she knew she had been whipped not so much as punishment, but as the erotic spectacle she presented to his lecherous gaze.

A curious kind of pride enveloped her in the knowledge that she had this power over men. Trussed and bound, whipped and clamped, she excited a monarch's prick to a massive erection and made the spunk in his balls boil like lava.

He held his cock in one hand, rubbing the enormous pinkish-brown mushroom of the head. His fingers stroked her cleft and when he removed the metal from her pinched flesh the blood rushed so fast into the tiny veins that the pain doubled. Tears streamed down her face. He caught one on his finger and transferred it to his thick lips. Then he lifted her hips as far as her chains would allow and impaled her on his cock, driving it up into her.

It was thick and very long, the tip alone distending her till she moaned. Somewhere a drum was beating steadily and the king performed in time to the rhythm, entering her, then withdrawing, then entering again, forcefully parting the tender walls of her channel till the circumference and length of his formidable shaft stopped her up entirely.

The drumbeat quickened. Rashad panted and she responded to his furious onslaught. Pain was forgotten and she ground her clit against the slippery cock as it plunged in and out. She was sweating, her bruised body on fire, her loins aching for the bliss of release, and she cried out as he thrust again and again. She squirmed in her bonds and came, inner muscles sucking his seed-filled shaft into her body. He gave a great roar as his semen pumped from him. He slumped for a second, then slowly withdrew his shrinking phallus and let her down.

The journey from Quexol to the highlands had been arduous. Early on, Merrisan and Phila had suffered the misfortune of being ambushed by brigands. They escaped, but lost their horses and some of their equipment. They continued on foot, scorched by the sun during the day and chilled by frost under the black velvet canopy of night.

'Blow this for a game,' Merrisan grumbled as they struggled up a rise, her feet slipping on the black volcanic shale.

'We've kept Welgard,' Phila reminded. It was her turn to carry it slung across her back. She liked the sensation, for it promised that soon she might be able to free her beloved princess.

Merrisan had entered her life like a lightning bolt, her energy, her untamed spirit and her glorious physique captivating her. They were lovers, comrades-at-arms, devoted to one another, their love likely to last till death, but Phila worried about Varna and longed to see her again. For this she would endure any hardship.

Yet even here, even now, when they were about to face the greatest peril yet, she admired Merrisan's body clad in supple leather, the taut shoulders and arms, the slim waist and boyish hips. Her thighs were strong and shapely and Phila wanted to touch between them, finding the thong that covered her slit, pushing it aside and exploring the warm damp folds that guarded the clitoris.

But Merrisan was caught up in their task. She paused in the shelter of a rock, leaned against it and dragged out the dog-eared map. 'We're on the right track, according to this. I think these are the slopes of Bald Spur. Can't you sniff a change in the air? Doesn't primordial instinct whisper, "There be dragons?"'

'I know. I feel it, too. And it's not only in the gut. There's the odour of sulphur and occasional rumblings below ground.'

'That must be Firestorm snoring in his sleep.'

Merrisan tucked the map away and they squatted in the lee, out of the wind, sharing the last pieces of meat from a deer that had fallen to her crossbow. They had cooked and dried it and it was still edible. With this and the plentiful supply of water gushing from mountain streams, they could go on for a lot longer. It was as well, for the folk in surrounding villages had been cowed and uncommunicative, fearing Firestorm's reprisals.

'You don't want to go messing with the dragon,' the headman had warned them. 'Stay away, for he's a canny one and knows everything that goes on in these parts. He don't like being disturbed. It isn't his time for feeding yet, and when it is one of my daughters is to be taken to him, tied up outside his den and left there to satisfy his appetite. That'll be a proud day for our family.'

'To lose a child like that? Are you mad?' Phila had challenged, but he simply looked at her uncomprehendingly.

'It will save the village,' he declared. 'What greater

honour can a man ask? Get you gone. Leave us alone. Firestorm mustn't be angered.'

Phila picked up her cloak and prepared to tackle the next promontory. She wished it was over, nerves taut as bowstrings, half-expecting to come across the dragon round every corner. She was certain now that he was very near. She glanced at the stark outlines of the mountains all around them and shuddered. She clung to the rock face, creeping along a narrow ledge with a blue-hazed, echoing drop on the other side. The wind had risen, carrying the scent of ice. They were high now, nearing the ragged projection of Bald Spur.

'Gods protect us,' muttered Merrisan as they came out in a small plateau.

It was bare of grass, and scorched tree stumps surrounded it like an army of skeletons. The crag rose sheer, and at its base, yawning like a great black mouth, was the menacing entrance to a cave. The Stygian gloom was lightened momentarily by a sullen orange glow.

'Firestorm's lair,' Phila breathed, needing to whisper, dread trailing cold fingers down her spine.

'He must breath out fire in his sleep,' Merrisan answered, and they edged round the rim of the clearing, a precipice on one side of them and the dragon's cavern on the other.

Phila was leading, but had no time to shout a warning as a noose came down over her head, past her shoulders, then drawn tightly to prevent her from getting at her knife. She heard Merrisan curse and turned to see that she was also roped. The thought of trolls or bandits flashed through her mind, but then she heard a familiar cracked voice and Rion was there, capering about, his expression one of unholy glee.

'Got you! Got you!' he shouted. 'You fell into my snare like a couple of plump partridges ready for the pot. You thought you'd left old Rion at Cragfor's to stew in his own juice, didn't you? Not so, my beauties. He's a mite too clever for that. He let you do all the work, finding Welgard and delivering it to him so that he could get his hands on the treasure.'

'You'll never have the nerve to fight the dragon,' Phila shouted, trying to worm her arms free.

'Who says I'll fight him? Though he'll be no match for Welgard,' the dwarf chortled, then dragged them to where a stake was driven into the ground, its iron chains stained with dark sinister patches. He was astonishingly strong for one so puny-looking.

'Wretched gnome,' Merrisan said grimly. 'What treachery is this?'

'No treachery. My right, that's all. I deserve the dragon's hoard. That's why I put up with Sandor's rudeness and bad temper for so long.' Rion hobbled round them, making certain they were unable to move, his grimy fingers using them with gross familiarity, pinching nipples and bottoms. 'This is where the virgins are left for Firestorm,' he vouchsafed. 'I suppose that state doesn't apply to you brazen hussies.'

'I've had men and found them wanting,' Merrisan answered crisply. 'That's why I prefer women.'

'I'm a virgin, if by that you mean I've never been penetrated by a cock,' Phila added.

Rion rubbed his hands together with glee. 'Excellent. Firestorm will eat you first. He'll be able to smell virginity a mile off.' Then he sighed and inserted a finger between her bound legs, wiggling it against her clit. 'A pity, for I'd like to poke my prick in you. However, I must save you for him. I've promised Leila a fine jewel from the treasure. She'll keep me to my word or beat me black and blue. Now I'll take Welgard.'

'Can you see it?' Phila faltered, completely unnerved. 'To most it's invisible.'

'I can see it,' he said triumphantly, and cut through the

leather that strapped it to her back.

'What are you waiting for? Challenge the dragon! Or are you afraid?' Merrisan shouted mockingly.

Rion looked around him uneasily. He part drew Welgard from its sheath, then gasped, shook his fingers as if burned, and let it slide back.

'What's the matter? Can't you handle it?' Phila sneered.

'It's Cragfor's fault. She said I could do it, told me secret ways underground by which to reach here, fast,' he grumbled, his eyes darting towards the cave mouth.

'She was lying,' shouted a voice from the darkness. 'Welgard can only be used by the pure in heart, and your heart is black as coal.'

'Sandor!' Rion exclaimed and dropped to his knees, shaking, the sword clasped in his hands.

The barbarian stepped into the light, a naked broadsword glittering in his fist. He looked larger than Phila remembered, his jaw bearded, his clothing serviceable. The broad girdle that supported his scabbard was of tooled leather, and there was the glint of fine mail under his jerkin. He tossed aside the wolf skin cloak and took off his helm. His hair straggled to his shoulders, and beyond.

'Up to your tricks as usual, Rion,' he said abruptly, then, as the dwarf shifted, 'One move and I'll split you like a melon!'

'Sandor – son,' Rion squeaked, grovelling at Sandor's rough-hide booted feet. 'How can you speak to me in that way? Would I do anything to harm you?'

'I've seen Cragfor since you did, and she's told me everything. I know you're plotting. I know you'd sell your soul to Lagras for gain. I know where Varna is, and I'm going to rescue her,' Sandor said, kicking him with a concentrated energy that brought howls from the dwarf's throat.

'Don't, don't!' he bellowed. 'Save your strength for Firestorm. You need his wisdom if your quest is to succeed.'

A fierce green flame flickered in Sandor's eyes. He picked up Welgard and strode to the stake. The long blade quivered in his grip as his muscles rose in ridges on his tanned arms. There was the clash of steel on steel and the chains dropped away. Phila stood free beside Merrisan, rubbing the marks where the links had bit deep.

'Well met, Sandor,' she said. 'You say you know where my lady is. Will you tell me?'

He smiled down at her from his great height, and his teeth gleamed white against that dark beard. 'Later,' he said. 'Even the rocks have ears and Lagras will be hungry for information.' He tested Welgard, balancing and turning it, and his smile deepened to one of savage joy. 'First I have a dragon to kill, after he's told me what I need to know.'

He raised his hunting horn to his lips and blew a loud blast. The sound reverberated among the crags and peaks, rising towards the heavens. The scree shook beneath their feet.

'Come on, Firestorm, you sluggard!' Sandor bellowed and blew the horn again, a long rising crescendo that seemed to pierce both cliffs and forests and earth.

The glow at the back of the pit-mouth brightened, became lurid and shot through with flames. 'Who dares disturb my slumbers?' rumbled a deep, drowsy voice. 'Is it time for the virgins? I'm not hungry. Go away.'

'Firestorm!' Sandor shouted, pacing closer to the cave. 'You coward! Face me, Sandor Deva, Durani Knight!'

A searing bolt of flame enveloped the entrance and the rumbling grew louder. Phila stood transfixed, clasping Merrisan's hand and staring as she saw movement behind the smoke and flames and heard that monstrous, echoing voice say, 'Oh, braggart boy! You'll regret this! Come then. Face me and tremble.'

Phila gasped as the cave mouth was blocked by the heat and fire exploding from the nostrils of the dragon.

Chapter Eleven

Sandor braced himself, legs planted apart, balancing his weight. He clenched both hands round Welgard's hilt, and waited.

The cave glowed with a weird phosphorous radiance, silhouetting the vast crested head and massive shoulders of the beast. Sandor's loins tensed and his bowels churned. He had fought giant tigers with teeth like sabres, rhinoceros with thick woollen coats and curly tusked, hairy elephants, but never, in all his experience, had be faced such a monstrous creature as this.

Gusts of heat wafted from its gaping jaws where enormous fangs exuded the foul stench of rotting flesh. As it advanced on bowed, greenish-brown reptilian legs, the great clawed feet crushed the skulls and bones littering the ground – human remains – all that was left of countless virgins. Firestorm belched out a further stream of flame and Sandor dashed to one side, arms braced above his head as he swiped at the scaly throat. The dragon bellowed as Welgard pinked him. The blood spurted. His head darted towards his assailant, snarling, eyes fierce pools of venomous rage. He advanced further from the sheltering cave and lashed out with his mighty tail. The ground juddered as it struck, gouging ugly gashes in the soil.

The tip caught Sandor with the violent sting of a bullwhip. It could have snapped his leg bones as it flung him aside, but he landed on his feet like a cat, instinctively retaining his grip on Welgard. The red mist of battle fury blinded him as he rebounded, striking Firestorm wherever he could. The dragon used his talons like swords. One curved claw flashed down, narrowly missing the part-healed wound in Sandor's upper arm; had the blow landed it would have torn it from its socket.

He knew he could not stand up against such enormous strength for long. The fight must reach a swift conclusion. Even Welgard couldn't perform a miracle, but it was making Firestorm suffer, its point piercing that tough scaly skin and making the creature roar with baffled rage and pain.

Firestorm was in the open now, his immense size dwarfing everything. Even while loathing him, Sandor was awed by this centuries old dragon with eyes that seemed to glare into his very soul. The beast's throat had darkened to angry crimson, contrasting with that lizard-like colouring.

Then the sky was suddenly blotted out as he unfurled his wings, stretched his neck, and in a great billow of flame, launched himself above the precipice and into the sky. As he gained speed the down-draught made Sandor reel. Everything blurred as the dragon passed over, the fire from his nostrils streaming, the sound of his flight echoing across the mountain peaks where the silvery snow turned pink and started to melt. Firestorm wheeled. He spread his wings to catch the thermals and swung his massive bulk round. He was no longer heaven-high but bearing down on Sandor, a glittering thing of scales and thunderous noise, slavering jaws and widespread talons.

Sandor stood firm, Welgard pointing upwards. Too late, Firestorm saw his intent. He spewed forth flame but Sandor withstood the blast. Carried forward by his own impetus, the dragon speared himself on the magic sword. It entered his throat, severing the jugular. Blood sprayed out, drenching the clearing and cascading in a hot flood over Sandor. He recoiled. Welgard was dragged from his hold, still buried in Firestorm's neck.

The beast roared his torment, fire and smoke pouring from his jaws as he crashed down, rocks and earth and the mountain itself shaking at the impact.

He threshed, his tail whipping, then lay still as his blood pumped from him, spreading into a dark red pool. His sides heaved with his laboured breathing, and his fleshy tongue lolled from between his fangs. Sandor leaned over him, but left Welgard in situ. Dragons were notoriously treacherous and Firestorm might be playing dead.

'You must tell me how I can rescue Princess Varna,' Sandor said sternly, the dragon's blood smarting like acid on his skin. 'Fulfil the prophecy. Cragfor has told me that you know how it is to be done.'

The dragon snorted, his wide nostrils still breathing out fire. 'You are the hero sent to slay me. I've waited for you too long. I'm tired and ready to join my ancestors,' he growled, his mighty head barely supported by that partly severed throat. Then he rallied slightly, the old light appearing in his eyes. 'I was a knight like you once, but ensorcelled by Cragfor. She left me here to guard the treasure which would one day belong to the she-wolf who'd save her country and baffle the wiliest warlock of them all.'

'But how am I to use this hoard? Lagras is powerful and owns half the known world,' Sandor demanded, bending closer to catch Firestorm's words, though the stench of the dying beast turned his stomach.

'Wake the Seven Sleepers,' the dragon muttered. 'They lie in the deep caverns below this mountain. Once mighty warriors, they too have been under a spell, sleeping for years, awaiting a blast from the golden horn hanging on the cave wall. Three blasts and they will wake, arm themselves and fight for good. Four blasts and they will cause terrible destruction. Wizards and sorcerers, enchantresses and witches have been trying to find them for aeons, but you are the only one who can do it.'

'How do I reach them?' Sandor's heart was heavy. Here was a further obstacle between him and his princess.

'Go through my cave and beyond, deep down into the earth's core,' Firestorm gasped, hardly able to draw breath. 'Whatever you do, don't let this secret fall into the wrong hands or everything will be destroyed.'

Then the great head drooped to one side as Firestorm breathed his last.

'That's it. He's gone. Oh, well done, my brave hero!' shouted Rion, scrambling down from the rocky chink where he had been hiding.

'What?' Sandor rounded on him, flourishing Welgard that dripped with the dragon's blood. 'You dare address me, vile toad! Firestorm was less of a monster than you.'

'But the treasure! You promised! It is mine by right!'

'Lies, all lies. Even now you don't change your whining tune, but I'll change it for you,' Sandor answered coldly. 'We'll view Firestorm's treasure together. You'll come with me into the cave.'

'We're ready,' Phila piped up, white-faced and reeling from the shocking conflict between hero and dragon.

'I owe you,' Sandor said. 'Cym has told me of your exploits.'

'My brother Jat. You've seen him? How is he?' Merrisan asked eagerly.

'He's alive, but Queen Naram's plaything. I know how much he must hate his slavery, and am sure he'll join us if he gets the chance.'

'That's wonderful news. At least he still lives. We'd hoped to have conquered Firestorm ourselves,' Merrisan said, then shrugged and went on, 'But having seen the monster's strength, I doubt we could have done so. I hate to admit this, but it needed male muscles to wield Welgard. You must always use it, discarding all others.'

Sandor looked at the agile girl with the honey-coloured hair and candid eyes and his cock stiffened. He was already aroused by the adrenaline that had pumped through his veins during the fight. Now he wanted to express the surge of power and energy that tingled along every nerve. But he knew full well that Merrisan lusted after those of her own sex. To her he was just a fellow warrior, nothing more, and his thoughts strayed to Cym. She had sheltered him when he escaped from Lagras, tended his wound and ordered her bravest men, led by Wicus, to ride with him into the remote regions inhabited by the wild tribes of the hills. These encampments, ruled by powerful chieftains, owed allegiance to no one, guarding their fortress strongholds against all comers.

But they respected Cym, her fame widespread. She was noted for fair dealing and bandits rode into Quexol in disguise to bring her their loot. She had decided that now was the time to call in a few favours and had travelled with Sandor, making her presence felt in the mountainous districts. So far Sandor had resisted her attempts to seduce him again, his mind fixed on Varna, but now he wasn't so sure, the pressure in his balls building, diverting him from thoughts of purity and faithfulness.

He strode to where the path wound down, steep and dangerous, cupped his hand round his mouth and gave a loud hail. Within a short while a head wearing a jaunty fur cap appeared and its owner scrambled up till she stood beside him.

'You've done it?' Cym cried, beaming at him.

'Yes.'

'I heard the battle and saw Firestorm flying. Ye Gods, what a fearsome sight! But I knew you'd best him.'

She came close and linked her arms round his neck. His prick swelled. She wore fustian breeches so tight they outlined the cleft between her labial lips, and a long linen tunic that cinched her waist and showed the deep V between her breasts. Her black hair tumbled round her shoulders, and her eyes shone with enjoyment of the adventure. She was armed to the teeth and ready to use her weapons ruthlessly, but just as eager to lay them aside temporarily and open her legs for him.

Sandor used his considerable willpower to resist her, saying, 'The cave. The treasure.'

'The Passion Stone!' Cym's voice rang out among the crags and she dropped her arms, though still pressing her body to his.

'And then to find the Seven Sleepers.'

She stared up at him quizzically, saying, 'I've heard of them. Warriors under a spell? A legend, surely? A fairytale to scare children.'

'Firestorm told me they exist and I believe it.'

'Shall I call Wicus and the men from the camp below? D'you want them to accompany us into the dragon's lair?'

Sandor rested his hand on Welgard's hilt, tilting it forward. He knew he could trust her, but was unsure about the rest. He couldn't begin to imagine the amount, but Firestorm must have held within his coils riches to addle a saint's brain and beguile even the most honest.

'A small group first, I think,' he said, and shouted across to where Merrisan and Phila awaited orders. 'Are you prepared? We don't know what we may find in there. As for you, Rion, here's your chance to see the wealth that's haunted your avaricious dreams, heating your cock more surely than the most alluring brown-skinned houri.'

The cave was pitch-black. Sandor used a tinderbox to ignite torches made of bound twigs, then led the way inside. The foul smell of dragon droppings thickened the air and they had to watch where they stepped. Firestorm had shown no compunction about soiling his own nest.

Then, a little distance in, the light caught on a great heap piled haphazardly on the boulder-strewn floor. Sandor stopped involuntarily and the others almost cannoned into him.

'The treasure!' Rion squeaked, losing his voice to pent-up emotion.

Sandor held a torch high, the light spilling over the heap. His eyes were dazzled by the fiery radiance as he stared at the dragon's spoils that spanned the centuries. Diamonds sparkled with white heat, rubies shone like blood, opals flashed in a myriad rainbow hues tangled with ropes of pearls. There were emeralds, amethysts and turquoise, some rough-cut, others fashioned by masters of lapidary into necklaces, torque's, rings, bracelets, crowns and pendants.

Among them were golden gem-encrusted goblets and platters, swords fit for a king's coronation, candlesticks, caskets, anything and everything which had appealed to the magpie mentality of Firestorm. And, set a little apart on a rocky pedestal, the biggest, most splendid jewel of all.

'There it is!' exclaimed Cym, sounding as if she couldn't believe her eyes. 'The Passion Stone!'

Sander took it into his hands. It was heavy and almost filled one of his large palms. He passed it to her. 'It is yours, Cym,' he said, his voice warm as the blood that pulsed in his groin.

'What about me? Where's my reward?' shouted Rion, making a dash for the pile and starting to tug at it. Gems cascaded down, tumbling to his feet.

'Leave it,' Sander commanded, but the dwarf's greed had given him almost superhuman strength and he threw off Sander's grip on his neck, struggling and fighting and stuffing his pockets full of jewels.

Suddenly a lilac cloud formed, elongated and balanced on its point like a spinning-top. It flashed so brightly that it lit up the cave. Then it was gone, vanishing like an extinguished candle with only the ghost of its glow hanging in mid-air. Cragfor stood on the rough floor, with Leila beside her.

'Get that repulsive little maggot,' the witch shouted, arm outstretched and fire shooting from her fingers.

'But you said... you sent me...' Rion gibbered, kissing the ground at her feet.

'It was better that I knew what you were about, scum,' she hissed. 'Couldn't have you telling tales to Lagras, could I?' She jerked her thumb at Leila while Rion cringed and wept. 'Tie him up. Whip him to within an inch of his miserable life, then hang him over the abyss,' she ordered. 'You can let him drop if you're in the mood.'

Leila picked him up and thrust him under one arm, then strode towards the cave entrance. 'Mistress! Goddess! Have mercy!' he wailed, till his voice trailed away and they were lost to sight.

Then Cragfor turned to Sandor, and he was overwhelmed by her beauty. He knew she was an enchantress, changeable as the wind. There was no telling which way she would turn, but just for the moment, he was in favour.

'Thank you for your aid,' he said, and bowed over her hand.

'There's no need to play the courtier with me,' she reprimanded, but a pleased smile quirked the corners of the cobalt blue lips that matched her hair. She smiled at Cym, saying, 'Hello, old friend. Shall we share this delicious morsel of manhood? We've both had him, one way or another. Let's do it again.'

'I'm willing,' Cym grinned. 'But he wants to save himself for Varna.'

'How trying,' Cragfor sighed.

'I must find her without delay,' Sandor butted in.

'Not so fast,' Cragfor said, her transparent silken wraps rustling as she closed in on him, touching herself lasciviously, pinching her nipples with azure fingernails and diving a hand down to caress her clit.

Sandor felt his cock straining towards his belt, damp

with longing, tormenting him with desire. What harm would there be if he indulged his lust? Varna need never know.

'You've found out where she is, haven't you?' he blurted out, trying to focus his thoughts on the princess.

'Being untrue to you, I shouldn't wonder,' Cragfor informed him languidly, her eyes slitted as she pleasured herself. 'She's on the Isle of Eblon, a slave in the household of King Rashad. He adores her and wants to marry her.'

'She'll never agree!' Sandor exploded, pain like a lance in his chest.

'Maybe, maybe not. She's already had a pirate.'

'You lie! She wouldn't! Let's go on and find the sleepers.'

He had to move or he knew he'd spend in his trousers, the witch's actions so lewd and explicit. Also her words made him doubt his beloved. If it was true that Varna was playing him false, then why shouldn't he give in to his base passions?

'Come on!' he cried, rushing past the treasure and taking one of the labyrinthine tunnels. Despite the flaring torch the darkness congealed around him. Was he on the right path?

'You are,' said a voice behind him.

He spun round. Cragfor smiled, yellow eyes dancing as if this was the most amusing of expeditions. A sudden awful suspicion halted him.

'Was it you who put a spell on these men?'

Cragfor laughed. It sounded like the tinkle of breaking glass. 'Oh, no,' she carolled. 'Blame one of Naram's forebears. They've always been a problem family.'

Now Sandor could hear the clink of armour and the whispers of his other companions. He wasn't afraid of what lay ahead, but it was encouraging to know support was at hand. He pressed onwards, the tunnel widening as it wound steeply down. The torchlight threw patterns on the walls. They were dry in some places, at others wet and covered in lichenous growth. The temperature remained the same, mild yet bringing Sandor out in a sweat.

Somewhere he could hear the drip, drip of water and suddenly, without any warning, the path finished at a wide ledge. They were in an amphitheatre designed by nature. The flickering, ruddy light of the torches was lost in the darkness of the roof. Sandor's feet struck rough-hewn steps leading down into the cavern where a waterfall sparkled, falling from a fissure into a rock pool.

And there they lay – seven armoured men on seven couches covered in animal pelts. They seemed to be sleeping normally, three on their backs, another on his stomach, one on his right side, one on his left, one partially propped, using his rolled cloak as a pillow.

No one dared speak. Even Cragfor was silent as slowly, almost reverently, they walked round the sleepers. Then, 'How handsome they are,' she murmured, her pink tongue licking over those deep blue lips. 'Noble of feature and giant of stature. Formidable allies indeed. Are you going to wake them, Sandor?'

'Yes, and their mounts, too,' he said, and nodded to where seven magnificent horses slept, some curled on the hay-scattered floor, others leaning against the stalls of the makeshift stable.

'That must be the magical horn,' Cym said, pointing to where it hung against the greyish, moss-spattered wall.

Sandor felt as if he was walking in a dream, a feeling of danger still lurking at the edge of his nerves. Yet excitement and a sense of occasion tingled through him as he lifted the instrument from its resting place. It was shaped like his own hunting horn, but made of gold.

Three blasts only, Firestorm had said. Four and these would be enemies, not friends. There was no room for error. Picturing Varna in his mind's eye, he lifted it to his lips. A clarion call awoke the echoes, ringing and ringing – a pure note that might have come from celestial plains. He blew it for a second time, then a third. The echoes died.

Then, as he watched anxiously, one of those still figures stirred. He was the biggest; a redheaded, red-bearded hulk. His brilliant blue eyes snapped open and he sat up, waking at once as a soldier will. He stared at Sandor, then saw the women and a wide grin threatened to crack his rugged face.

'What's afoot, friend?' he bellowed, his voice deep and far carrying. 'I closed my eyes to have forty winks and I wake to find you here. And girls, too. Better and better. Funny how one usually wakes with an erection. Which of you ladies is going to come over here and oblige me?'

Harness jingled and leather trappings creaked as the horses nuzzled the hay. The remaining warriors were waking too, yawning, scratching, knuckling their eyes and ogling the women. Cym and Cragfor were delighted with this reception, but Merrisan and Phila stalked forward and gave them a warrior's greeting, clapping them on the back.

'I'm Sandor Deva, and I need your help,' he said, addressing the redheaded man who appeared to be the leader.

'And I'm Lord Erek Ruadson,' he boomed. 'And these are my equals, princes and gallant soldiers. Tell us what you want and how we got here, for I don't really remember.'

'All in good time,' Cragfor gurgled, undulating her hips invitingly. 'I expect you're hungry.'

'I could eat an ox.'

'And thirsty?'

'I need a barrel of ale.'

'And some fucking?'

Erek roared with laughter and slapped her across the rump in a gesture of rough affection. 'You're right, darling. My cock's fit to burst.'

She wriggled playfully in his massive arms, and said, 'Leave it all to me. You shall have your heart's desire, and more, I promise.'

'But what of Varna?' Sandor snapped, interrupting them rudely.

Cragfor rounded on him, her eyes flashing dangerously, reminding him sharply of the serpent he had encountered in the forest – one of her many personas he was apt to forget when she was being charming.

'Stop fretting,' she said in that sibilant voice that made the hairs rise at the back of his neck. 'You'll get the chance to rescue your sweetheart, never fear. But first, I must see to the welfare of our warriors.'

She pointed upwards and twirled. The lilac cloud blotted out the scene. Sandor was enveloped in its whirl. He was blinded and deafened by the terrific rush of air, conscious of height and speed and a confused impression of everything gone mad. He grasped Welgard and hung on to sanity by a thread.

The whirling stopped. He opened his eyes. The cave was no longer there. He was standing in a long hall built of wood. A fire crackled on a hearth wide enough to take logs the size of a man, the smoke weaving upwards to disappear under a canopied arch.

'Welcome, hero,' said Cragfor, and now she was wearing silver chain-mail. Her breastplate enhanced the curve of her bosom. Her white tunic barely reached the wispy fair hair at her fork, and her long legs were bare to the knee where they met sandal-boots with wedge heels.

'You're always changing your colouring,' he said, for this time she was a pale shade of blonde, a smooth shining sweep of hair reaching her waist. Her lips and nipples were pink and her nails had an opalescent sheen.

'I know,' she said, giggling. 'Isn't it fun? Now come and sit with the others. There's plenty for all.'

'How do you do this?' he wanted to know, guessing she'd been at her spell-book again.

'I was trained in the arcane arts, but sometimes I use downright chicanery,' she admitted. 'The swiftness of the hand deceives the eye, my dear.'

'I don't think so in your case. You're a sorceress, through and through. That's why you detest Naram so much.'

'Sit, sit, and stop arguing. We're here to drain pleasure to the dregs. Forget everything till tomorrow.'

The sleepers, now fully awake, were making up for lost time. Seated on benches either side of a long trestle, they gorged themselves on roast meat, cramming their mouths full, then taking great gulps from tankards of ale. Cragfor had not stinted on the illusion, and the hall was hung with tattered banners and battle flags, crossed pikes and suits of armour. Anything, in fact, to make them feel at home. Minstrels strummed in a gallery that jutted out halfway up one wall. Big-bosomed serving wenches in tightly laced bodices hurried back and forth, bringing in more dishes piled high with food, giving little shrieks as they were goosed, warrior hands disappearing up the deliberately torn slits in their skirts.

Sandor was seated between Cym and Cragfor, and his hunger was enormous, yet as he ate he was aware of hands on his thighs under cover of the table. Someone, and he suspected it was Cym, was untying the thong fastening of his trousers, while someone else, probably Cragfor though she wore a look of tranquil innocence, was cupping his balls and playing with them. He took a long pull at the ale in his goblet, and then gave up the struggle. Tidal waves of pleasure washed over him as Cym lifted his cock free and, while she rubbed the engorged shaft, Cragfor spread his pre-come over the tip and fondled it.

He was aware that the warriors were pulling the wenches across their laps and dragging aside their velvet stomachers to kiss and suck at the ripe dugs. Erek had a girl astride his lap. Skirts thrust back, her thighs were stretched wide as he poked his meaty prick into the wetness of her cunt.

Sandor closed his eyes. He knew it was witchcraft, knew it was wicked, but couldn't resist as orgasm seized him and flung him to the stars.

'Cafless, what in Izar's name is going on? The city's in an uproar, and I hear there's trouble in Trokles,' Lagras stormed, his face contorted with rage.

The captain dropped to one knee, his helmet under his arm, his other hand on the pommel of his sword as he stammered, 'I'm doing my best, sire. Insurrection is rife and though I've had a hundred rebels crucified along the highway, still the malcontents ambush and kill our soldiers.'

'Where are they coming from? Who is behind it?'

Lagras was slumped on his magnificent throne, a slave-girl on either side, but even the attentions of their agile fingers on his crotch did little to alleviate his worry and tension. His empire seemed to be crumbling about his ears, no matter how many troops he dispatched against the agitators or how cruelly he punished those he caught. Chedon's drugs no longer seemed to be the answer. Though distributed among the populace as was customary, they appeared to have lost their potency.

'I've searched everywhere. Tortured and questioned prisoners, but haven't been able to drag information from them,' Cafless replied from his submissive position. 'All I've succeeded in finding out is that it began in The Rookery, that seething hotbed of strife where the criminal element hang out.'

'Send in more guards! Burn it to the ground! Slaughter everyone in it!' Lagras thundered, pushing the girls aside, getting up and taking to a worried pacing over the marble floor. He stopped in front of Cafless and jabbed a finger at him. 'You'd better do something quickly or I'll have you hung, drawn and quartered as a traitor... in public!'

'Ooh, that sounds interesting,' trilled Naram, walking in with Jat crawling behind her on a lead. 'Can I watch?'

Lagras glowered at her, his mood in no way improved. He blamed her for the troubles. 'Be careful it isn't you being executed,' he snarled. 'Your powers seemed to have deserted you, sister. You can no longer see in your scrying-glass. Who's causing this upheaval, eh? And where's Varna?'

'How should I know?' she answered pettishly, glowing like a malignant comet in her black spangled robe. 'You can blame no one but yourself. Had you not gone soft over Varna it would never have happened. You should have whipped, pierced and branded her into submission, then dragged her before the priests and forced her to be your wife. You'd have quickly tired of her then and life could have gone on as before. But, oh no! King Lagras had to fall in love in his declining years. It's pathetic!'

'Watch your tongue, you proud bitch!' Lagras commanded. 'Use your wits to get us out of this mess.'

'Someone is tampering with my sight,' she yelled, stamping her foot in rage. 'And what about Izar? Has she withdrawn her protection?' Then, seizing a jewel-handled rod, she belaboured Jat with it.

He bent over, manacled hands flying to protect his bare cock, receiving more marks on a back already latticed with fiery lines. With each fresh stroke, the whippy rattan cane bit into his martyred flesh.

'Izar is not answering my prayers,' Lagras said sombrely. 'No matter how many new-born infants I sacrifice or how much virgin blood I pour on her altar, the goddess remains silent.'

'You must have displeased her, brother,' Naram answered huskily, her breasts swinging as her arm delivered each downward lash.

Lagras stood watching his queen take out her frustration on Jat, and heat crept into his genitals, stronger than when the slave-girls had fingered him. Today his fancy was for the princely young man – so anguished yet unable to control the desires Naram's beating aroused. Jat's cries were half-pain, but mingled with a dark skein of pleasure that Lagras recognised. Though he clasped his penis it poked through his fingers, upstanding, its wet tip dancing to the rhythm of the blows. It became larger, stiffer, ready to discharge its load.

Lagras moved in for the kill. Only through the act of sex could he forget the disasters that beset him, and that for a moment only.

'Bend over,' he shouted, positioning himself at Jat's rear entrance.

High up in his tower, Chedon indulged in a paroxysm of mirth. His crystal ball showed him the king and queen rapidly losing their grip, both of them using Jat to satisfy their lusts. Wiping the laughter tears from his eyes the wizard finished stuffing his belongings into a carpetbag. The hour was almost come, and he didn't want to be anywhere in the vicinity when Varna, the Seven Sleepers and their army attacked the palace.

His last act as astrologer, necromancer and producer of narcotics which, unbeknown to Lagras he had been diluting with a harmless stimulant for weeks, was to concentrate his will on keeping the shroud of darkness over Naram's quartz skull.

Then, still chuckling, he escaped by the network of passages and winding underground tunnels which would lead him to Cym's headquarters, where she worked, night and day, among the insurgents, clearing the way for Sandor's return with Princess Varna.

Fireworks made a brilliant display against the night sky. Rockets shot up towards the moon, leaving a trail of fiery blossoms, and others exploded in clusters of stars, reflected over and over in the still waters of the bay.

Those who could had found places at the ship's rail. Varna had no such problem, her seat reserved next to Rashad's ebony chair.

'Isn't it beautiful?' he exclaimed every time there was a whoosh, a bang, and the deck was lit up briefly. 'My pyrotechnicians have excelled themselves, clever fellows indeed. D'you know, they are working on the development of a weapon that could fire missiles, they call them "bullets", with all the speed of an arrow, using the exploding powder with which they make fireworks.'

'Fascinating,' Varna replied, and yawned behind her hand. It was amazing that one so childish could be an emperor almost deified by the people of Eblon.

The party was in her honour and held aboard the king's own galleon, *The Golden Lady*. He could have endowed it with a more warlike name, but she had quickly discovered that he was a sentimental man, given to generous gestures as long as matters went as he wanted. She'd gone along with this. There was no point in antagonising so rich and influential a ruler.

Now he leaned over and kissed her lips, saying, 'I might have named this vessel for you, moon of my delight. My choice was aptly prophetic. This is our betrothal feast and soon you will bear my name, as you now bear that slave bangle.'

Varna placed her hand over the gold band encircling her wrist. This was the least of her worries, but marriage to him would put an entirely different perspective on matters. He had been obsessed with her from the start and Fareshah, that knowledgeable eunuch, had advised her to use this to her own advantage. She had listened to him and learned valuable lessons. At first she had tried to involve Rashad in her plans, but though he listened indulgently, all he really wanted to do was explore and take his pleasure at her every orifice.

His existing wives were jealous to the point of being dangerous, and Fareshah took her under his own protection, holding the highest post open to a eunuch. There were always petty squabbles taking place among the various factions, and the other eunuchs were a troublemaking lot. Varna realised she had been fortunate to find such an ally as him.

As time passed she found herself losing her grip on reality. Every luxury was hers to command, accept freedom, and she had to keep reminding herself that this was not forever. She still had to be reunited with Sandor, fight Lagras and go home to Trokles.

So she pleasured Rashad, entertained him with demonstrations of her prowess, agreed when he wanted to see her in armed combat against his champions, beat them and accepted the victor's wreaths made up of gems instead of laurels, and then regaled him with tales of derring-do. He loved to lie with his head in her lap, caressing her while he listened. Once it would have gone against the grain to pamper a man who had enslaved her, but now she bided her time, exercised and kept her body honed for the moment she was sure was coming. She would be ready.

The Golden Lady was a pleasure craft, unarmed and designed for trips round the harbour when the king was in a nautical mood, or parties such as this. Its poop deck was carved and gilded, its sails of purple cloth decorated with Rashad's coat-of-arms. They had dined below in the huge stateroom, and later this had been cleared for dancing, musicians playing stately measures. Then up to watch the fireworks, and now mountebanks arrived using the deck as a stage; a troupe of deaf mutes who were remarkable acrobats, then a fire-eater, a snake charmer, and a juggler who tossed innumerable coloured balls into the air.

Varna found this even more boring than the fireworks. And she was finding the feel of Rashad's plump, sweaty hands on her intimate parts nothing short of nauseating. He liked her to be naked, but tonight she was wearing a midnight silk gown that clung to her body. It was slashed to the hips, showing her shaven mons, then swirled back into a raggedly pointed overskirt hitched high at the back. Rashad had insisted she wore boots of supple leather that reached the apex of her thighs, the inner rim brushing against her lower lips. Intrigued by her independent air and foreignness, he allowed her to wear a rapier, hoping that she'd draw it and duel, a spectacle that excited him to crisis point. This had been a step in the right direction, and it comforted Varna to rest her hand on the basket-hilt. For that she could endure a hundred nights of his kisses.

Then, with a clash of cymbals, a radiant figure sprang from behind a curtain and swirled into a dance, while the music tinkled in those strange cadenzas that reminded Varna of gypsy songs, odd and mystic, every note embellished.

The dancer wore floating blue robes shot through with silver, moving with the grace of a butterfly. She bent at the waist, gorgeous limbs gleaming through the gauze. Her chemise was cerise, nipples denting it darkly, and her skirt rode low on her undulating hips, displaying a diamond in her belly-button. Raven ringlets flowed to the slender shoulders and lustrous eyes shone over the edge of her veil. Her hennaed feet were bare and anklets adorned with silver bells tinkled as the dancer gyrated wildly to the throbbing of the drums. She fell to her knees and arched her spine, her hands at her mound as she moved frantically, bringing herself to ecstasy.

Rashad nodded and said to an equerry, 'Throw her a bag of money,' then he beckoned her to his side, slithered low on his spine, tossed back his feathered cape and opened his pantaloons.

'Kiss it,' he ordered.

The dancer sank between his beefy thighs, then glanced at Varna. With a gesture calculated to keep the royal robes open over the erect cock, she pushed a screwed up scrap of paper into Varna's hand. Then, tossing back her veil, she lowered her face to the king's crotch, ran her tongue-tip over the glans and made him moan.

Puzzled and in no way envious of the dancer's task, Varna kept the note in her palm but succeeded in reading it.

I'm Cym, a friend of Sandor's. Be prepared for action.

Varna's heart seemed to stop, then went galloping on. No one was looking at her, all attention focused on seeing his majesty achieve his climax. He expected nothing less, convinced he had the stamina of a bull and could service dozens of women, one after the other. Varna knew this was far from the truth but no one was allowed to think it, let alone voice it.

She so much wanted to prise Cym from Rashad's prick and question her. Was Sandor close? When would he attack? She could hardly sit still for excitement. Maybe tonight she'd see her lover again. An hour – maybe less – and her ordeal would be over.

Cym was accomplished at fellatio, and soon Rashad could no longer hold back, pumping his hips while she worked diligently on his shaft. He groaned as he came, his foaming essence jetting out, overflowing from the corners of her mouth. Varna saw her throat convulse as she swallowed some of his seed.

The crowd was slightly inebriated and the sight of their emperor being sucked off by the dancer roused them to a frenzy of desire. Fareshah orchestrated a scene that might amuse them.

He clapped his hands and two strapping women in short kilts and body armour entered, dragging a reluctant slave-girl between them. They seized her by her wrists, and tied her to one of *The Golden Lady's* masts, pressing her breasts against the wood. She was fastened securely, arms strained above her head, legs spread round the post, her white buttocks parted to show the cloven purse of her pudendum. She was auburn, and her bush had a ginger tinge. She was crying, tears of humiliation and fright running down her cheeks.

Varna could no longer feel pity. She had seen this repeated so many times and invariably the victim ended up enjoying herself, just as she had done. Fareshah was a past master at demonstrating the dichotomy between pain and pleasure. The girl must be a newly acquired slave. She had an innocent air and a slight body, though her breasts were well developed. But Varna's nerves were on edge. She was sure something was about to happen, and exchanged a glance with Cym who crouched at Rashad's feet, limbs like coiled springs.

'How many strokes, sire?' Fareshah said, deferring to the king.

'A dozen should soften her up nicely,' he replied, reaching out a lazy arm and running his fingers over Varna's nipples. She could not help her wanton flesh from crimping, two tight peaks emerging through the midnight blue silk.

She looked at the girl's vulnerable buttocks. The crowd went quiet and, into that hush came the whistling sound of a whip. A muffled grunt betrayed the force of that first blow. The girl writhed, rubbing her nudity against the smooth mast. Her pelvis lifted as she sought pressure on her nubbin. The lash landed again and Varna's insides churned as she saw the second welt branded across the lower part of the cringing bottom cheeks, only the crease between remaining unmarked.

Rashad's guests broke into a roar, urging the eunuch to continue, and he glanced at the king.

'Let Varna do it,' the monarch decreed. 'I've seen her take punishment but it would amuse me to see her meting it out.'

She wanted to refuse, longed to take a stand against this despot, but Cym made an almost imperceptible gesture and she realised that her obedience was vital in that fraught moment. She stepped towards the slave-girl and held her hand out for the whip.

Without giving herself time to think, she thrashed her, again and again, hating not the helpless girl but those who had tormented and shamed her, and even herself who had learned to take pleasure in this perverted pastime. Her victim screamed, then hung in her bonds, sobbing piteously. The crowd were urging Varna on, nearly hysterical.

They were making so much noise that even the guards on duty did not notice the sleek black vessel that crept closer. It was only when a sickening crunch shook *The Golden Lady* from stem to stern as grappling irons bit into her timbers that anyone realised the ship was under attack. Men started to swing across the rigging, long-knives gripped between their teeth, landing on the deck and holding all at sword-point.

Varna spun round and saw Sandor hurl himself on Rashad and clamp an arm round his throat, and heard him shouting, 'Tell your men not to resist and no one will be hurt. We've not come to harm you, merely to treat with you and demand the return of Princess Varna.'

Chapter Twelve

'But you can't do this!' Rashad spluttered, helpless in Sandor's stranglehold.

'I already have,' he answered, with a flash of even white teeth.

Varna wanted to pinch herself to make sure it wasn't a dream. He was there, *really* there! Devastatingly powerful, towering half a head over the tallest of Rashad's men, while the breadth of his shoulders made them seem puny by comparison. His long dark hair escaped from under his turban-wound helmet, his cuirass was of chaste iron, worked in patterns of gold, the leather jerkin, the velvet breeches and black top boots, proclaimed that he had come up in the world, or been a most successful raider.

Her heart flipped and her breasts rose and fell with agitated breathing, nipples chafing against the silk. She burned to touch him, to feel his mouth on hers, but was suddenly shy. His bearded chin and moustache made him look older, sterner. She trembled as she imagined what he would do when he found out she'd been letting other men use her body.

Rashad's guards stood motionless, looking to him for orders, scared of their grim-faced attackers. The troupe of entertainers was jubilant. They had been a part of the plot, led by Cym, distracting attention so that the black craft was unobserved. She went over to them, exchanging congratulations, then freed the slave-girl from the mast.

'Your highness,' Varna heard an instantly recognisable voice say, and then Phila had her arms round her, a tearful young amazon who kept repeating, 'You're safe. I can't believe it.'

'Where's Merrisan?' Varna asked when she had recovered a little.

'On the mainland. At our headquarters, training a raw bunch of women recruits. We found Welgard and searched for Firestorm. Sandor escaped from Lagras and killed the dragon. Then Cragfor arrived and we woke the Seven Sleepers and Lagras's days are numbered and soon we'll be back in Trokles and...'

'Slow down, there's so much to take in,' Varna laughingly protested, and looked over at Sandor again and the magnificent sword, shining blue-silver in his hand. 'Is that Welgard?'

'It is. He doesn't use anything else,' Phila rattled on enthusiastically. 'We're going to win. Erek the Red, that's Lord Ruadson, the leader of the seven, is rallying troops from all over the place. It's amazing just how unpopular Lagras is. All it needed was a bunch of warriors, like Sandor and Erek and the rest, to forge a fighting force to be reckoned with.'

'Sandor's wonderful but, oh, Phila, I haven't been true to him,' Varna confessed, with a catch in her voice.

'I shouldn't worry about it,' she replied with a grin. 'From what I gather, he hasn't exactly been celibate. There was Cym, for example, though she now seems enamoured of Kron.'

This name startled Varna, a guilty pang stabbing her, adding to the pain when she thought of Sandor coupling with another woman. 'The pirate?'

'Oh, yes. He turned up and joined our merry band of pilgrims. He told us you'd been sold into Rashad's seraglio.'

'Did he say it was he who sold me?'

'Yes. At least he was honest in that and said he was sorry about it.'

'Where is he now?' Varna didn't like to dwell on the

confrontation when Sandor found out about their intimacy.

'That's his ship,' Phila said, pointing to the black craft that clung to *The Golden Lady* like an ardent lover.

'*The Raven*?'

'That's right.'

'And he's...?'

'Securing Rashad's palace.'

Varna was given no time to speculate on these extraordinary revelations for the king spoke again when Sandor released him. 'What d'you want?' he growled, and pulled his feathered cloak round him with a regal gesture.

'I told you. I'm recruiting an army to march against the Valdivians. We want bowmen, swordsmen, and cavalry. Are you with me or not?'

'Lagras is invincible,' Rashad stated, and several of his ministers nodded in solemn agreement.

Sandor laughed grimly. 'We'll crush him like a cockroach. Will you side with us?'

Rashad's eyes darted from his guards to the collection of hard-bitten men who had taken *The Golden Lady* with consummate ease and the minimum of fuss. 'And if I do lay my life on the line, for believe me, Lagras is unforgiving and I should die most horribly if you fail, how will it profit me?'

Sandor gestured, and one of his lieutenants brought over a saddlebag. Sandor tipped out a shimmering stream of gems on the deck near the king's feet. Even Rashad gasped.

'They're incredible,' Rashad gasped, nonplussed by this splendid gift.

'And there's plenty more where they came from. Do you agree to my proposal?'

'I must consult with my generals,' said the king, but the gleam in his eyes as he gloated over the treasure showed he had already made up his mind.

Then Sandor looked at Varna for the first time and she melted under the ice-fire of his gaze. 'You will free the princess,' he said, and she felt faint as his arm came round her, pulling her against the hardness of armour, the hardness of male muscles and, below his waist, the hardness of his erection.

'But I wanted to marry her,' Rashad bleated, though running the gems through his stubby fingers the while.

'She's already wed to me,' Sandor said firmly, astonishing her. 'Not in a temple maybe, with a lot of mumbo-jumbo mouthed by a priest, but by the law of nature. I took her virginity.'

It was as if there had never been anyone else – no beatings and purging and plugging, no agony and ecstasy, no other man anywhere near her, save Sandor.

Lured by the promise of wealth unconfined, Rashad had decided to become their ally and treat them as honoured visiting dignitaries. After the signing of agreements, feasting and toasting and the provision of beautiful slaves for the relief of Sandor's cunt-starved soldiers, Varna took him to the villa Rashad had given her in a private part of the palace grounds.

It was a lovely building with an unrivalled view of the sea, and on this starry night and in the company of the man she loved she felt that she moved in a beautiful dream. The moon poured bars of quicksilver over the surface of the pool, and it was a warm night, the air filled with flower scents and the sound of a fountain.

'My lady! Heavens, what has been going on?' exclaimed Otka when Sandor and Varna came in, arms entwined. 'And who is this man?'

Varna laughed happily, embracing the comely woman who had been her gaoler, but was now her personal maid and confidante. 'Let me introduce you to Sandor Deva.'

'The one you've spoken of so often? But what of King Rashad?'

'It's sorted,' he said, his deep voice booming across the femininely decorated chamber. 'We shall be returning to Valdivia very soon, there to put an end to Lagras and his evil régime.'

Otka fluttered her hands and expressed concern, till Varna put her arms round her shoulders and consoled her, saying, 'It's true. We're slaves no longer. Now leave us. We have a lot of catching up to do.'

Hardly had Otka left the room when Sandor clasped Varna to him and kept on kissing her, his newly grown beard tickly but soft. She freed her mouth, straining back to stare up into his face, laughing and crying, feeling that she would die of joy. Then she buried her head against his chest, inhaling the odour of him – horse and leather, chain-mail and sweat, feeling his hands repossessing her. Questions would follow soon enough, but now all that mattered was the lifeblood rushing back into her, waking her as if from a drugged sleep. This was real. This man was her husband. All that had gone before was nothing but a strange and very terrible nightmare.

'Damn honour and chivalry, the sleepers and Lagras. This is what I came for,' he muttered, cupping her buttocks in his broad hands and pressing her against the solid bough of his cock.

Her pulse rushed. The sensuous ache in her cunt could not be ignored. He lifted her and carried her to the bed. Her hands tugged at his clothing, unbuckled back and breastplate, unbelted his tunic, opened his breeches. She drove a hand inside, her palm closing over the helm of his stiff, upward curving prick. He peeled down her bodice, exposing her breasts and sucking hard at the nipples. There was a savagery about him absent the last time they made love.

She stayed his hands, looking into that unsmiling face

and saying, 'You're different.'

'I'm no longer a boy.' His fingers dug into her breasts, leaving marks. 'I've learned about myself, and women.' He tore at her skirt till it hung in tatters. He stared at her denuded mound and the little gold hoops in her outer labia. 'They've shaved you.'

'It's the custom here,' she replied, and her clit swelled as he eyed her hairless cleft.

'And the rings in your sex and that bangle on your arm?'

'Are symbols of slavery.'

'Take them off,' he commanded.

'Not yet,' she said. 'Later, perhaps.'

His fingers touched her cleft, circling the smooth lower lips and the jewels adorning them. 'This isn't how I remember you,' he said.

'But you still love me?' she asked, freezing inside. It would be unendurable if he did not.

'Yes, forever. But I want you to tell me what you've been doing with other men, and to show me.'

'Show you?' Her thoughts were whirling, this request taking her by surprise.

'How do they excite you? Is it through pain or submitting your will to theirs?'

'But, surely you don't...?' she started to protest, then stopped, reading a new hunger in his eyes. Her hand was still in his breeches, and his cock had increased in size as if he had tapped into a part of his nature she had never realised existed.

He wanted to dominate her, to prove his mastery, and she was more than willing to have him do so. 'Don't pretend you haven't been whipped and fucked by others,' he said, and the timbre of his voice sent thrills through her, connecting with her cunt. 'There's Kron, to name but one. He boasted of it, gave me all the details, kept on and on till I threatened to slit his throat if he so much as mentioned you again.'

'He doesn't mean anything to me,' she said, relieved that this secret was out.

'I understand, Varna, though I found it hard to begin with. He's no threat to me, and anyway he's in cahoots with Cym. They suit each other well, a pair of lawless rascals. But I still want to know what excites you.'

'Well, sometimes Rashad liked to tie me up,' she proceeded haltingly.

'And Lagras?'

'Him, too.'

'Go on. I've been Lagras's prisoner, don't forget, and seen the things he does to his slaves. Can you really tell me that you gain enjoyment from such treatment?'

'Not at first, but I learnt how to.'

Varna reached for a cabinet by the bed, opened a drawer and took out chains, cuffs, a ball-gag and a whip. She held them out to him, but he frowned and shook his head, then suddenly pulled her naked body across his lap. She hung face down, her breasts dangling. She was conscious of many things; his aroused cock poking from his breeches and pressing against her belly; the strong, musky scent of him; and the exposure of her buttocks, already quivering in expectation.

His first blow shocked through her, a stinging smack administered with the full strength of his sword-arm. Her bottom clenched of its own accord, but she could not escape, howling as she rocked at the impact of his second slap. Then, sex warmed by the heat sizzling through her rump, she ground her clitoris against his thigh, trying to contact his penis. Its length stretched out hard beneath her, but she couldn't quite angle her body for maximum pleasure. Each burning slap engendered greater desire in her. She was more in love with him than ever, though he was a novice in this way of arousal. She wondered if he would always be like this now, or would the gentle lover return, once he had experimented with the darker side of sexual enjoyment.

'You want this, Varna,' he said, and these were the first words he had spoken since starting to chastise her.

'Oh, yes. It makes me long to come.'

He covered her backside with fiery slaps, then turned her around and stared into her eyes, and she knew he saw the tears of pain and the heat of passion, inexorably intertwined. She sat astride him, and he massaged the soreness from her rump, then slid his hand into her crack, finding the slippery moisture of her love-juice and bathing her delta. She sobbed quietly, and he moved a finger over her throbbing bud and she gasped as climax overwhelmed her.

Letting her finish, bringing her down gently, Sandor flipped her over on her back and knelt between her legs, impaling her on his erection. She was still contracting and her inner muscles grabbed at his cock gratefully, needing something huge to clench round. He started to move, clutching her breasts as he powered his hips in a ceaseless rhythm. Varna's clit was still thrumming and she pressed it to the base of his cock at every forcible stroke, but before she could reach a second orgasm she felt it twitch, pulse hard, then pour out its libation.

'We don't need bondage and whips,' she whispered into his ear as he lay heavily across her prone body. 'We have a greater gift, that of love.'

'Oh, I don't know,' he grunted, teasingly. 'I may have to discipline you now and again, you headstrong wench.'

And Varna sighed, breathing in the mingled scents of their bodies and running her fingers through his hair, happier than she had ever thought possible.

The peace of Udin's celestial castle was rudely shattered when a chariot bowled through the open door where he had been standing but a few moments since, admiring the sea of clouds solid as snow on mountain peaks.

He had retired to his throne that headed the large table, the company served by his nine daughters, the glorious warrior maidens who fetched dead heroes from the battlefields on the backs of their chargers. Armour set aside, they were scantily clad, moving with grace and allure, bringing in ambrosia and mead and every perfect fruit of the forest – ones that were always fresh and never decayed.

'What's the meaning of this? Why did you send that mincing popinjay with a message to attend you?' demanded the charioteer, hauling on the reins of four griffins, part eagle, part lion. They glared around them with fierce red eyes, opened their beaks and hissed, as aggressive as their mistress.

'Someone talking about me?' Asvald said sweetly from his place on Udin's right hand, adding, 'Goddess you may be, but you always were a foul-mouthed slut, Izar.'

'Shut up, fool! Why speak to the monkey when the organ grinder's around?' she snapped nastily.

'He was following my instructions. We need to talk,' Udin said sternly, and the clouds turned from billowing white to storm grey. Thunder echoed in the distance and a single fork of lightning filling the Great Hall with a zigzag of blue.

Izar alighted from her chariot, and the goblin slaves who formed part of her retinue gentled her bad-tempered steeds. She stalked towards Udin, her generous breasts thrust forward, her robes floating round her legs showing disturbing flashes of her milky thighs. Her arms were in constant graceful movement, a pair sprouting from each shoulder. She was stunning, a magnificently evil deity who breathed sexuality from every pore. She paused, reached out and traced Udin's cock through his robe with a pointed red talon.

'You have a divinely wicked touch,' he conceded, his

penis swelling. 'But no more! I've never had you and I never will.'

The woman seated beside him sprang to her feet, hackles rising. 'Husband, did you have to invite that depraved creature here, to besmirch our hearth and home?' she said, her voice having a nagging edge.

A well-built, fair-haired lady, she was the goddess of marriage who wouldn't even give credence to the notion of adultery, though Udin was forever proving it to her.

'What's the matter, Frodis? Afraid he'll stray again?' Izar said, her voice heavy with honeyed malice. 'He has a wandering eye and an insatiable cock. He should keep it in his breeches. It's got him into a lot of trouble. Witness those strapping daughters, born to him by the earth-mother.'

'Don't fret, my love. This is no concern of yours,' Udin put in quickly, attempting to pacify his wife.

'It is when that shrew contaminates the place,' Frodis sparked up, her own children seated around her while she did her best to ignore his bastards.

'Who are you calling a shrew?' Izar shouted, swelling to twice her size, her snake-hair writhing.

'You!' Frodis yelled, losing her poise. 'And take those animals of yours away. They're defecating on my carpet.'

Izar laughed and the storm broke, rattling round the hall to which there seemed to be no end and certainly no ceiling. 'What's wrong with a dollop of shit?' she roared.

'Udin! Do something!' Frodis implored, deeply mortified.

He sighed, that mighty, all-powerful god who could cope with anything except trouble with his women. 'Izar, I say this to you, once and once only. I forbid you to help King Lagras. Now take your disgusting beasts and get out of here.'

'You have the audacity to forbid *me* to do something? How dare you?' the goddess raged, her eyes shooting fire, her skin glowing with it, the serpents in her hair coiling and testing the air, tongues flickering.

He rose, a towering figure in purple and gold. 'I dare because I'm in charge. No god is mightier than me. If you disobey I'll have you cast into the deepest regions of outer space, there to burn in the everlasting fires of the bottomless pit, tortured by demons. While you scorch they'll rouse you to unspeakable lust, a lust that will never, ever be satisfied.'

'You can't do this to me. Lagras is my vassal. Valdivia has been mine since time immemorial.'

'And I'm pledged to aid Princess Varna. You must obey.'

'You can't make me!' Izar challenged, thunder-balls exploding as she fired them from twenty fingertips.

'Don't push your luck. Now get out,' Udin replied, and struck the floor beneath her feet with his rune-carved spear. A vast crevasse opened up and, with a shriek, she disappeared within it, her chariot, griffins and goblins tumbling after her.

Lagras stamped into his private temple. He was bloodstained and battle-sore. His forces had clashed with Varna and her army on the Plains of Asgrid and been vanquished, beating a hasty retreat to Quexol, with her in hot pursuit.

Now, eyes flashing, face grim, he bore down on the priests huddled near Izar's altar, shouting, 'Why aren't you propitiating her? Where are the virgins I ordered? Get on with it. There's no time to lose!'

Naram glided from behind the hangings, wearing transparent black, with a diamond tiara on her flaming red hair. She was as beautifully turned out as if going to a ball, and Jat walked beside her, a leash attached to the ring in his frenum.

'You lost again, I presume?' she said, halting before

Lagras and caressing his tangled beard lovingly. 'This is getting a habit. Soon you'll have no men left.'

He gripped her hand in his leather gauntlet, dragging her harshly against the armour covering his chest, hoping to hurt her nipples. 'I refuse to surrender,' he bellowed. 'They're using magic against me, potent magic, and ours has failed. Why is this, Naram? Why doesn't the goddess answer my prayers?' He flung Naram aside and glared at the high priest, ordering, 'Bring in the virgins.'

Six young women were herded through a door by Aswad and Rana. Lagras looked them up and down as they stood before him, heads held high. They were not slaves, but daughters of prosperous merchants, government officials and the like. They varied in height and build and colouring, but each was a picture of girlish perfection.

'Cafless!' Lagras called and immediately the leader of the Cutha Lancers stepped forward. He looked exhausted, his armour battered, his uniform muddied.

'Sire,' he answered, summoning the energy to click his heels together.

'Give them to your men. I want to see them defiled. Right here, in front of Izar's altar.'

'Oh, good,' Naram exclaimed, tugging at Jat's lead and drawing him closer so that she might touch his stretched prick. 'We don't seem to be having any fun lately. You're always so bothered, Lagras, deep in discussions with your generals or off campaigning.'

'Don't you realise the gravity of the situation?' he growled, striking his fist into his palm and pacing like a caged tiger. 'We've been beaten on every front, on land and at sea. Every state in my empire has risen up against me, and Valdivia is in enemy hands since this last battle. Quexol is all I have left.'

'What will happen to us?' she asked, her violet eyes wide with apprehension.

'I don't know. Izar has deserted me. All that remains is to die nobly.'

'I've no intention of dying,' she retorted heatedly. 'It's not quite over. Sacrifice the virgins and then, if Izar doesn't perform a miracle, we can always use him as a hostage,' and she jerked on Jat's lead.

A sardonic smile curved Lagras's lips. 'That's true,' he said. 'Well done, sister. If they want the young man to live, then they must let us go. But first, the virgins.' He signalled to Aswad, and the slave-master kneed the girls to the floor. Then Lagras addressed his bodyguards, saying, 'You've fought like lions and deserve a reward. Take these girls and do what you will with them. I want their maidenheads as a gift for the goddess.'

The soldiers perked up, no longer weary, circling the young women and pulling at their clothing, exposing firm young breasts, dimpled buttocks and slender thighs. The men lined up to take their turn, but several at once was allowed, a single girl taking cocks in her hands and another in her mouth, while a third was pushed into her love-tunnel and a fourth past her anal ring.

Lagras waited with cruel lust for the struggles, the screams, the weeping and wailing. He was disappointed. If there were any cries at all, then they were ones of pleasure. The guards were hungry for that sweet flesh and took the girls any which way; on the temple floor, over stone benches, pressed upright against the walls. Those men who were still waiting their turn shouted encouragement to their fellows, rubbing their cocks and exciting their balls, organs straining from codpieces and lacing.

Still no protests and hysteria, no pleas for mercy. 'I think they're enjoying being ravished, sire,' Cafless said, almost apologetically.

'What!' Lagras growled, his face like thunder. 'Are there no virtuous maidens left in the city? Were these longing to lose their cherries? What's the world coming to?'

'Blame the war, majesty. Uniforms excite the female population. They love soldiers,' Naram put in, by way of consolation.

'It's disgraceful. Have they no morals? Virgins are supposed to sob and scream. It's traditional,' he declaimed indignantly.

'There's blood, sire,' Cafless said, and pointed to where white semen mingled with pink as it trickled down the legs of some of the girls.

'Right! Gather it, soak cloths in it. Burn it on Izar's altar,' Lagras cried frantically.

Varna, covered with sweat and dust, led her cavalry through the great gate of Quexol.

They had not had to attack the heavy teak portal with siege-engines. Cym's cohorts had opened it from within, and others to the north, east and west. Quexol was theirs for the taking, the last bastion, the final obstacle overcome in their struggle to defeat Lagras. Proudly she rode under the mighty stone arch, and Sandor jogged with her on his huge white charger.

'Not long ago my father's head adorned a pike up there,' she said, pointing towards the battlement above them.

'Soon it will be Lagras's,' he replied grimly. 'If that's what you want.'

'Maybe,' she said. 'I can't yet believe he won't give us the slip.'

So many weeks of gruelling fighting, for the Valdivians had been tough and their leaders shrewd veterans. Every province, each town and port had been hard won. News had come through that Trokles was free, and this had given Varna a tremendous boost, driving her on to the last battle.

There they had clashed, Lagras's mighty army and her own, on the Asgrid Plain where once the Northlanders had suffered a crushing defeat. Now nothing stood in Varna's way and she entered the Valdivian capitol with her troops marching behind her and the cavalry prancing ahead. It was a proud moment and, 'Oh, father, dear father, I hope you are watching this,' she prayed within herself.

Surprisingly there was no resistance. No soldiers in evidence, no sentries or watchmen. Presumably they had all been recruited to take part in the battle and fallen on the field, and if a skeleton force had been left behind, then Cym's hellions had taken care of them.

The citizens stood thick on either side of the broad central road, watching the impressive cortège pass. They were silent at first, fearful, expecting the city to be sacked, its men slaughtered and its women raped. But Varna had taken the precaution of having Cym inform all she could that their conquerors would be merciful.

Word spread like wildfire and a few people raised a cheer. This was taken up, and a volley of applause greeted Varna. When she reached the plaza outside the great temple she dismounted and climbed the steps, then turned and addressed the sea of faces, all watching her expectantly.

'Citizens of Quexol,' she cried, her voice ringing out across the sunlit square, disturbing the pigeons, which rose, fluttering, from cornices and roofs. 'You have nothing to fear from us. Our mission is a peaceful one. I shall appoint a governor for Valdivia, someone elected by yourselves, after which I'll return to my own country and hope that we may live in harmony henceforth.'

'What of the tyrant, Lagras and his demon sister?' demanded a belligerent youth, leaping up on a balustrade and waving his burly arms.

'Give 'em to us!' the people howled. 'We'll deal with

'em!'

'I can't allow mob rule, but never fear, justice will be done,' she promised. 'They shall be tried by a just body of men. You have the word of Princess Varna of Trokles.'

'All right, we trust you,' the young agitator declared and leapt down to join his mates who thumped him on the back, proud of their spokesman.

Varna swung up into her saddle and, 'To Lagras's palace?' Sandor asked, his eyes hard as steel.

'To the palace,' she said.

The huge building appeared to be deserted, the guards on duty having fled. This, more than anything else, was indicative of how far Lagras had fallen from power. At one time no one would have dared leave their posts.

Sandor grasped Welgard's hilt, stalking cautiously, a coterie of handpicked fighters with him. 'Be careful,' he advised Varna. 'He's a wily one.'

'I know,' she answered, naked blade in her hand, sandal-boots making no sound on the polished onyx floor. The silence was eerie.

They proceeded through the passages and reception rooms and then became aware of noises issuing from the temple. They froze, each warrior alert; Merrisan was holding her bow, Phila a long-knife, and the rest were armed with swords.

Incense thickened the air as they crept closer. The sounds were recognisable as those made by several couples in the throes of copulation. Varna and Sandor exchanged a glance. The atmosphere was redolent of sex. Then he pushed aside the silk curtain that lay between them and the altar. She stopped short, biting back an exclamation of surprise. The guards were there all right, but too pre-occupied with thrusting their cocks into the orifices of a collection of young females to notice their sudden arrival.

Lagras saw them, however, and drew his sword. 'We're

under attack, you dolts!' he raged. 'Cafless! Do something!'

With an oath he flung himself on Varna. Her arm shot out in a reflex action, her blade a part of it. The swords touched, sprang apart, touched again. The tempered steel rang. From the corner of her eye she saw Sandor disarming Cafless and his sheepish men, and subduing Aswad and Rana. Then she concentrated wholly on fighting the man who had slain her father, but for all her skill speed and tenacity, Lagras beat her sword aside repeatedly. A heavy blow knocked her blade from her hand and she knew she presented a wide target, immobile and defenceless.

'Die, bitch!' Lagras snarled and lunged at her.

She sprang back and, bending swiftly, retrieved her fallen weapon. Anger gave her renewed strength and she rushed on Lagras, gashing his forehead with a sweeping blow, the blood dripping into his eyes. Half-blinded, he attacked and feinted, their feet stamping up and down the floor as they lunged and parried, stunning the onlookers into silence. Lagras made a wide arc with his blade, caught it in one of the curtains and brought it crashing down. It tangled round his feet and, as he struggled, Varna wrenched the sword from his hand and sent it spinning off into the distance where it landed with a clatter.

She threw herself on Lagras, kneeing him in the groin, her blade raised. A moment more and it would have fallen across his throat, nearly severing his head from his body.

'Stop!' Naram shouted, her voice quivering.

Varna rose slowly, the point of her weapon nicking Lagras's neck, warning him not to move. 'What have you to say?' she cried, her breathing uneven from the struggle, her voice hoarse.

'Watch out!' Merrisan shouted. 'She has Jat!'

Varna shifted her gaze from the king to his evil queen,

and saw that she had a dagger directed at Jat's heart.

'One move and I'll kill him,' Naram warned. 'I demand a safe passage out of here for Lagras and myself. If you refuse or in any way harm my king, then the boy dies.'

Varna didn't know what course to take. She couldn't let Merrisan's brother die, and yet to have Lagras walk away was unthinkable.

The matter was taken out of her hands. Merrisan notched an arrow in her bow and let fly. The iron head sliced neatly through the leather thong attaching Jat's cock to the queen. He flung himself on Naram and wrested the dagger from her, then held her down, ignoring her as she spat and clawed and screeched.

Sandor marched towards her, seized her by the hair then propelled her to one of the pillars. He forced her to face it, hacked strips off the damaged curtain and knotted them round her wrists, then did the same to her ankles so that she was spread-eagled. Her gown ripped like paper when he tore it from her body, her elegant shoulders, back, buttocks and thighs exposed for all to see – and punish.

'Stop!' Lagras cried, hands held to his bleeding head wound. 'She's my queen!'

'She's a witch, an exponent of the black arts,' Sandor answered sternly. 'She has used others mercilessly. Now it's her turn to be a slave, at the whim of anyone who fancies to use her.' He swung round to where Jat was embracing his sister, and said, 'You've suffered in Naram's hands more than most.'

Jat had torn off his bondage straps and, though still naked, presented a proud figure. His eyes went over the helpless woman, and though she hissed threats, he seized the whip that had been taken from Aswad and paced the distance between them.

Lagras, already manacled, stared across in frustrated rage. 'This is all your doing, you Trokles vixen!' he grated, and Varna felt a rush of fear and something else she didn't want to name as she read the clear message in his dark eyes.

'You robbed me of father and country,' she retorted. 'Like you, I'm of the blood royal and was duty-bound to fight for my freedom. Wouldn't you have done the same?'

'Oh, yes,' he said with slow deliberation. 'I would and I *shall*. You may think you've beaten me, but no one conquers Lagras. I'll move heaven, earth, and hell, the stars, the moon and the sun, to reinstate myself and take back Valdivia. So beware, princess.'

Just for a moment she felt once more the charismatic attraction of the man, his darkness, his ruthless arrogance, his physical presence that robbed her of her will and made her think of nothing but sex. Had things been different, had they only fought on the same side, then who knew what might have happened between them. He could have shared her throne, her life, her soul.

Then a piercing scream rent the air as Jat struck Naram, the whip coming down to cut into her flesh. She bucked against her bonds, and a long red welt bloomed on her right buttock. Somewhere in the background Merrisan shouted encouragement and Jat laid on the stripes vigorously. It was as if he was avenging himself for every insult, beating and shameful exhibition he'd been made to endure at her hands.

Her trussed body arched and twisted as far as her restraints would permit. She flung back her head and yelled, and Jat lifted his arm and walloped her till her white flesh was scored with crimson lines, crossing, re-crossing, marking her from slim shoulders to the backs of her thighs.

Varna watched without pity. The woman deserved all she got, and Jat merited this reward. His cock was erect now, a natural hardness without the aid of leather thongs to maintain it. He cast the whip aside and ran his hands over Naram's fiery stripes, then pushed his fingers between her bottom crack. When he withdrew them Varna could see them glistening with Naram's love-juice. He smiled broadly and jabbed his fingers into her anus, then her vagina. She moaned, lifting her pelvis up against him, absorbing his touch and wanting more.

He bent at the knees a little and, taking his cock in one hand, thrust it into her, standing straight when it was firmly lodged and moving her helpless body up and down on the slippery shaft. She cried out in ecstasy, and Jat pumped harder.

'Make me come,' she wailed frenziedly.

Jat slid a hand round her belly and found her nubbin. His middle digit frigged it as he moved his prick within her, faster and faster till they both reached the peak and shuddered into climax.

'Oh, brother, my dear Jat!' Merrisan exclaimed joyfully. 'She's not done you permanent harm. I was so afraid for you.'

'Indeed not,' he answered, his flaccid cock slipping from the queen's cunt. 'I learned a lot from her. What will happen to her now? Can I have her as my odalisque?'

'I've promised the populace that she will be tried, along with Lagras,' Varna said, suddenly bone-weary and needing to be alone with Sandor. 'She'll be imprisoned here, and until the time comes for her trial, I see no reason why you shouldn't have use of her.'

'What of her powers of witchcraft?' Sandor asked, not taking his eyes from either of the prisoners.

'Chedon has seen to that,' she replied. 'He's put a block on her powers, Lagras's too, with Cragfor's help.'

'That hideous hag!' Lagras spat to show his contempt. 'Are those your only magical practitioners, Varna? A toothless old busybody and the spawn of an ogress and a troll?'

'I have the protection of Udin,' she answered, sheathing

her sword while Sandor gave orders for their captives to be taken to the dungeons.

'Udin!' Lagras declared scornfully. 'You really believe he helped you?'

'I know it,' she answered, then passed a hand over her eyes, suddenly dizzy.

Sandor caught her as she stumbled, lifted her in his arms and strode off to find shelter for the night with Cym at *The Three Doves*.

The silky white curtains stirred a little in the breeze blowing in from the lagoon. It carried the scents and sounds of Ciophos, a city celebrating a double event – the marriage of Varna to Sandor, followed by their coronation.

She lay in the nuptial bed of the great royal chamber and moved herself carefully, so as not to dislodge his cock. He had taken her several times now as her lawful husband, and she wanted at least a couple more orgasms before they slept.

'What a day,' she whispered, deciding to talk so that he didn't doze off. 'Weren't Phila and Merrisan splendid as my squires of honour?'

'Indeed, they carried out their arduous duties without a hitch,' he agreed, his hands moving over her breasts in that firm but gentle way she loved so much, this giant warrior treating her as if she was made of thistledown. Not always, of course. There were times when she demanded harsh sex, performed on the spur of the moment.

'Now I shall lose them for a while. They're off adventuring again,' she said regretfully, almost wishing she could saddle-up and go with them.

The night sky beyond the windows lit up. King Rashad had provided the fireworks with Fareshah's help, and they were still going on, amusing the innumerable guests and the jubilant people of Ciophos.

'Cragfor can probably see them from the Forbidden Mountain,' Varna said lazily, running the tip of her tongue round the rim of his ear. 'A pity she didn't stay for the wedding reception.'

'Erek went with her. Did you notice?'

'Who could fail to? Their lovemaking is so noisy! Does she intend to make him lord of her domain?'

'I think so,' Sandor said, pinching one of her nipples till she nearly screamed with pleasure. 'She's told me she wants him to help her guard Firestorm's treasure, some of which I've left in her care. But whatever, he's certainly found a novel use for the helve of his battleaxe.' He chuckled and thrust a finger into Varna's cunt and worked it into the juices, imitating a wooden dildo.

'How rude!' she squealed, laughing at the thought of the witch and the warrior and the games this uninhibited pair would play together.

Then he suddenly became serious, throwing back the light quilt and fingering her labial lips where jewels flashed amidst the fringing of dark curly hair.

'You still wear these,' he said, watching her reaction closely. 'Why?'

'Because they look pretty and feel exciting,' she answered quietly, reaching down and turning one of them in the sweetly engorging flesh.

He touched her arm, naked like the rest of her, apart from the slave-bangle. 'And this? I thought you would have thrown it away by now. You have gems aplenty.'

Varna sat up, her fingers smoothing the metal which bore Rashad's crest. The bangle had never left her since it was first fastened on. 'Be patient with me on this one. Call it superstition or what you will, but I wear it to remind me of how easily it could happen again.'

'But Lagras and Naram are in exile, sent far away to the terrible icy regions of Antica where few strangers survive the cold, the blizzards, the wild beasts and ferocious cannibals who inhabit the frozen wastes.'

'They aren't the only sorcerers and wickedly greedy people in the world,' she said.

She looked into his eyes, but did not waver. There was no way she was going to tempt fate by becoming too sure of her position as Queen Varna. Destiny had a nasty habit of catching the unwary off guard, just when they thought they were safe.

Exciting titles available from Chimera

1-901388-20-4	The Instruction of Olivia	*Allen*
1-901388-01-8	Olivia and the Dulcinites	*Allen*
1-901388-12-3	Sold into Service	*Tanner*
1-901388-13-1	All for Her Master	*O'Connor*
1-901388-14-X	Stranger in Venice	*Beaufort*
1-901388-16-6	Innocent Corinna	*Eden*
1-901388-17-4	Out of Control	*Miller*
1-901388-18-2	Hall of Infamy	*Virosa*
1-901388-23-9	Latin Submission	*Barton*
1-901388-19-0	Destroying Angel	*Hastings*
1-901388-21-2	Dr Casswell's Student	*Fisher*
1-901388-22-0	Annabelle	*Aire*
1-901388-24-7	Total Abandon	*Anderssen*
1-901388-26-3	Selina's Submission	*Lewis*
1-901388-27-1	A Strict Seduction	*Del Rey*
1-901388-28-X	Assignment for Alison	*Pope*
1-901388-29-8	Betty Serves the Master	*Tanner*
1-901388-30-1	Perfect Slave	*Bell*
1-901388-31-X	A Kept Woman	*Grayson*
1-901388-32-8	Milady's Quest	*Beaufort*
1-901388-33-6	Slave Hunt	*Shannon*
1-901388-34-4*	Shadows of Torment	*McLachlan*
1-901388-35-2*	Star Slave	*Dere*
1-901388-37-9*	Punishment Exercise	*Benedict*
1-901388-38-7*	The CP Sex Files	*Asquith*
1-901388-39-5*	Susie Learns the Hard Way	*Quine*
1-901388-40-9*	Domination Inc.	*Leather*
1-901388-42-5*	Sophie & the Circle of Slavery	*Culber*
1-901388-11-5*	Space Captive	*Hughes*
1-901388-41-7*	Bride of the Revolution	*Amber*
1-901388-44-1*	Vesta – Painworld	*Pope*
1-901388-45-X*	The Slaves of New York	*Hughes*
1-901388-46-8*	Rough Justice	*Hastings*
1-901388-47-6*	Perfect Slave Abroad	*Bell*
1-901388-48-4*	Whip Hands	*Hazel*
1-901388-50-6*	Slave of Darkness	*Lewis*
1-901388-55-2*	Darkest Fantasies	*Raines*
1-901388-53-0*	Wages of Sin *(Mar)*	*Benedict*
1-901388-54-9*	Love Slave *(Mar)*	*Wakelin*
1-901388-55-7*	Slave to Cabal *(April)*	*McLachlan*
1-901388-56-5*	Susie Follows Orders *(April)*	*Quine*

All **Chimera** titles are/will be available from your local bookshop or newsagent, or direct from our mail order department. Please send your order with a cheque or postal order (made payable to *Chimera Publishing Ltd*) to: **Chimera Publishing Ltd., PO Box 152, Waterlooville, Hants, PO8 9FS**. If you would prefer to pay by credit card, email us at: **chimera@fdn.co.uk** or call our **24 hour telephone/fax credit card hotline: +44 (0)23 92 783037** (Visa, Mastercard, Switch, JCB and Solo only).

To order, send: Title, author, ISBN number and price for each book ordered, your full name and address, cheque or postal order for the total amount, and include the following for postage and packing:
UK and BFPO: £1.00 for the first book, and 50p for each additional book to a maximum of £3.50.
Overseas and Eire: £2.00 for the first book, £1.00 for the second and 50p for each additional book.

*Titles £5.99. All others £4.99

For a copy of our free catalogue please write to:

Chimera Publishing Ltd
Readers' Services
PO Box 152
Waterlooville
Hants
PO8 9FS

Or visit our Website at:
www.chimerabooks.co.uk